FLIGHT OF THE LADYBIRD

TIM HOLMES

Published by HGA Publishing

Paperback ISBN - 978-1-7397999-2-2
ePub ISBN - 978-1-7397999-3-9

Cover design and layout by Spiffing Publishing

1

There was no significance to the exact day that Jean de Villeneuve first tapped the keys of his Olivetti, only that it had taken him so long to embark upon his story that many doubted he ever would, such that the impulse that morning to sit down and write even took him by surprise. He blamed the months of procrastination on "sheer, cursed laziness and a fearful reluctance to dig up the past." His editor was inclined to believe him, but not before threatening to abandon Jean and his "wretched oeuvre," as she chose to describe it.

Paris was shrouded in thick fog on that November morning. Jean slipped into a dressing gown, lit the stove, and rubbed his hands over the flame before placing the coffee pot over it. Grabbing a cigarette, he opened the doors onto the narrow balcony, stepped out into the darkness and gazed down four floors to the street below, sipping his coffee and drawing deeply on his cigarette. They are all so busy, so damn busy down there, even at this God-forsaken hour, he thought, before shouting out into the freezing darkness, "Enough, enough of this damn stupidity. I will, I will write your story, my Coccinelle. I promised you I would, and I will. You'll see."

He closed the doors to the balcony behind him, put a match to the gas fire in his study, plucked the cat off his chair, sat down, stretched out his bad leg and fed a blank sheet into the typewriter.

*

Ma Coccinelle – Before the Beginning

"Mon beau colosse qui protege tout mes secrets" – my beautiful giant which guards all my secrets – that's what she called the sweet chestnut tree by the rough path in the forest above Rosis, the village in the mountains where she hid for a while when not scurrying about the Caroux and the Montagnes Noires carrying messages or provisions for us and other colleagues.

I spotted her there in her private hideaway one day during a moment of relative peace, if you can call it that. She was perched high up in the tree's canopy, leaning her back into its vast trunk, balancing on a bough, her legs wrapped tightly around it as if she were riding bareback. She was scribbling in a notebook, the same tome from which I will now base this story. She kept it in a cavity in the tree's trunk, wrapped in a black sheep's fleece for safekeeping.

Towards the end of those three terrible years, once the imminent dangers of the Occupation had vanished and the Nazis had retreated, she recovered her memoires – which by then had grown to three volumes – and entrusted them to me. As she handed them over, she announced that they were a gift "which only you deserve to have" – words which I shall never forget. I wondered later whether it was some sort of gesture on her part to disown those years, to separate herself from them as if the sinews of guilt still plagued her. Perhaps because I was a central part of her life during those years, she felt I should become their custodian as if she no longer wished them to taint her existence. But I couldn't be sure.

And so it was that I'd hidden a part of her life away

in a box in the bottom drawer of my desk and never been motivated to look through it, no doubt afraid of what I might find. I never pondered to any great length why I'd been given the notebooks until several years later, at an anniversary lunch in Paris with other comrades, she asked me if I would write her story. Her request shocked me at first although I'd always been tempted to do something of the sort.

And now I had her permission after all these years, to resurrect those memories, to bring those days back to life as best I could. It terrified me. How could I ever do her justice? I wasn't sure. It bothered me for months, almost a year – but I'd have to start somewhere, sometime.

Her name is Coccinelle. That was her alias, her nom de guerre, and the name I eventually came to know her by. But that name soon became too much of a mouthful so we abbreviated it to "Nelle" and it stuck. The name she'd been born with was Marie-France Champuix, but that is a different story and another life apart.

We named her "Coccinelle" for an obvious reason. In the early summer of 1943, she caught us unaware by emerging stealthily out of the holm oak woods and wild box and broom scrubland of the rugged Caroux massif in which we were camped. It was the location where we'd decided to hide out near the Mont de l'Espinouse, at the southern confines of the Massif Central, a safe enough place to rest for a few weeks. How she'd ever managed to find us was a small miracle but a credit to her innate derring-do. She arrived furtively as one might expect, eyes wide and fearful, catching us by surprise despite our lookouts. She was dishevelled and practically in rags, limping, and with a soiled, spotted scarlet scarf wrapped around her as if she were hiding a scar on her neck. She had her hands held up high above her head. When she approached me, I noticed she had a ladybird poised on the end of her nose, which refused to fly away.

At first, I failed to recognise the pitiful figure. Only a few minutes or so later did I realise who she was. I'd been warned of someone who might arrive wearing a red scarf. I was shocked at the immediate thought that she could only have come in search of me. Whatever powerful emotions we might have felt at the time upon encountering each other again in this unlikely location, we both hid the fact from the start – that is, that we'd been close friends since our lycée days, and what's more, lovers or flawed lovers for a few years thereafter.

The full-blown invasion of France by the German army in May 1940 had put an end to any plans we had for a future together. We were obliged to go our separate ways. I'd heard rumours of what had happened to her in the spring of 1942 but they seemed so improbable, that I dismissed them. If such hearsay were true, I might so easily have denounced her outright and arrested her myself. Instead, I found myself suffering a conflicting and compelling urge to protect her, whatever falsehoods had been spread amongst friends and enemies. I wanted to be the first to hear her truth, her side of the story. I was adamant that my comrades should not condemn her unequivocally before I'd given her the chance to confide in me.

After some initial interrogation, our group concluded that she could be trusted, and that she was indeed the new liaison contact who we'd been expecting.

We directed her to sit down amongst us, keeping our weapons close by just in case. She was starving and begged for food. Before we provided her with a bowl of soup, we joked and laughed at her ladybird and removed it from her, passing it around from hand to hand amongst ourselves as if we each wanted a share of the luck it might bring us. Most of us were acutely aware of the cultural significance of a ladybird. In retrospect our laughter was inappropriate and was not something I'm proud of now, since she was in a poor state, and took it badly. We had no idea then of what she was going through. I continued to hide my feelings and remained aloof at a time when she would have wanted all the love, reassurance and comforting I could provide her.

Both the black-spotted scarf wrapped around her neck with its bright scarlet hue and the presence of the ladybird on her nose, gave us a convincing reason thereafter to name her "La Coccinelle," the ladybird. Had she flown in to bring us luck and grant us a wish, just when morale was low and things were becoming unpleasantly tough – we were starving, we'd run out of munitions, and one of our combatants, Bruno, was badly injured? We soon looked to her as our good luck charm and to be frank, we needed some female company too. Little did we know how much more she would have to offer, let alone why. But that would remain our own particular secret, just the two of us.

This will not be an easy story to tell and yet I can feel her hand even now, resting lightly on mine, urging my fingers along the keys, the sweet scent of her parfum still lingering about me in the room where I sit, the memories of "Coccinelle la Combattante," my ladybird Resistance fighter, stirring my thoughts, always haunting my conscience. Est-ce que j'ai vraiment fait mon maximum? Should I have done more for her? Could I have been better?

Rue de Buci, PARIS 6eme

November, 1973.

2

Three of them worked in unison that night – two lookouts both armed, and the other carrying a brush and a pot of paint. They crouched under the oblong shadow cast by the moonlight upon the graveyard wall, waiting for their moment. Earlier, they'd expressed their fears that the night was too bright, but the order had come from on high and had to be heeded. Two dogs barked at each other over in the far corner of the square where the church stood, a square building surrounded on all sides by grave stones and cypresses. One of the men stirred the pot of paint. It was to be bright red tonight but the choice of colour was circumstantial – whatever they could get their hands on. In this hamlet, Saubon-le-Duc, there were three houses to be condemned. Two in a single street by the church, the third on the edge of the village, on the road to Meursault. All three front doors were to be daubed with a large letter "C" – "C" for "Collabo," collaborator, the occupants waking the following morning to a new life with two choices which required their immediate attention – to flee or to face the likely consequences of a summary judgement.

Whatever choice was made, the accused was doomed, their lives turned around indefinitely with a perilous, uncertain future ahead of them. From the beginning of the Nazi Occupation of France, people from all walks of life were confronted with relentless and conflicting choices – ordinary people often faced with unordinary, impossible decisions. If you made the wrong one, you paid for it, often with your life. In truth, you were probably damned either way.

On this night, Marie-France Champuix, living in the outskirts of the hamlet with her parents, was deemed to have made the wrong choice. She'd been denounced to the authorities by an anonymous letter – a surprisingly common occurrence at this time – and bearing in mind the severity of her crime, the local Resistance, who'd intercepted the message, took it upon themselves to mete out their own version of justice before the locals or the gendarmerie could get to her. But that was only the beginning.

There were inevitable dilemmas to one aspect of how one lived one's life in Occupied France in those years, which only the current circumstances of defeat and occupation could have fomented – to resist or not to resist. Amongst those who chose not to resist there were also choices – to hide away and wait, or to cooperate and collaborate.

Resisters were more likely to believe they had little or nothing to lose, and a certain reckless free spirit pervaded their decision-making. The choice to take up arms against the enemy either directly, or indirectly assisting those who did, was the most extreme of choices and in reality only a small proportion of the population joined the official Resistance. By contrast, for those who risked losing much more – their dignity, a family, children, a home, a job, a business, for example – they were faced with different, more considered choices. Most people chose the passive route, the one of least resistance to the invaders, which meant living a discreet, unobtrusive life "waiting" patiently until the occupying forces would be driven out, neither resisting nor collaborating. In some cases, their very inactivity risked them being tainted with the brush of collaboration. And then there were the others, the collaborators, those who chose to cooperate with the enemy, and some in open support. That avenue carried its own risks for which many were to suffer in a purge of vengeance towards the end of the war as the German army fled France.

Despite all which one might have read or heard of the many hundreds of thousands of heroes of the French Resistance, in reality "attentisme," or "waiting" was the route which most French citizens pursued in the years from 1940 to 1945.

Marie-France had fallen somewhere in between these grave choices, leaving her in greater jeopardy than most. She had a predictable but promising future ahead of her, such that she might have much to lose, and yet potent feelings combined with pressing circumstances had conspired to drive her several months earlier into the arms of an officer of the German Wehrmacht. Additionally, her natural instincts for the preservation of the unborn child she knew she was now carrying compounded the predicament in which she found herself. Apart from this one faux-pas on a beautiful, star-filled night during the last few days of 1941 near the Burgundian town of Chalon-sur-Saône, when and where it had all begun, she might well have considered that she had everything to lose by falling in love, and might never have come close to contemplating such a thing. For sexual liaisons with the enemy were viewed as collusion, and to many, the gravest, most undignified form of collaboration, especially for a woman of standing in the largely patriarchal, rural society which existed at the time.

Having completed the painting of a bold "C" upon the doors of the two suspected collaborators in the heart of the hamlet, the group moved down the road towards the more substantial manor house owned by the Champuix family. The double iron gates to the courtyard were wide open to the street. The men painted the "Cs" on the iron panels below the railings on both gates, so that they might be seen when passing along the lane in either direction. Too much paint having been employed on the brush for the first gate, parts of the "C" began to drip down the gate leaving a pool of blood-red paint on the gravel driveway. They were more sparing with the use of their paint on the other gate. Once the mission had been accomplished, the group dispersed into the shadows, covering their tracks as they'd been trained to do.

Marie-France's parents were woken at dawn by shouts and a rap at their bedroom door.

"Monsieur Henri, monsieur, I beg you, wake up, wake up. Come quickly. You must come and see what has happened."

"What is it?" Monsieur Champuix bellowed from his bed before opening the door to Laurent, one of the winery workers.

The look of urgency on Laurent's face was enough for Monsieur Champuix to reach for his dressing-gown and slippers and race down the stairs, rushing out through the front door and across the courtyard towards the entrance.

He stood in front of the gates. "How is this possible?" He stood back and rubbed his chin. "But who is responsible? And why? Laurent, let us look for paint, black paint, in the stores somewhere and paint over it. I'm sure we'll find it there. Please get rid of it as soon as you can. Immediately. Paint over it twice if need be." They headed off together towards one of the barns to look for paint.

After searching for a while, Laurent sat down on the edge of a low work bench and sighed. "But who would do this? It must be a mistake. They've got the wrong house. We are not collaborators. No one here is a collaborator. Okay, we gave those German troops a little wine last week to mind their own business. But everyone does. That's not collaboration. It's protection."

"I fear that we have enemies, people who wish to do us down. Our competitors even," said Monsieur Champuix, shrugging his shoulders.

"Our rivals wouldn't do that, surely."

"You'd be surprised. In these strange, hard times, people will do anything. Everyone is living on the edge, and many, many are in a much worse state than us. Someone has found a way to bring shame upon us, to denounce us, and for a reason we do not yet know. When we have found the black paint and removed the evidence … by the way I think the paint may be in the east barn … I'd like you to gather everyone together, to explain what has happened, and begin by making some tentative enquiries."

"I'm sure you will be careful, but I would advise you not to make any accusations too quickly," said Laurent. "Some of our staff, especially the ones who are not locals are, how can I put it, restless. They may move on at any time at the slightest sign of trouble and we cannot afford to lose what few workers we have."

"I have no intention of doling out any blame now. I will tell them what has happened and it will serve as a warning for everyone to remain vigilant. And I will of course discuss it with my wife and my children. Everyone needs to know."

"Should we not nevertheless make some enquiries or investigations?" Laurent said.

"I don't know. I need time to think. I'm inclined to think it best that we deal with this on our own. We should not involve the police or the militia. Is that understood, Laurent?"

"It is understood, sir, yes. Certainly no militia," Laurent said, nodding.

3

The Champuix's home, which also served as a winery, overlooked vineyards on two sides, for Saubon-le-Duc was one of the so-called "wine villages" of Burgundy, abutting the better-known vineyards of Meursault which for centuries had produced a white Burgundy wine of world renown. Domaine de Champuix was a family-run estate with an established reputation, comprising a total holding of thirty-eight hectares, enough to provide a comfortable living for the family. They'd been growing grapes for six generations, supplying barrels of mature wine to a "negoçiant" in Beaune who carried out the bottling on their behalf. The family owned small parcels of vineyards in the vicinity of Saubon-le-Duc and in some of the better regarded premiers crus of Meursault which had, only a few years earlier, acquired the esteemed status of "appellation d'origine contrôllée" with some of more famous "lieu-dits" (sites) permitted to be marked on the label as a Premier Cru. It was not lost on the astute Monsieur Henri Champuix that the occupying Germans, under the terms of a recently negotiated requisitioning agreement, had been forbidden to sequester such bottles. So as not to incur the wrath of whichever regiment had been billeted locally, most of the winemakers of Burgundy supplied what was requested within reason, holding back the most treasured bottles as best they could, as well as those labelled with the name of a Premier Cru vineyard. Apart from local consumption, much of the trade headed north to the restaurants of Paris or south to Lyon much as before, and the smaller but esteemed export trade continued too, not least to Germany and Switzerland, and when possible, to Great Britain.

The middle-aged Henri Champuix was assisted in the cellar by his son Marc and younger daughter Eloise, with additional cellar hands employed at harvest time for the winemaking. Laurent acted as the foreman and took overall charge of the running of the estate, operating under Monsieur Champuix's orders. Marie-France preferred the outdoors. The work of the vigneron was her role of choice, managing a small team of helpers tending the vines in several different plots in various locations. She had been tempted by other occupations even though women were expected to marry, stay at home, provide food for the table and attend to the wellbeing of the children. Her early tentative interest in a career in the family business had undoubtedly delighted her father although her mother had more traditional views, insisting that being their first-born she should have a choice, including that of being a housewife, as she herself had chosen. To her father, being born a Champuix, son or daughter, required obligations to the family business as if it were a duty and non-negotiable. It was nevertheless a commitment which Marie-France wasn't always happy about. At times she might grumble with her father for forcing it upon her, for that is how she saw it when life became hard. In better times, she relished the independence she found tending to the vines, which she managed with a fervour and an undoubted skill from one harvest to the next. She'd only spent a few years in the job before the arrival of the German army on French soil changed everything.

She'd met Jean de Villeneuve while at secondary school in Beaune. Always top of their class, their academic prowess and natural willingness to learn brought them together early on. His parents were both professors at the nearby Université de Bourgogne in Dijon, and Marie-France believed that must have contributed to Jean's love of learning. His general knowledge exceeded the bounds of the school curriculum in every respect and Marie-France soon fell in love with his wild imagination, enthusiasm for life and intellectual curiosity, claiming that she was never bored in his company. His parents were both members of the Parti Communiste Français (PCF). Although it had recently been banned, this fact hadn't affected their son's fascination in Marxist-Leninism. To Marie-France, his politics seemed both novel and exciting although the news of his political persuasions was met with caution by her parents. But any negative feelings were partly counterbalanced by relief, since Marie-France had not previously shown much interest in men, let alone maintaining a bona fide relationship.

Jean also shared an enthusiasm for the outdoors although he had no knowledge of or interest in grape growing. His preferences were for rock climbing and cycling. Even so, he agreed during the summer of 1940 to help Marie-France in the vineyards at the Champuix domaine, before intending to continue his studies in October at the prestigious École Normale Supérieur (ENS) de Lyon, reading politics and administration. During that time he lived with the Champuix family in an outbuilding, and was employed with other workers as a hired hand in the vineyard.

Jean and Marie-France had formed a relationship over that tumultuous summer of 1940 as the German army invaded France through the "impenetrable" Ardennes, as Pétain had described it, outflanking the defensive Maginot line – a ferocious "blitzkrieg" of infantry and tank battalions which marched rapidly and relentlessly west and southwards, reaching Jean's home town of Dijon by 17th June. An armistice was signed five days later, which resulted in only half of France being occupied, thus maintaining a degree of neutrality and independence but leaving a defeated French army of 1.8 million soldiers to be rounded up as prisoners of war, many of whom were eventually deported to Germany. It was a year of tremendous upheaval and migration on a massive scale for those who lived in the northern half of France, although the Occupation affected and troubled every citizen across the nation in one way or another – even the amorous young couple working at Domaine de Champuix who from day to day read the fear and anxiety in their parents' eyes.

A new French collaborationist government was formed for the unoccupied southern zone, situated in the town of Vichy in the centre of France and overseen by the Maréchal Philippe Pétain, the victor of Verdun. The Armistice was signed between the defeated French General Huntziger and the German General Keitel among others, on June 22nd 1940.

Jean and Marie-France never saw or heard a German soldier until early July, when it appeared that the construction of the dreaded new Line of Demarcation was going to split them in two, if Jean were to continue his studies further south in Lyon. Such a barrier would also divide France into two halves, the occupied and the unoccupied, touching every aspect of daily life. The full impact of this and the effects it would have on Marie-France and Jean initially passed them by. The first signs that grave changes were taking place was when Marie-France heard that the bridge across the banks of the River Saône in the nearby town of Chalon had been closed one morning, while German soldiers erected an official crossing point. On Marie-France's side, the north, France was governed directly by the military occupiers. And from the south bank of the river, unoccupied France was governed by the Vichy Government. This half of France was known as the "Zone Libre" and encompassed most of southern France from the Swiss border south of Geneva near Gex to the Spanish border in the western Pyrenees by the town of Arnéguy. Apart from dividing its people, the economic effects on the south were drastic. The Germans had occupied the richest agricultural lands and the most essential industrial hubs of France. Three quarters of French grain and potatoes were grown in the occupied zone and most of France's steel and coal was produced and mined there respectively. The result was that life became considerably harder for those living in the south.

Despite this, Jean's desire to return to his studies in Lyon, a city situated in the southern "Zone Libre," overrode any other considerations. That meant he would have to change and register his new address and head south as soon as possible before it became impossible to do so, and before the September harvest – parting from his parents and home in Dijon, and Marie-France and her vineyards in Meursault. Once this unnatural frontier had been established, word soon got about that it was an arduous task simply crossing the Demarcation Line, requiring an identity card (Ausweis) or a free-movement card (Passierschein) which necessitated an interminable web of formalities and intimate investigations into one's personal life. These passes were difficult to acquire, and many who were desperate enough to cross the line began to do so illegally, facing the risk of being shot and killed. The 1,200 kilometre frontier was heavily guarded and patrolled by troops with guard dogs, with surprisingly few locations where it was possible to cross. And much of the border was mined. Access points, always on roads or lanes, comprised a barricade wrapped extensively in barbed wire, a barrier, an administration hut with a Nazi flag pole, a red, white and black painted sentry box, and a large warning notice stuck to a board by the barrier. To the frustration of the locals, they were often closed, and opened only according to the whims of the local "Feld" or "Kreis Kommandanturen" responsible for cross-traffic over the new border.

Such restrictions on the free movement of citizens made life very difficult, especially if one relied for a living on the commercial transaction of goods and services. The line was drawn out arbitrarily with no respect for local boundaries or the prevailing topography, such that a farmer might find half his fields in the "Occupied Zone" and the rest in the "Zone Libre," or the children of a village might find themselves separated from their school on the other side of the line. Forty-one "départements" were occupied entirely and a further dozen partially. France became a divided country as a result, but it wasn't long before a network of smuggling rings sprang up, run by defiant young men keen to improve their incomes. Contraband included anything from basic foodstuffs to fuel, spare parts and eventually arms and people. Others who crossed were desperate locals, keen to keep in touch with nearby relatives or friends who'd been cut off from each other through no fault of their own.

Marie-France found her relationship with Jean severely curtailed both by their distance apart and the new frontier imposed upon them, which she was now unable to cross at will. Their encounters came to a halt, and with the breakdown of the postal service until the end of September, communication with him had been impossible for a few months. In that same month the "inter-zonal" card appeared, also known as the family card, replacing the common written letter with a few pre-printed words which you could highlight or delete, allowing for a frustratingly brief communication – not at all satisfactory for the pining Marie-France.

Not surprisingly she'd considered opportunities for crossing the line to be with him. The frontier was only twenty-five kilometres south of Saubon-le-Duc, and Lyon was a further 130 km south from there, which would take her, she calculated, three full days on a bicycle to reach him. She had a friend who'd crossed at night in that way, and another who'd crossed the Saône in a friend's rowing boat. She enquired from her father whether she might hide away in an empty wine barrel on their next trip to Lyon, but he'd forbidden it. After April 1941 she'd heard that specialist border guards had taken over from the Wehrmacht and crossings had become considerably more dangerous.

It was often the subject of extensive arguments around the

Champuix dining table. One evening Henri Champuix spelled out his views.

"You will not risk your life and abandon your duties in the vineyard to reach your boyfriend under such precarious circumstances. I forbid it. Besides, you'd never get back home again."

Her mother argued differently. "But Henri, how is she expected to love this man if she never sees or hears from him? Goodness knows, he might have given up on her by now and met a fellow student. Who knows what will befall them?"

"It is this cursed war, not me who you must blame," Henri said.

Marie-France's mother, Clémence, flung her arms into the air. "And what of all those refugees travelling back home to the north, and our French soldiers and foreign airmen trying to reach safety? They must be crossing the line. I've heard that there's a repatriation pass some can get hold of. People are crossing the line. Why not Marie-France? The butcher told me he has friends helping people across every day. Besides if you live near the line, you can get day passes. What of that?"

"I forbid it. Besides, who is to run the vineyard in her absence? No one can replace Marie-France. She knows every corner of our vineyards and the team love her ... even worship her. It would be a disaster. We risk losing the business, our living, the house, everything. We must stay together and help each other. What about that boy in Meursault? François Lebegue's son. He's a decent chap. An expert grape-grower too. What's wrong with him? He's a better bet for a boyfriend, surely."

Marie-France sat up straight hoping to appear more assertive. She leant across the table, staring wide-eyed at her father. "I love Jean. And I will see him if I can, if only for one weekend. This is my life, not yours."

4

The vines flowered in late May in most of Marie-France's vineyards, the dates of inflorescence in each dependent on their altitude, aspect and orientation to the sun. The months of June and July were customarily occupied by tying up or pruning overly vigorous shoots. On one of those mornings, one of Marie-France's vineyard helpers handed her a letter as they were preparing for the morning's work, explaining that she'd been handed it while cycling to work with instructions to pass it on. Marie-France opened it and read it immediately.

My Dear Marie-France, *15th July 1941*

MOST URGENT AND PLEASE DESTROY AFTER READING

I hope you receive this letter. I entrusted it to a university friend who said she could get it across the line for me through another friend, and then possibly another, so it might take some days or weeks. Such is life under this insufferable regime.

Some bad things have happened and I have taken some big decisions. This has been forced upon me but I have also been overcome by a great desire to fight for my country and to destroy the enemy whenever I find an opportunity. Do not be afraid. But poor, dear Papa has been arrested for demonstrating one night and since, as you know, he is a member of the PCF (which incidentally was forcibly disbanded in September last) and communists are seen as the enemy, often by our own people, he is likely to be deported to Germany. I cannot begin to imagine what his fate will be. Maman tells me that the Friedmanns, colleagues in Dijon, have been arrested, just for being Jewish. They also face deportation for hard labour, I hear, in the hellish factories of the Ruhr. There is talk of more of these "raffles", round-ups and deportations happening. Such is the way things are going.

I am informed that the Nazis have now began an invasion of our brothers' lands in the Soviet Union. Operation Barbarossa. It began on June 22nd, a massive invasion, three million of the bastards heading east and all despite the Molotov-Ribbentrop non-aggression Pact. So, I am joining the beginnings of a Resistance cell under the FN in Lyon to fight the fascist pigs. It's official, the Nazis are now our enemies too. The Front National is our local Resistance movement, it's political but also military, established by the PCF, but it is for anyone to join and shortly I will be actively pursuing and killing the enemy. I will avenge for the wrongs done to my father. I can't wait. This also means that I have abandoned my studies for now. I see it as the beginning of something more important, to fight for freedom, workers' rights, and my country.

What does this mean for us? I know that must be your first thought. I honestly cannot tell you. I'm afraid that this wretched war has dealt a sledgehammer blow to our relationship, which precious as it is, has barely had a chance to flourish. It is a most cruel fate and heaven knows where I shall be, but not with you. We can be sent anywhere to fight the enemy, and all is so secretive. You only know what you have to know and nothing more. You must understand that. All I know is that we are being rapidly re-organised under different leaders, groups and cells to carry out acts of sabotage against the enemy.

I think of you often and wonder how you are in your vineyards. But do not be tempted to come looking for me, whatever happens. It will be too dangerous. Everyone in my group must designate a next of kin. These are my mother and you. When my time comes, you will hear of it. Needless to say, I hope such a thing never happens and we will meet again soon.

Until soon, my dear, with all my love and best wishes,

Jean

Marie-France folded the letter, returned it to the envelope, and placed it in her pocket. Her eyes glazed over, a vacant feeling of disbelief took hold of her. She sat down on the wet earth and buried her face in her hands, releasing a whimper of despair. She sat there at the foot of a vine, weeping discreetly until a colleague walked up and placed a hand on her shoulder.

"Bad news, Marie-France?"

At first, she was unable to reply, then she looked up. "Terrible news. This war. I haven't yet lifted a finger against the enemy. I have only seen and heard of far off battles, not even that, just small skirmishes, and yet this feels like much more, much worse."

"I'm sorry you are suffering."

"Thank you, but we are all in pain in one way or another. What will become of us? How will it all end?" She buried her face again in her hands.

Her colleague placed her hand on Marie-France's shoulder again. "My Léonard says we will defeat the Boches. The Americans and the British will arrive to drive them out. And our brave French Resistance too. But how long we will have to wait, I do not know."

Marie-France stood up, wiped the tears away with the back of her hand and went to address her team. For the moment she was resolved to continue her work in the vines. That was the best she could do, the best distraction, the most rewarding outcome despite all that was going on around her. As she worked the rows that morning, she wondered how she might reply to Jean. But what could she say, even if she had an address for him? For his own safety, and hers, he'd deliberately left no means of communication. She was angry with him too, and that was perhaps not the best way to approach him. He had surely lost his father. He was going off to fight somewhere, God knows where. And how? As far as she knew, he knew nothing of guns, grenades, explosives, ammunition, nothing martial, nothing which might destroy the enemy. Except he could climb a telegraph pole and cut a wire or sabotage a vehicle. She knew of people who'd begun doing that. She wondered whether she could do that too.

The summer of 1941 passed by without a word from Jean. Since mid-May, goods and services were granted free passage across the Demarcation Line and Marie-France accompanied her father to Lyon delivering wine on a number of occasions, hoping somehow that she might hear a word of Jean or find the right opportunity to meet. On one such visit to Lyon they stayed overnight with her father's parents while their vehicle was being repaired. She had often visited her grandparents as a child and presumed that now that she was a little older, she'd find them more interesting. Over dinner they were particularly eager to talk of the war, and learn of her work in the vineyards. They asked about Jean and she informed them of his latest activities. Was she going to join him and become a "frondeuse" they wondered, but she had to ask them what that meant.

"Are you going to rebel against the Occupiers and their wretched rules and stipulations? We need our young to start fighting in whatever way they can," her grandfather said, to her surprise.

She laughed at the proposition. "But I have vines to attend to, and responsibilities to Papa. I can't just run off and take up arms. We can't leave the fruit on the vine. We have harvests and a business to run. But I *have* thought about it, I assure you."

"Passive connivance is not good enough. There are things you can do without prejudicing your work with the vines. An active contribution is still possible. Get onto your brother about that too. For example, last week, we had women protesting here at the main station, lying on the railway tracks to stop the deportations to the camps. That's all good protest," her grandfather said.

They talked all night of the war and how it had made life so much harder. Shortages of meat and dairy products had hit them particularly hard. Cigarettes, sugar and coffee were now almost non-existent, the German troops having "stolen" their share, as her grandparents put it, although the official word was "expropriation." As the food queues grew, so did the resentment. It was clear to see throughout her time in Lyon, whether it was hastily prepared posters glued to telegraph poles or flyers on noticeboards which she'd spotted in the streets or conversations overheard in the cafés. "To Live under Defeat is to Die Every Day," was one such poster which forced her to stop and think. Another "Think French, Act French." Her grandparents told her of the French police's "Renseignements généraux" which had resulted in the creation of the "brigades spéciales" to work hand in hand with the Gestapo and SS on rounding up known Communists, Jews and other so-called "undesirables," placing them in camps around the country, ready for deportation to Germany and eastern Europe.

The conversation became more frank and livelier after dinner when Grand-père fetched a bottle of marc de Bourgogne which he seemed intent on finishing that evening. By this time, Grand-mère had made her excuses and gone to bed.

"I thought you would be pro-Vichy but you seem so eager for me to resist. Are all your facts and figures and information tonight an attempt to urge me to join the Resistance?" Marie-France said, addressing her grandfather.

"It is true. I am inclined to tolerate the Vichy, but not the German army. Vichy appeal to the traditionalist right, the aristocracy, our Catholic faith, and they embrace authoritarianism. They are distinctly rightist without being fascist. And they're intent on cleaning up the lassitude, secularism and hedonism which France has just suffered from under the Third Republic. Pétain has refused to create a single party state, he supports the Church and loathes too much liberal modernisation. He stands for old France, but not fascism. That is important," Grand-père said.

Marie-France's father's views were hardly any different. "The time of the Third Republic was a dark time for France, the time of 'la décadence' when the French showed signs of a moral decline and society undoubtedly became degraded. We needed a change, although we were not expecting this one, to be sure." He sighed and took a sip of the grape spirit.

Grand-père stretched out his legs and cleared his throat. "Yes, and now we have Joan of Arc as our patriotic symbol, our national symbol of a united, patriotic France under the 'Révolution nationale.' The motto of 'Travail, Famille, Patrie' has more poignancy for to-day's times. Don't forget, we've worked the land as a family for several generations. The true symbols of France are 'la Terre' and the peasants and noblemen who toil in our fields. There's a lot to be said for the Vichy regime's support for people like us working the land."

Marie-France sat up, prepared for a fight. "Vichy's nationalism seems very exclusionary, and very inward-looking to me. Now we have forced collaboration, and a government which is antisemitic, anti-communist, anti-Freemasons, Anglophobic and xenophobic towards Spanish republicans especially. I'm proud of the fact that my Jean has joined the Resistance, and is hopefully fighting for a better future, freeing us from the yoke of Nazism."

"Are you sure you know what he is really fighting for? For a Communist France, do you think? Henri said, becoming increasingly red in the face.

"He says above all that he is fighting against the Nazis and fascism. I'm not sure if he's a true Bolshevik though. I know you may think of these resisters as dangerous, treasonable, political subverts and all communists as anarchists, but one day you'll see them as patriots and even Gaullists. I know you don't like him, but I don't care," said Marie-France.

Her father put his glass down. "Don't forget that he's abandoned you for his party and the cause. He's not good enough for you. You won't see him again, I'm sure. They say they will have interned over 10,000 Communists by the end of this year. At least Jean isn't Jewish otherwise he'd risk languishing in the central transit camp at Drancy, to be sent east to Poland for hard labour. You'd never see him after that. They say that's where they're all being sent. Pour souls. Just as well my mother-in-law has passed away. She was a quarter Jewish, I think. But you'd never have known it."

"Did you ever know the rest of her family?" asked Grand-père.

"No. There weren't really any to know. She was an only child. I'm glad Jean's not British either, not that Marie-France was ever going to end up with a 'rosbif,' even though we did send her to our agents in London for a year to learn some English. But not to find a suitor, it must be said," Henri said.

"I enjoyed my time in London. They're good agents with good sales in Britain. What is so wrong with the British?"

"They're not to be trusted. I'm fairly happy that Pétain and our Prime Ministers Laval and Darlan are Anglophobes after what the British did or more likely didn't do for us, abandoning us at Dunkirk with their evacuation in May last year and then two months later sinking our Mediterranean fleet at Mers-el-Kébir in Algeria. The British really are our relentless, 'eternal enemy.' Mark my words, although those aren't exactly mine," Henri said, wagging his finger.

Marie-France looked puzzled. "Why did they sink our fleet?

They are our allies?"

"Because they didn't want our ships falling into the hands of the Germans. Killed almost 1,300 French sailors for the sake of it," Henri said.

Grand-père groaned and downed his glass. "A 'racially degenerate, mixed race' is how Béraud described the British in that *Gringoire* newspaper, the other day. Anyway, the British now support de Gaulle in London and the Free French. There is no longer a British ambassador for France. Are they really coming to save us? I doubt it."

"Why should they? Perhaps the Soviets will come, now that Hitler has turned east," said Marie-France. "And by the way, the Communists are the largest group filling the ranks of the Resistance, in case you didn't know."

"Heaven forbid that we should have the Soviets here. Collectivised vineyards. Could you picture it? What nonsense," Grand-père muttered.

Henri stood up, as if he were preparing his last words before bed. "I'm concerned enough by organised labour, the CGT workers' union, but I can see with all their nationwide organisation, their secret cells, that the Communist supporters in France are well placed to resist the Nazis. But I wonder for how long ordinary citizens will endure the savage reprisals which the Gestapo are starting to carry out in retaliation for these sabotages on their troops. Let's be frank, these resisters are a ragged bunch of misfits, a mixed bag from no particular background, or religion, or profession or even ethnic group. De Gaulle fears the Communists most, yet he claims to be the true voice of Resistance France. But true, it is the Communists who are beginning to resist most and he'll need to come to terms with that."

"Who knows where things will go? Time for bed," Grand-père said, shuffling towards the door. "Finish off that bottle if you wish, you two."

5

After what seemed like a long week, Marie-France rode into Chalon-sur-Saône to meet a girlfriend. The 1941 harvest had been planned for mid-September and she was determined to get out a bit and see her friends before the most intensive time of the year for her. The harvest could last six weeks. It was a long two hour bike ride but she enjoyed keeping fit and it was a fine day for a morning out, and a worthy distraction from the daily grind. They agreed to meet at the Café du Paix in the centre of town, for the simple reason that sitting in a café named "Peace" in a time of war amused them both, and neither had been there before.

Although older than Marie-France, Antoinette was a chum from her school days who'd set up a business working from home, making curtains and household furnishings. Marie-France arrived early and sat in the corner waiting for her. The café owner had informed her that the coffee she requested would be revolting, although claiming with a shrug that some people still drank it. She opted for a glass of local red instead. She picked up a newspaper from the stand and gazed half-heartedly at the headlines whilst allowing herself to be distracted by her fellow guests.

For the first time, she was able to observe officers of the Wehrmacht in close proximity. Whatever evil they might be capable of, they appeared to be doing their best to disguise it today. She observed their polite requests and courteous gestures towards the locals around them. They seemed keen not to offend anyone. For a moment she imagined what they might look like wearing civvies. In better days these four men sitting around a table might have amounted to nothing more than cultured young German tourists enjoying a holiday in Burgundy. The sight of them in their perfectly pressed uniforms, shining buttons, and polished knee-high boots seemed so incongruous. The lugers strapped around their waists were presumably loaded and lethal, but Marie-France ignored that fact for a blissful moment. One such officer walked up to the bar and ordered their drinks, enunciating in a perfect French accent. He turned around, caught Marie-France's eye and smiled at her as he waited for the wine to be poured out. She averted her glance coyly. She supposed that they were off duty, although soldiers never switched off, surely. But even *they* needed a rest, some relief, a respite from the threats, intimidation and killings which filled every hour of their miserable day. They were at war, everyone was, although today didn't seem like it.

Antoinette walked in, removed her hat, apologised briefly, placed her shopping bag on the chair opposite Marie-France and ordered a glass of red from the bar. She too reflected upon the unusual guests sitting at the table in the opposite corner. The fact that Antoinette shared the same feelings caused them to giggle, if surreptitiously. Marie-France had to lift the newspaper to hide her face.

"What lovely uniforms they wear," Antoinette said, with barely a guilty thought.

"It's the men behind the uniforms who are catching your eye. I can tell," said Marie-France.

Antoinette leant across the table to whisper. "Well, don't you agree that they are good-looking too, especially the blue-eyed, dark-haired one, don't you agree? And they are hardly much older than us. In their mid to late twenties, I would say."

"Maybe, but how many of our brothers and sisters have they

killed? Don't forget that. It's easy to become engrossed. I guess because it's a novel thing having soldiers in our cafés, let alone the enemy's men. Let's change the subject before we attract their attention," Marie-France said.

"Have you heard from Jean, then?"

"Not a word. He may as well not exist. I don't want to talk about him."

"Anyone else in your life, then? And stop staring at them."

"Is that what I was doing?" Marie-France said, surprised.

"Yes, you can't help yourself, can you?"

"What about you? How is married life with François?"

"A bit boring, but he has a good job, so we're fairly comfortable except for food. We have no food."

"*Boring*? You've only been married for two years. François isn't boring. Remind me what he does."

"When I said 'boring,' I didn't mean François, I meant our lives at the moment. He's a manager at the iron foundry. You know that. At least he's on this side of the Demarcation Line, north of the river."

"Must be nice to have a man to share your bed with every night. Jean was working at the domaine over the summer, but he slept in the workers' quarters. Never with me. It was difficult to enjoy a night together."

"Did you *ever* sleep with him?"

"A little, but not nearly enough. We stole moments when we could. But we will, if we ever do see each other again."

"Do you think it may be finished?" Antoinette said.

"I think we may be finished, yes. I'm sad about it. At first I was angry, then I came to see and understand his thinking, and I felt sorry for him."

"But he left you in the cold. Do you miss him?"

Marie-France leant into the table as if she were about to reveal a secret. "Quite honestly, I'm not sure. I certainly miss someone. I'd like to have a man by my side. We all would, wouldn't we? So many women have lost their men, especially those who had soldiers or those who volunteered to fight. There are loads of widows out there now."

"And a shortage of good men."

Antoinette smiled and got up to order two more glasses, avoiding casting an eye in the direction of the officers, who were getting up and preparing to leave. The girls stayed a further hour and shared a slice of apple tart together. Antoinette walked with Marie-France to the edge of town before pushing her off on her bicycle on the road back towards Meursault. Before she set off, Marie-France conceded to Antoinette that she was lonely, and shed a tear over her shoulder as they hugged each other goodbye.

*

They repeated their encounter again a fortnight later on the eve of Marie-France's harvest. This time as she approached the same café, she heard a piano being played. The doors and windows were open and the sound filled the street. It was uplifting to hear such a beautiful melody, one which she believed she recognised, its familiarity testing her memory. It was one of Debussy's Preludes but she couldn't be sure which one, but what a gratifying, serene experience, and most unexpected. She parked up her bike next to a small military vehicle by the entrance. Antoinette was waiting for her at a table. When Marie-France sat down, her friend pointed towards the piano player.

"It's the same dishy officer we saw before, the dark-haired, blue-eyed one. Do you remember?" Antoinette said.

"Yes. Is that pastis for me? Thank you," said Marie-France as she pulled a chair out to sit down. Before she took her seat she went up to the bar to ask for a large glass of water. There weren't many people in the café but enough to suggest that the piano player had attracted an audience.

"Apparently he comes in here often to play, as this is the only piano he can find which is in tune. He paid for someone to have it tuned last week."

"Was he a concert pianist in another life?"

"No, he's not, but this is where it gets spooky … he's a winemaker with an estate in Germany somewhere. Can you believe it? His family are winemakers and live in a great big Schloss overlooking the Rhein."

Marie-France laughed. "You're joking."

"About the Schloss, yes, but the barman says he really is a winemaker in Germany, and he just wants to go home."

"Then he should," said Marie-France.

"You can't just desert. You know you can get shot for that. By a firing squad no less," Antoinette said.

"Well, let's enjoy our pastis and a free Debussy concert. What's your news?"

They stayed another half an hour and left before "the pianist-winemaker" had finished his informal concert – for that was what they now chose to call him. Marie-France headed back home a little later than usual that afternoon, estimating her arrival home for supper at around 7.30 p. m. The road was mercifully flat between Chalon and Chagny and the traffic was almost non-existent. A gentle breeze helped her along. She gazed left and right at the fields of waving sweet corn, and the buzzards above her, gliding on the thermals, calling out with their shrill cries. As she reached a minor crossroad and braked, she began to wobble, her rear wheel losing traction and forcing her to dismount. "Damn, a bloody puncture. What am I going to do?" she said. There was nothing to be done but walk or cadge a lift, so she began to walk.

The first car which passed by slowed and stopped thirty

meters ahead of her. It was a German military vehicle. When she reached it, the driver got out, lifted his cap and introduced himself in perfect French. She felt like blurting out, "Ah it's you, the 'pianist-winemaker,'" but stopped herself. He introduced himself as Lieutenant Johann Schräder.

"May I offer you a lift, Mademoiselle? I see that you have a puncture. I am heading towards Dijon, if that is any help to you."

"No. But thank you. And besides, that is not allowed," Marie-France said abruptly.

"There are no rules against it, unless of course you have personal objections, which I would completely understand."

Marie-France stood holding her bicycle with both hands, contemplating the lift she had been offered by a German officer. She peered down at her unsuitable shoes then gazed at her watch. It was nearly seven. She couldn't walk. It was impossible.

"Perhaps you could take me to within a few kilometres of my house. And I will walk the rest. I should not like to be noticed or found out. It would not look right amongst some people. You understand, I'm sure."

"I understand that too. I have a camouflage tarpaulin under which I'm sure you could hide if we should pass anyone on the way. I use it to cover the vehicle if I suspect enemy aircraft are passing overhead."

"Where is it?"

Lieutenant Schräder opened the rear of his car and removed a folded camouflaged sheet, holding it up for her to see before tossing it into the passenger seat. He placed his hands on his hips and smiled at her as if it were now up to her to respond. "I think that will work, no?" he said.

Marie-France nodded, and walked towards him, offering him her bicycle, which he picked up effortlessly and placed on the rear seats. He opened the passenger door for her.

"Is it your day off or something?" she asked, as he started the engine and they moved off.

"We have time off occasionally although I had business in Chalon and I now need to report to base in Dijon."

"I heard you playing the piano in that café."

"That is my real reason for travelling to Chalon. My excuse is that I am verifying the crossing point in Chalon, which I did do, in case you should be reporting on me for neglecting my duties." He laughed at his own comment.

"I won't be snitching on you, don't worry, especially as you have been kind enough to offer me a lift. Is that what you do in life? Piano playing, I mean. Or are you a military man through and through."

"No, I am not a military man, and certainly not a distinguished one. I'm not even a military man at all. I just enjoy the piano and it helps me forget where we are and what we are doing here."

"But you are an officer, so you must have had some training, some experience too."

"I did what I had to do to please my father mainly, who also went to war, the last war, although I don't believe he cares for any of this Nazi stuff either. I'm a reluctant soldier, I assure you, merely carrying out my duties and wishing that this war will end peacefully and swiftly and that I can return to Germany as soon as possible, unscathed, and having avoided killing a single Frenchman, or woman, for that matter. My wish is to leave France untouched and return home to my farm, my estate and my life before this Hitler monster took over our country and ruined everything for us." His words and the way he iterated them sounded like a chant as if he'd practised it a hundred times.

"Is that what you say to every French person you meet?"

"If they ask, yes. Because it is the truth. I am not a Nazi and I wish to have nothing to do with this war. Perhaps I am weak to have been carried along by it. Would you have escaped and run off somewhere and risked being shamed and disgraced and called a coward? I don't think so."

"Probably not."

"We are all in this, whether we choose it or not, and it is most regrettable."

"What do you do when you are at home?" Marie-France asked.

"Our family are farmers; well, more precisely, grape growers and winemakers. I'm a winemaker."

"Me too, my family too."

"What? Here in Burgundy?"

"Yes, of course. I will show you some of our vineyards on the way. We can stop if there is no one about. In fact we start the harvest tomorrow. Would you like to taste the grapes too? You'll know as well as me, if they are ripe enough to harvest."

"We grow Riesling and only Riesling in the Rheingau. You grow Pinot Noir, Chardonnay and a little Aligoté, and some Gamay in the south, if I'm right. I suppose my father will be picking soon too. We also make sweet wines, incidentally, which we harvest as late as mid-December. About ten percent of our production is late harvest. Sweet wine is fashionable in the Rheingau now, although we always used to make fine dry wines as in Alsace."

"Not in Burgundy. We only make dry wine at our estate. Premier Cru Meursault. We just happen to own mainly white wine vineyards. But I do make some Pinot Noir for a friend down the road in Chassagne and we own a little Pinot Noir vineyard in Santenay."

Marie-France turned her head briefly to take a closer look at him. She smiled and chuckled to herself. Fancy meeting the enemy in such a way. And a few years earlier he might have been a visiting wine student at Dijon University. She'd met a few of those, although she had to admit that the Burgundians were a parochial lot. As far as they were concerned, Burgundy was the only place in the world which made wine. Whatever they did in Bordeaux or the Rhône valley was of little interest to them, let alone what happened outside France.

The lieutenant suggested that German wine regions were much like that too – parochial and fiercely competitive. For the first time Marie-France began to feel relaxed, although it felt strange at first. Yet after a while he made her feel perfectly at ease. Chatting about wine with him was such a pleasure. As far as she was concerned, "wine-speak" was an internationally fluent language without borders, and brought only pleasure and fascinating exchanges of information. After all everybody had their own style to imprint on their wines beyond the basic, accepted practices. Marie-France always found it interesting to learn what others were up to in the vineyard and in the cellar. Such a bloody shame, this damn war, she thought. It was the only obstacle which seemed to divide them, and so cruelly and unnecessarily.

Marie-France asked him to slow down as her vineyards came into sight and pointed to a place to stop under the shade of a couple of old plane trees. "Let's get out. I'll walk with my bicycle from now on. But first, let's pick some grapes so we can taste them. I'm looking for the right balance of sugar and acidity … well, you know what we're looking for, don't you?"

They wandered through the vineyard together, picking and tasting individual grapes, spitting out the pips as they walked through the rows, chatting as if they'd worked these same vines together since childhood.

They reached the brow of a low hill. "Such a fine spot here, with lovely, gently rolling hills and stone walls everywhere," Johann said, waving his hand across the landscape. "The vines are such a beautiful colour too. I'm lucky to be posted here, but who knows where we will be sent next? Everybody's terrified that we'll be going to the eastern front to fight the Bolsheviks. That's a fate worse than hell, I'm told, not least in winter. I keep having these nightmares of Napoleon's troops retreating through the heavy snow, mile after mile, until each soldier, one after another, drops dead and is lost and buried in the vast, anonymous landscape of snowdrifts and iced-over rivers, to be forgotten about for ever."

"Goodness. That sounds most morose. Don't you have better dreams than that?"

Johann laughed loudly. She remarked to herself how much pleasure it had given her to make him laugh. "But you know, it was only 130 years ago. Heaven forbid that we should ever suffer that now. It was a foolish, avaricious move by Napoleon and now our 'great Führer' is leading us all down the same mortal path. Heil bloody Hitler. Such foolish hubris." He stamped his boot on the stony soil in anger.

Johann paused for a moment and looked earnestly at her. "Sorry, I should be going on my way now. I shouldn't have said that. We can be court-martialled for such insubordination to our dear Führer." Johann had spoken with such disgust that he took Marie-France by surprise, but after everything he'd been saying during their short journey in the car, it was clear that many Germans had no truck for this war, let alone for their leader. She'd heard that before but couldn't quite believe it.

They walked back to the road. He mounted and started his vehicle, and shouted above the rumble of the engine "Goodbye Marie-France. It was a pleasure to make your acquaintance."

"I know where to find you. Café de la Paix," she shouted back. He nodded and smiled. She lifted her hand to wave and then thought better of it and smiled instead.

Marie-France continued on her journey back to Saubon-le-Duc, with their encounter, their conversation, his words, spinning about her head as if it had all been a mirage. She thought of him again that night as she lay down to sleep. Such encounters were improbable, impossible, forbidden. Anyway, she thought, he'll be off and away soon. She'd never see him again.

6

After the fermentations had completed, Henri declared the 1941 Burgundy white wine harvest only "passable." It was good enough to quaff and enjoy within a year or two but no better than that. It had no chance of entering the annals of outstanding vintages.

"Luckily we aren't in red wine territory. Friends tell me that it was a tough one for Pinot Noir growers this year," Marc said. "I think we'll sell off all our Santenay to the negoçiant. Not worth putting our name on the bottle."

"We can only do our best with whatever mother nature throws at us and remember, and I think you forget Papa, that we have shortages of copper sulphate and manures, there are few horses to plough, and we can barely muster half the labour force we need to do a complete job. And now the negoçiant has told Laurent that he can only allocate a mere half of the bottles we need for him to bottle the 1940s and half the 1941 whites," Marie France said.

"What we really need is this bloody war to end and for things to return to normal," said Marc.

It was Marie-France's busiest time of the year, with the harvest often not completing until October. She could take it easy immediately afterwards while her father and brother occupied themselves with the winemaking, but in these days of shortages of everything, an extra pair of hands in the cellar was much appreciated. She'd been down to Chalon twice since meeting her winemaking-pianist, but had not spotted him. Chance encounters were the only possibility, a most unsatisfactory, but suitably cautious situation. She had talked to Antoinette of her puncture and subsequent adventure. Antoinette remained the only person to know, not that there was much to tell, let alone to incriminate her. Both knew that fraternisation with the enemy could be a risky venture but, with so few men about, the temptations remained everywhere about them. They'd witnessed many women of their age being wined and dined but assumed they'd been obliged to turn to prostitution to live the sort of life they were once accustomed to. So many had lost the financial support of their husbands that they risked severe poverty. Even for the pleasure of a generous meal, an hour or two spent chatting with a German soldier was appealing. Temptation was never far away. And there were plenty of bars and restaurants which catered exclusively to German officers and their female companions. Something to eat other than bread and soup, some male attention and a few glasses of champagne were hard to resist. It was the women who worked in the bars and cafés who remained most exposed, and in the larger towns, singers, performers and actors – anywhere where there was entertainment and a nightlife.

But Marie-France had no intention of getting caught up in such circumstances. When she thought of seeing Johann again, and that wasn't often, she considered a picnic amongst the vines or a bike ride into the Côtes, somewhere far away, and beyond the gaze of prying eyes. Meanwhile she would occupy herself with the life she'd chosen. The busy task of pruning the vines would soon be upon them and that could last well into late February.

Her brother had lent her the small van on occasions to collect and drop off vineyard workers when the weather became too cold for them to cycle to work. She made a point of passing by the café on a number of occasions using the same vehicle. On one such journey into Chalon she spotted a vehicle similar to the one Johann had been driving. She parked outside the Café du Paix, hoping to see him. Then again she wondered how wise she was being. Could such actions awaken suspicions? He was playing the piano so she ordered a drink and sat at a table nearby. She took a few sips of wine but, without Antoinette to talk to, she began to feel awkward. She lit a cigarette and drew on it heavily. How could she let Johann know she was there waiting for him? An immediate feeling of guilt overcame her. This is so inappropriate, and so wrong, she thought. What would Papa think, let alone Maman? It would be best if she left. It was an impossible situation. She got up from her chair, inadvertently knocking it to the floor in her haste. Johann stopped playing, turned around and smiled as if he knew she was there all the while. Marie-France paid for her drink, bid the barman adieu, and walked out.

She sat in her van finishing her cigarette, feeling stupid and wondering what to do next. At least it was dark now and there was less of a chance of being recognised. But with so few people about, familiarity would soon be hard to hide. She should be making the most of the long, dark November nights – but how and where would they ever meet again? And she didn't fancy hanging around on street corners like a whore. It was too risky. Someone might spot her.

Johann came out of the café, nodded at her as if to say farewell, and got into his car. Marie-France started her engine and headed off towards the road out of town. A pair of headlights not far behind her reassured her that he was following. She stopped just beyond Chagny in the same lay by they'd stopped at before, under the plane trees. She spied him in her rear mirror, removing his cap, straightening his hair and then getting out of his car. She lowered her window and he peered in.

"I'm low on fuel. That's why I've stopped," Marie-France said, in a trembling, barely audible voice.

"Yes, of course. That's an excellent reason for stopping, but the official reason is that you have broken down and you have stopped me to ask for a helping hand. I'm repairing your vehicle. Let's open your bonnet. And I'd better sit in the driving seat with a puzzled look on my face." She laughed at his unexpected pragmatism. Perhaps he'd already rehearsed the scenario a hundred times.

They sat together in her van in the darkness, an unusual situation for both of them, they admitted, and laughed about it before either of them spoke.

"I'm glad you stopped. I'm assuming you wanted to see me if that is not too bold a presumption," said Johann.

"I missed hearing the piano. We have one at home, but no one plays these days." It was the best answer she had for him under the circumstances.

"Is this how people have to meet during a war? I suppose it is," Johann said.

"Only because you are supposed to be the enemy."

"Do I feel like the enemy to you?"

"No. Apart from your uniform, which I think suits you, by the way."

"It's not really me though, is it? Picture me in some dirty trousers, a sweaty shirt, a sun hat and a pair of secateurs in my hand, if you can. That's me," Johann said, smiling.

"I know, but it only makes it so much harder. We could be close friends, and yet there's such a high price to pay."

"I must force myself not to think of you. But I'm as lonely as you are when we are not in each other's company," Johann said.

"I honestly can't decide if that's a good thing. My sensible side says I should not even look at, let alone talk to the enemy. My other side says something else."

Johann leaned towards her. "What does it say?"

"I think I should be going now. I have to be careful how far I travel. Fuel is hard to come by. But this is one way to meet, if you really want to continue meeting."

"I have a fuel can in the rear. We always keep a spare. Don't worry. I'll top you up just enough for it not to look too suspicious."

"But how do I communicate? How do I know when you will be at the bar?"

"I will make a point of being there Mondays and Fridays, 5 p.m. How about that?"

"But that makes it too regular, too suspicious and too much like a rendezvous. Everything must be spontaneous. I will have a think. I'll decide on a better plan, but we can try next Monday."

"Hopefully then." Johann clasped her hand briefly.

A small truck passed by, slowing as it passed and then accelerating away swiftly. Marie-France got out of her vehicle while Johann collected the canister of fuel to fill her up.

"Will it always be like this every time we meet? I feel nervous and on edge, wondering who might have spotted us. I hope not. I hope no one recognised my van. It's a worry, isn't it?"

7

A loud knock at the door wakened Marie-France. She sat up abruptly.

"Where are you? You're late. What's going on? You've missed breakfast."

It was already 9 a.m., daylight streamed through a gap in the curtains, and Marie-France had overslept. "I won't be long, Pa," she said.

"It's not the first time you've overslept this month. What's wrong with you? It's the tenth day of December. We're starting the pruning in the 'Les Charmes' vineyard, remember?"

The days had got colder. They were in for another hard winter, she was sure of it. Getting up in the morning had got tougher and working in the vineyard required determination and stamina. Winter had hardly begun and yet she wished for it to end. At least they had the cuttings in the vineyard to burn to keep them warm but she could only make use of their heat during the breaks. They filled braziers at the end of every dozen or so rows and huddled around them at frequent intervals to warm their hands, drinking a warm tea with a splash of grape brandy added. Those who weren't wearing gloves were worse off, but didn't seem to care. It was long, repetitive work, which left your hands aching at the end of a day. It was the task Marie-France liked least, but it was important work and its accuracy and precision determined the success of the following vintage, as long as mother nature also played her part.

She had heard nothing of Jean, not so much as a rumour, nor a letter. Apart from a few locals of her own age whom she met in nearby Meursault or Puligny, her better friends had become those with whom she shared her day – her vineyard team. During the long, dark evenings she played cards with Eloise and Marc, who occasionally invited friends for a drink or, if Marc had shot a few rabbits, he invited neighbours for supper. They lived as much as they could off the land. Their staples were rabbit, pigeon and occasionally woodcock and quail. Her mother tended a vegetable garden behind the kitchen, well protected from frost and pests behind a high stone wall, where they also grew soft fruits and kept a few chickens in a coop along the back wall. Marie-France looked after the apple, pear and cherry trees in the orchard beyond, and at this time of the year, a few well stored apples or pears off the fruit storage trays in the barn were a treat. Much of rural France lived like this, war or no war. The major cities suffered the most from the shortages because they had nothing to grow themselves, but everyone lacked the most treasured, imported goods such as tobacco, sugar, tea and coffee, and of course fuel and coal for home heating. Many suffered from the cold during the particularly harsh winters of 1940/41 and 1941/42. The Champuix had plenty of firewood from their forested land to warm the house in winter, with the sawing and splitting taking up a large part of the day. Much of the wood was given to staff and helpers during the winter as a gesture of gratitude for the year's work. The Champuix could never be accused of being poor employers. To the contrary, they were considered generous and compassionate.

One morning in mid-December their breakfast was disturbed by the arrival in the courtyard of two German army motorcyclists followed by an open-top lorry with a dozen troops seated in its rear. A staff car followed, with a driver and an accompanying officer. Henri Champuix opened the front door and walked out onto the front steps.

The officer spoke first. "Good morning, I'm sorry to disturb you, sir. We have instructions to search all farmhouses, barns and outhouses in the area. We are looking for three Resistance fighters. Have you seen them? I should remind you that if any are found on your premises, you will all be arrested and risk deportation to Germany."

Marie-France immediately recognised the stark and purposeful voice, and shuddered at the thought. This was her winemaker-piano player in action, which authority, orders and duty had transformed into someone completely different. And yet he was polite and business-like. He then spoke in German, presumably giving orders to his troops. She heard the clatter of heavy boots on the cobblestones through the open front door.

Marc went to the front door and spoke up. "What if these boys are found and we did not know anything about it? It's impossible to keep an eye on all our barns and land every minute of the day. Besides what did these Resistance people do?"

"It is your duty to guard all of your property in such circumstances and to be aware of strangers and stowaways. Do you know where they are?" Lieutenant Schräder asked again.

Marc raised his voice. "No, sir, I do not. I've never seen any Resistance fighters. We are grape growers and winemakers here, simply carrying out our daily tasks. This is Burgundy, for heavens sakes. We make famous wines here."

"Please, we do not want any trouble," Henri said.

At that point Marie-France appeared at the front door. Lieutenant Schräder blinked and stood upright when he saw her but otherwise managed to disguise his surprise at encountering her. He doffed his cap and apologised for the disturbance once more then turned to his troops and barked an instruction.

"I have asked my men to be thorough but at the same time to

respect your belongings. Nothing is to be overturned or damaged. You may accompany us if you wish. First, please, we wish to search the house, and the cellar and attics too."

"What have these people done? Are they dangerous? How should we approach them?" Marie-France asked.

"I may as well inform you, as you will hear soon enough. They are responsible for derailing a troop train south of Lyon. They were captured and interrogated but escaped while being transported to Lyon for execution. The punishment is the death penalty by means of a firing squad for such offences against the Wehrmacht. One and possibly two more are thought to be heading home to Dijon, which is why we are searching all this area."

Marie-France drew a short breath and remained speechless for a second, hunching her shoulders, wrapping her cardigan more tightly about her, then placing her hands in her pockets. The hunter and the hunted. She knew the former but perhaps she knew both of them. No, it couldn't really be Jean. She replied as appropriately as she could.

"We will be prudent, then." She smiled briefly and walked back into the house.

"My apologies for the inconvenience, mademoiselle," Lieutenant Schräder said, but he wasn't sure if she'd heard him.

Marie-France made herself scarce whilst Lieutenant Schräder carried out his duties, commanding his troops into one room after the other, finishing with the barns and the winery and adjoining sheds. While he was peering into each of the vats, he announced to Henri that he was a winemaker back home. A short but civil conversation ensued. By the end of the search Henri found himself shaking hands with the German officer who'd also professed a great enthusiasm for the wines of Burgundy.

"I look forward to tasting your wines one day. Let us pray for better times," Lieutenant Schräder said upon mounting his vehicle.

They left the courtyard leaving behind a cloud of oily-blue exhaust.

"You were very polite to him, Pa," Marc said later.

"He was to me too. Did you catch that he was a winemaker himself? There is a friendship to be found even amongst the enemy, extraordinary as that might sound to you. Besides he was most considerate. I have heard of others suffering a lot of damage and unpleasantness with these searches. I consider that we were lucky. We could have suffered a right old ransacking."

"Perhaps so, but he's still a bloody Boche, isn't he?"

That night Marie-France walked out into the darkness, circling the courtyard and then out into the barns and the winery, unlocking and then locking each door as she passed through. She sat down on a bench in the workers' sleeping quarters and lit a cigarette. If Jean would sleep anywhere at the domaine, it would be here, somewhere familiar, somewhere he might even consider his home. She walked in silence around the premises, although she had a great desire to shout out his name, but decided it would be foolish. No one else in the family had seemed to consider whether Jean might be one of the two or three on the run. But then again, perhaps she was simply being fanciful. If this whole incident today had proved one thing, it was that she still cared for Jean. And above all she missed his laughter, his gaiety and his enthusiasm for life.

8

Jean was nowhere to be found. Night after night Marie-France checked the outhouses for any signs of him. Now that it had snowed, he was unlikely to risk leaving his footprints in the vicinity for anyone to follow. After a week, she came to the conclusion that the one place he would never come to was Domaine de Champuix. It made perfect sense. He would never risk implicating them all. He knew the penalty for harbouring a Resistance fighter, knowingly or not. She pondered the fact that she'd truly lost him, at least for now, and even considered that he might never return. The odds of surviving doing what he did, had to be less than fifty-fifty. One day she'd hear the awful news that his body had been found in a ditch, cruelly tortured, so bruised that he was barely recognisable as the Jean she once knew. That sort of thing was happening increasingly. And for what? Wasn't it better to keep your head down and get on with one's daily life like her brother Marc, who from time to time stole fuel or broke into German warehouses for food. These were minor infractions, which if he were careful would frustrate the enemy but reduce the risk of being caught unless you were unfortunate.

She thought of Johann too, who appeared to be doing much the same thing – tolerating an equally detestable and heinous situation in which he wished to play no part and in which he did not believe. She equated his vilification of fascism and Nazism to that of Jean's similar revulsion for it. Was Johann such a bad person because he'd been caught up by the Nazi draft and forced into serving in the Wehrmacht? She'd read of far worse people, real Nazis who worked for the Gestapo or the SS regiments. They were the real, fanatical enemy. Even her father had seen through Johann's uniform, aided almost certainly by Johann's genuine interest in the wines of Burgundy and their shared career choices as family winemakers.

"Even Germans in uniform can be courteous and well-mannered," he told his children later. "That officer caught me by surprise. He was educated and knowledgeable too. And his French was impeccable. It is a great shame that we are at war with people like that."

"Yes, I think you're right. I don't think he cared for what he was doing at all," Eloise said. "He'd rather have been doing what we're doing, just getting on with our lives and making wine, don't you think? I thought he was rather attractive. I'd have gone out for a drink with him if he'd taken his uniform off."

Marc laughed. "Don't tell Ma that, she'll kill you."

Marie-France kept her mouth shut, but she managed a smile and a nod. Only one person in the Champuix household, Marie-France's mother, Clémence, would not hear of the Germans being spoken of in the house. Her only brother's death at the battle of Verdun after a particularly fearsome German bombardment on the French line a few weeks before Christmas 1916 – the battle's 25th anniversary was almost upon them – could never be forgotten nor forgiven. Her loathing of the Germans endured and she remained forthrightly unrepentant.

If Marie-France's sister thought Johann was attractive, then perhaps he must be. She even said so. She knew it was a ridiculously spurious pretext for allowing her feelings to wander. But Eloise had barely ever shown a flicker of desire for any man and now she'd willingly go out for a drink with Johann. It was absurd, Eloise had always had high standards, but to be fair she barely knew the man. It was simply a fatuous first impression.

Marie-France saw Johann once more before Christmas, combining their encounter with a drink with Antoinette at the Café du Paix beforehand. She informed her father she needed to collect a few hundred rootstocks from their supplier outside Chalon and borrowed the small company lorry for the purpose. She decided to confide in Antoinette by revealing her affections for Johann. She badly needed someone to talk to about him and hoped Antoinette might be a reliable barometer. She began by confirming that she believed she'd lost Jean forever. There was no chance of him returning and anyway she'd now found an affection for Johann. If Antoinette was surprised at Marie-France's new found desire for their winemaking-pianist in uniform, she didn't show it.

"I'm not condoning it, but ordinarily I would," Antoinette said. It was the best she could come up with in that moment. "Let's get another drink before we go on."

"You don't approve uniquely because of the circumstances?"

"Yes, that's correct. The circumstances. Otherwise, I would. You could get yourself into terrible trouble if you got caught. Think of how it will affect your parents, the family business, the family name, let alone the misery and indignity you will go through yourself. You'd have to leave here. Is it really worth it?"

"But if we don't get caught, and are extra vigilant? There'll be no fraternisation at all in public. All will take place under a veil of secrecy, to be revealed when this war ends."

"I think you're being naïve. Are you really that bored and desperate? There are other decent boys around, aren't there? Why him? I mean, I kind of get it. He's very handsome, his family do what you do, he says he's not a Nazi, he's obviously had the same sort of education as you, he seems very gentlemanly and you seem relaxed when I've seen you with him, which isn't often to be frank.

You probably have other things in common too. But, but, but." Antoinette lifted her hands, then clasped her head and looked Marie-France straight in the eyes.

"So you wouldn't see him any more? It's different for you though. You've got someone. I'm lonely. I don't have anyone. There's not much love at home, you know. I want a man to do things with. I need a man. And I don't get on with Ma like you do with your mother. I can't talk to her about it. I'm Papa's girl and Ma knows that. I think she's often jealous of me. Pa much prefers spending time with me than her. And besides I want something more going on in my life. I'm bored and fed up. I need excitement, something to get up for."

Antoinette leant across the table. "You'd certainly have an adventure with him. But where are you going to hide out? In cold, old abandoned barns, frolicking about in the damp hay with all the rats scuttling about you. How romantic is that?"

"A hotel is out of the question unless we elope and head for somewhere no one knows us. But I don't suppose he has time off like that," Marie-France said.

"A romantic weekend up in the Savoie somewhere. No. It's all too whimsical to me. I'm sorry, darling, but I don't think it's a good idea however much you crave him. And he is delicious, I grant you that, but even so. And how do you know he even wants you?"

"Because we've talked a lot. It's obvious. But he no doubt has the same reservations as me. He's not stupid. He needs to be careful too."

As Marie-France finished speaking, Johann ended the piece he was playing. She hoped this would be an opportunity to engage.

"Do I have any requests?" he said, turning on the stool and glancing towards them.

"Yes, a few Beethoven sonatas," Marie-France said without hesitating.

Antoinette left the café shortly afterwards, leaving her friend to enjoy Johann's piano playing.

Marie-France went up to the bar, sat down on a stool and ordered another drink.

"You're the Champuix girl, aren't you, the one who works in the vineyards?" the barman said.

"Yes. You want some of our wines?" Marie-France replied, smiling.

"Could do. What price?"

"Whites only, same price as the one you're serving, I expect. Ours is just as good. The standard Bourgogne Blanc, I suppose." Marie-France glanced towards Johann. "Do you pay that German piano player? He's very good. He's always in here, isn't he."

"You mean, Johann. No, we don't pay him, but I let him play when he wants as long as its Chopin or Debussy. We don't want any German stuff, not that I'd know. He's a good guy. Very friendly. I don't really see him as the enemy. He told me he just wants this war to end, like we all do. He says they're billeting him elsewhere soon. After Christmas, I believe. Do you play? We'll need a new piano player soon."

Marie-France didn't think to answer the barman's question, but she wasn't going to play the piano for him. Instead, she paid her bill and told him she'd drop off a free sample bottle for him to try after Christmas, turning to glance towards Johann as she left.

There was still snow on the road in parts, but she was in no hurry and drove cautiously, the headlights lighting up a lonely path in the darkness ahead of her. A fox froze in the headlights then crossed over into the woods and disappeared, but otherwise there was little to see, the traffic at this time being mercifully light. She stopped on the side of the road in their familiar location and waited, allowing the engine to run to keep her warm. She went over that afternoon's conversation with Antoinette while she waited, at one point wondering whether she shouldn't continue on her journey. She shifted into first gear and started off. As she did so, a pair of headlights loomed up behind her.

A man wearing the familiar uniform of a German officer walked up to her and greeted her. She pulled down the window. "I'm sorry I kept you waiting. I have some brandy to warm us." He reached for the bottle in his overcoat and showed it to her. He stretched out his other hand into her cab and wrapped his arm around her shoulder briefly.

"That'll be nice." Marie-France hesitated and smiled before continuing. "I think you should follow me. We're too visible here and I'm driving the company lorry this time. I could be seen. There's a track through the vineyards just up here on the right, and there's a dense copse we can hide in."

This time Johann joined her in the cab. He removed his cap but it was too cold for him to remove his overcoat. Marie-France was wearing two wool sweaters, a short sheepskin coat, gloves and a bonnet which covered most of her hair. As she removed her gloves, he clasped each of her hands in his to warm them. "Here, take a swig of this," Johann said, removing the cork from the bottle with his teeth. He moved himself closer to her so that they were pressing up against each other.

"Oooh, that feels good." Marie-France handed him back the bottle and he helped himself. "I know what you are going to say. You're being sent away, aren't you?"

Johann looked surprised. "I was going to tell you, but not right away. It's too depressing." He took another slug of the brandy.

"Nothing much to lose then, if you're disappearing next week." Marie-France said, and kissed him on the cheek. She then sat back and stared at him. He placed both his hands around her head and drew her to him. He kissed her tenderly, then she leant back into his arms.

"Hold me tight, don't let me go. I want to feel you all around me. I'm so dreadfully sorry you are leaving. Do you have to go? I hope they don't send you anywhere horrible."

"I might be leaving but it doesn't mean 'goodbye.' I know where you are. I will find you again one day."

"War is so cruel. I've already lost someone. I don't want to lose you too."

"Here, have another swig of this," said Johann.

Marie-France undid the buttons of her coat, sat up and rubbed her cheek against his. She grabbed his hand and placed it on her breast. "Hold me tightly. Very tight." They embraced again, this time more fervently.

"You will be at home for Christmas, I suppose," Johann said.

"Yes. You are invited to join us."

He laughed. "Thank you. I can't though. I presume you are joking. That would be impossible."

"You have the invitation. I know you can't come. All my wishes would come true if you could. Peace tomorrow. You for Christmas. Haha." Marie-France reached into her coat pocket for a handkerchief and blew into it daintily. She leant her head into Johann's chest and warmed her hands between his thighs. "I'm at the bar again just after Christmas. I said I'd drop them off a sample bottle of our wine. It's much better than the one they serve at the moment. Let's agree a day and time to meet. Is that possible?"

"I expect so. Let's say 4 p. m. on Thursday at the bar and or 5 p. m. here. Wait, if I'm not around."

*

They met again at the bar on the appointed day and time, and reconvened later in the copse by the vineyard.

"We leave tomorrow. We are heading for Metz, but I

don't know more than that. I fear the regiment will head east. Reinforcements are needed. I've brought something to eat and drink. Our last supper, some cheese, bread. I'm afraid I don't have much time."

"How much time?" Marie-France asked.

"One hour at most."

Marie-France led him to the back of the lorry, opened the doors and gestured to him to step up into the rear. She removed her coat, threw it to the floor, lay down on it and invited him to join her.

"We need to be careful, if we are to go the whole way," Johann said, as he started to undress her.

"I know. We don't want an accident. I'm very certain I'm at my least fertile at the moment. But I can never be completely sure."

"You are perfectly sure?"

"Yes and no. I can't guarantee one hundred percent, but I'm fairly certain. Shall we not risk it?

"We will risk it. I will try to withdraw at the right moment," Johann said, and continued undressing her.

Marie-France then undressed him slowly, and taking their time, they made love, laughing at the plumes of condensation which their warm breaths generated in the freezing, humid air. They lay there in each other's arms without saying a word, listening to the frequent gusts of wind brushing and whistling through the pines around them. Johann covered them both with his coat, but eventually the cold got to them.

"One more time," Johann said. "Let's enjoy one more time." They made love once more, this time more vigorously.

"Let's dress. It's too cold, isn't it? Marie-France said, after they'd lain in each other's arms for several minutes. "Just a moment. I'll light this lamp and brush you down. I washed out the rear this afternoon but I expect it is still dusty and we don't want your uniform looking a mess." She lit the lamp. "Let's have a look. You need to straighten your tie. Otherwise you look fine." She patted his back and brushed some straw off his arms.

"I'm not one for long goodbyes," Johann said. "It only makes leaving worse."

"Here, I have something for you to keep." Marie-France produced a small photograph which her father had taken of her working in the vineyards the year before. Johann gave her a long hug, kissed the photograph and placed it into his breast pocket. They jumped out of the back of the lorry and Johann walked towards his car. They embraced one last time and he set off down the track. Marie-France waited ten minutes and then drove off slowly, keeping the revs deliberately low. When she reached the main road, a motorcycle passed her and slowed. She decided to act as if nothing were out of the ordinary and continued on her way following the motorcycle. She soon realised that it was her brother, Marc. Marie-France had ten minutes to prepare a set of answers for the likely interrogation which would ensue once they reached the house.

"What were you doing down that lane?" Marc said when they were home.

"Probably the same thing you were doing in Chalon or wherever you were," Marie-France said.

"I won't tell our parents if you won't," Marc said.

"Why, what were you doing which was so bad, Marc? Are you hiding something?"

"Nothing important."

"I didn't know you had a girlfriend."

"Not exactly a girlfriend. A girl, yes. A starving girl. Not someone Maman would approve of. But keep it to yourself. Since you're being so secretive, were you with Jean?"

"Yes. I was with Jean. With Jean. Not a word, I forbid you, right?"

9

In February 1942, Otto von Stülpnagel resigned as the overall German military commander of France and was replaced by his cousin Carl-Heinrich. The former had objected to the increasing reach of the Gestapo and its programme of mass executions. He believed it was better to manage the French people with a lighter hand, for example by relaxing the rules regarding the crossing of the Demarcation Line, which had caused so much misery. The appointment of his cousin by contrast heralded a time of greater violence and tumult.

The months after Christmas were not an easy time for Marie-France. By the end of February, she had begun to feel sick in the mornings. On informing Antoinette at one of their rendezvous at the Café du Paix in Chalon, it became clear to Marie France that she might be pregnant, although such a thought had never occurred to her until that day.

"You did it with the piano player, didn't you?" Antoinette asked.

"Why do you automatically assume I'm pregnant?"

"Because if you've been waking every morning for the last few weeks and feeling sick, it's called morning sickness and it's commonly related to pregnancy, that's why."

"But I thought we were being so careful."

"You did, then? You slept with that German officer."

"Yes. I slept with Johann, but from now on, if I really am

pregnant, it is Jean's child. Do you hear me, Antoinette? I slept with Jean. The child is Jean's. Are you clear about that?"

"I am. But don't tell anyone else who the real father is. It's not something to be proud of, and you'll be doomed if anyone finds out."

"I'm not stupid. I won't be telling anyone. I'll go to the doctor just to be sure."

"We need to have a chat about what you're going to do. I'll order us some more wine at the bar. That doesn't do any harm but I'd stop smoking if I were you. Some people say it starves the baby's brain of oxygen and stunts the foetus's growth. A wise mother once told me that, so I'd advise you to stop both smoking and drinking."

"Keep your voice down, for God's sake."

"I suggest you make an appointment to see the doctor next week or in a few weeks if the sickness continues. I can recommend you one here. Don't go to your family doctor as the word will get around far too quickly."

Marie-France cycled home that afternoon in a daze. If she really was pregnant, how was she to let Johann know? Would he want to know? The child would probably never know its father. The thought of that made her weep. Tears streamed across her face as she raced home battling the headwind. And what would she do about her parents – strict, upright Catholics? It wasn't as if she were ready to marry Jean. She guessed that would only make it worse in her parent's eyes. Their reaction would be blunt and unforgiving. The thought of it was too much to bear but she'd have to tell them before her pregnancy became noticeable. Feeling nauseous she dismounted when she reached a crossroads, and rushed to the ditch at the side of the road, leant into it and was promptly sick. She sat by the side of the road to compose herself, but her stomach ached and her body felt weary. She had to force herself to get up and continue the journey.

Marie-France was dreading her visit to the doctor. Antoinette had arranged it and agreed to accompany her. They'd planned to meet at the café first, and walk to the surgery from there. On the way, Antoinette went over all the questions which Dr. Fortant might ask her, some of which she warned, might be intrusive and embarrassing. And how much of the truth was she prepared to reveal?

"You can use my address, not the domaine, although the doctor will surely know your name. But what can you do?"

"Thank you. I'm not sure how honest to be with him."

"Be prepared to tell him when the date of conception was. That's the first point. These days with all that's going on, they'll hopefully not insist in knowing who the father is and I would just say "Jean" if you have to give a name. You can say he's in the Resistance and doesn't want to reveal any details. Some doctors are sympathetic to that. But you never know. A lot of doctors are Vichy sympathisers and that might bring out a lot of legal shit. Let's hope he doesn't report you."

"Do you know this doctor?"

"No. I've never met him."

"I thought you said you knew a doctor."

"I think the more anonymous the better. Don't you?"

It was thirteen weeks since Marie-France had slept with Johann. They reached the surgery and sat with two young women in the waiting room, both accompanied by their mothers.

When she was called in, Marie-France sat with a nurse and provided the details she'd already rehearsed, including her name, address and profession. The nurse then disappeared into another room. Marie-France, tearful, looked across at Antoinette.

"All will be fine. Try not to worry," Antoinette whispered.

Eventually the doctor entered, introduced himself without smiling, and went over and sat behind his desk. "So you're three months or more pregnant."

"Yes, thirteen weeks, I believe," Marie-France said.

"A few questions. Have you missed any of your periods?"

"Yes."

The doctor wrote a few words in his notes. "Are your breasts tender or sore? And have you been feeling nausea or sickness? They are all early symptoms of pregnancy."

"All of those symptoms, yes. I'm feeling both of those symptoms."

"You can have a urine test if you wish but it'll be expensive."

"No, I don't want any tests."

"Any excessive fatigue, mood swings or food cravings?"

"Yes. Sometimes. When will I start showing a bump?"

"Generally after about eighteen weeks. That would be mid-May in your case, but it can be earlier." The doctor scribbled down a few more notes. "And how do you want to manage this?"

"What do you mean?"

"For example, where do you want the baby delivered? At home in Chalon? These days we have maternity wards in hospitals, even in Beaune. Some people prefer that. How are we to register the birth certificate? The child will need a family name."

"I'll have to think about that."

"You certainly will, Miss, especially since your story hardly adds up. You say that you are a single woman. Are you aware of the law in that regard? I'll clarify it for you."

"Thank you."

"Although we are presently just within the occupied zone, there is talk of the Vichy introducing new family legislation in April. If you should decide to travel south, it will apply to you. That law becomes effective in a few weeks' time. A few things you should know. First, abandoning the family unit is punishable by a prison sentence. Secondly, married women committing adultery is a breach of the law … the wives of our current prisoners of war for example who might entertain the idea of an affair are likely to fall under the Vichy spotlight. That will be punishable by law. And thirdly, divorce during the first three years of marriage won't be allowed, even for adultery. And as for abortion, our Vichy government decreed on 15th February that it will be a crime of treason against the State."

"I see," Marie-France nodded. "Is that all?"

They returned to the café for a pastis. She'd already decided that the doctor was a "ghastly, puritanical, fascist pig" when he was interviewing her, and she used the same words to describe him again when discussing the appointment afterwards with Antoinette.

"So abortion is out of the question," Marie-France said.

"Have you considered abortion? It's illegal but it's worth considering."

"It's a bit late for that now I've registered with that nasty doctor. He'd most likely report me."

"I wouldn't worry about him. I don't think he was nasty, he was just brutally honest, impersonal and not in the least compassionate. There are ways around all of that legal stuff, I'm sure. He probably sees quite a few pregnant women. He'll be repeating the same old mantra to all of them."

"He made me feel like I was a prostitute, insinuating that I was comparable to the 800,000 desperate, man-less housewives of our POW soldiers."

"Anyway. I'm afraid it's the price you pay. So what next?" Antoinette said.

"I'll have to tell the parents. Eloise first, then Maman and then Papi. I don't think Marc will care."

10

At breakfast towards the last few days of April 1942, a family crisis erupted, which continued well beyond breakfast – the turmoil filling the whole day and spilling over into lunch and dinner and into the night. Henri Champuix announced gravely to the family that the letter "C" had been daubed in red, twice, one on each entrance gate of the Domaine de Champuix, and that someone, somewhere was under suspicion of collaborating with the enemy.

"We have been accused of being collaborators. Go and see for yourself if you don't believe me. Laurent is out in the road painting over the mess. I will get to the bottom of this. And if any of you know why or have the slightest suspicions, I should like to know. And are we all accused collectively or is it just one of us they're targeting? I need to know that too. Any ideas or suspicions, and I should like to know, please."

Clémence picked up her coffee and walked towards the door announcing she was returning to her bedroom and did not wish to be disturbed for the rest of the day.

"Poor Maman, she looks so shocked. And on top of the news of your pregnancy last week, it's too much for her," Eloise said, staring at Marie-France. "Is this all because of who you slept with, Marie-France?"

Henri rose from the table. "Enough. Enough. I will not have such talk in the house. If there are things which I need to know, you will come to me first and discuss it. Is that understood? I will have no direct accusations against members of the family, especially without the slightest evidence or proof."

Marc cleared his throat. "Let's be clear, the Maquis aren't going to punish us because of Marie-France's dalliance with Jean who by all accounts is a member of the Resistance anyway. They couldn't care less whether she's married or not, although I expect that's Maman's problem, what with all her Catholic stuff. Something else is going on. And sometimes they make mistakes. Apparently two other houses were stigmatised in the village last night. News will soon get around. Most likely it has nothing to do with us."

"Nevertheless, we remain a marked house," said Henri.

Marie-France returned to her bedroom and sat on the edge of her bed. She held her head between her hands. "What am I to do? What am I to do?" she whispered to herself. Was it the doctor spreading malicious gossip about a suspicious pregnancy, or Antoinette who'd denounced her in disgust? She'd heard of friends turning on friends and accusations erupting out of petty vendettas among rival families. People did it for money too. Out of hunger and desperation. It had become common enough. Or had Marc spotted Johann's car pulling out of that mud track? But at least he'd stuck up for her earlier. If he knew, he wasn't going to betray his sister. But someone knew. Or perhaps it was nothing to do with her. Could it have been Marc who was guilty, fraternising too enthusiastically with the Germans and their prostitutes? Maybe it was both of them. Her main concern was that someone had spotted her with Johann. But no one could prove it, surely. No one. She was certain of that. No one knew but Antoinette. Only two people knew that Marie-France had brought shame upon her family – herself, Antoinette and the person who'd chosen to report her, if that were not Antoinette. And whoever they were, they'd surely acted with a firm conviction and a determined sense of purpose. "Surely no one would want to cause me so much misery," she whispered.

She felt the same way in the morning. "No one does that to me. No one does that to me," she whispered repeatedly although she wanted to shout it out loud. "I'll leave. Best that I leave. I can't stay here any longer. Things will only get worse. Dear Papa will never forgive me," she said to herself. She began to make a pile of the essentials she would take with her: the book she was reading, the framed family photograph on her bedside table, a diary, warm clothes, her identity card, ration book, a small bag of toiletries and some food, which she raided from the larder in the kitchen. And lastly, she picked up a stash of bank notes which she'd kept at the back of her cupboard. Her plan was to cycle to Antoinette's, cross the Demarcation Line somehow, and then head for her grandparents in Lyon. She had to hope that they would let her in. Phoning them from home was too risky. She would then give birth to the baby in Lyon and live there with them. It was the only realistic plan.

Marie-France walked out of the house before daybreak, her belongings strapped to her back in an old hiking sack of her fathers. She peddled out of the hamlet onto the main road to Chalon and didn't look back. She'd woken early that morning fired up with a sense of determination to carry out her plan as best she could. She found herself thinking for the first time about the future of the unborn child she was carrying and the sort of life they were going to live. There were two of them now and she'd strive to provide the best for both of them. She acknowledged feelings of anger too, although she wasn't absolutely clear where they were coming from or against whom they should be directed, or why – perhaps a sense of injustice and frustration. Yes, she was angry with the absurd social conventions, the bigoted moral attitudes, the short-sightedness, the intolerance, the inability to see beyond the obvious. And above all the frustrations and impediments which the war inflicted upon personal lives. All of those feelings propelled her southwards that morning with a cool, gentle breeze at her back.

She reached Antoinette's house, the knock at the door catching Antoinette by surprise so early in the morning. She hadn't got dressed yet and peered through the window to see who it might be. Her husband, François, had already left for work at the iron works and she was busy clearing the remains of his breakfast such as it was.

"I can offer you my mother's jam and one piece of bread, and a strange tasting coffee," she said, before questioning why Marie-France had arrived so early at her house. Having described her circumstances, Marie-France asked how easy it was to find someone to help her cross the Demarcation Line without the necessary pass. She'd thought of stealing her father's tradesman's pass but that would only have made a bad situation worse. And what was she trading? Freedom?

"I won't stay long, but I need somewhere to stay. I feel like a fugitive now and it's something I'm finding really hard to get used to," Marie-France said. At that point she broke down and sobbed uncontrollably. "Oh my God, what have I done? Everything's such a mess. A terrible mess. What am I to do? It's desperate. My whole life as I've known it has gone. It's disappearing every minute of the day."

Antoinette placed her hands under Marie-France's armpits and lifted her out of her seat to hug her. She wrapped her arms around her, and held her tightly as she might a child. "You're going to be okay. Remember, you're such a resourceful, resilient girl. You always have been, and now you'll need to be so more than ever. If anyone can do this, it's you. I've never, ever needed to worry about you. You're such a strong, brave person."

Marie-France slumped back into her chair, still sobbing. "But I've suddenly realised I've lost all my freedom. D'you know what I mean? I'm being hunted like a doe. I'll have to hide away for months, possibly years in a deep, dark forest. I can't bear thinking about it. It's horrible." She wiped her tears away with her hands.

"And what's even worse, I'm pregnant. I'm pregnant. And what about my baby? What a life for my baby. I can't believe this is happening to me."

"It'll all be over soon. All you did was sleep with a lovely man who happens to be a German soldier. Perhaps you're missing him too. That's nothing to feel guilty about. You're such a purist. I know you wouldn't have done any of this unless you truly believed in him. I know that because Jean was your first, your one and only. You never exactly slept around, did you? Never, ever."

Marie-France nodded. "Do you think I'll see either of them again? They're soldiers, they're right in the midst of battle. And what's even worse, they're fighting each other. How crazy is that? How can they both possibly escape a soldier's death?" She wiped her eyes on her sleeve. "Poor bastards. What is all this for?"

"Let's get you settled. I'll make up a bed for you. We'll need to hide your bike. We'll park it inside. I'm sure François won't mind for a few days."

"I think Grand-père has a telephone. I need to contact them. I need to know that they'll have me and the baby. You know I plan to stay with them? They don't know that though. They have a big house in town. They've got a basement. I'll have the baby there. No one will come for us there. I can hide away in Lyon until this war is over. I'll tell them that the baby is Jean's. That's what I told my parents too. But someone obviously believes they know otherwise or they wouldn't have painted those big red 'C's on the gate"

"I wouldn't worry now about who betrayed you. The important thing is to get you to somewhere safe. Then you can have your baby in relative peace. François and I will put out some feelers to get you across the line, along with your bicycle and luggage. You can trust François, I'm sure of it. I already have an idea about how to cross. Probably not over the river here though. It's too well patrolled."

Antoinette went into the centre of town to the post office and put in a call to Hervé Champuix. She was brief and to the point, following the instructions Marie-France had suggested, explaining that their granddaughter would be arriving by the end of the week, most likely by Friday evening. To every question which was asked, she replied that Marie-France would be able to inform them upon her arrival. She also suggested that it would be kinder to Marie-France if they were not to make further enquiries with her parents and to wait to hear what their granddaughter had to say first.

When Antoinette returned and confirmed the conversation she had had with her grandfather, Marie-France expressed her gratitude, certain in the knowledge that Antoinette could not have betrayed her. "You're a good friend, I won't forget how you've helped me out," Marie-France said.

The following afternoon Marie-France crossed the Demarcation Line over the bridge at Chalon-sur-Saône showing a forged day pass to the border guards. François had decided it was much the easiest and surest way across since, for a small sum, he could easily acquire such a document for her in a few hours. Antoinette had provided her with a tarpaulin for overnighting which she strapped onto the rear of her bicycle, and a water bottle, a precious loaf of bread, some boiled eggs and a cured pork sausage which she stowed in her backpack. Marie-France was sufficiently familiar with the route so as not to require a map although they went over a list of the main towns and landmarks the night before, all of which she could expect to pass through on her journey. They estimated it would take her three days and three nights. Marie-France was perfectly accustomed to overnighting outdoors and the prospect did not daunt her in the least. By now the days had become longer and warmer, and cycling would be easier. Her only fear was rain or hail and the subsequent wet and the cold. She decided by far the best idea would be to cycle on minor roads to the point of exhaustion or until it became too dark to see, such that when she'd found a suitable wood to hide in, she would fall asleep immediately, having first tucked into the meagre rations she was carrying.

On the second night she took fright when she thought she heard voices nearby in the woods. She sat up and listened. She decided it was most probably wild boar or deer. Before she settled down again, she pulled out the family photograph from her ruck sack and placed it on a log beside her. "Tonight, the family will protect me," she said, staring at it. She felt a tear run down her cheek as she laid her head down again.

On Friday afternoon she managed to enter Lyon on a minor road and find her way to her grandparents' house without being stopped and asked for any form of identity. She knew she needed to ride purposefully through the back streets avoiding the main checkpoints. Additionally, she was fairly certain that the Vichy government had a different set of passes and ration books to those of Occupied France, a small detail which had been overlooked and which might have led to her arrest. She made a mental note to clarify the matter with her grandparents upon her arrival, for housing anyone without the correct passes would also lead to their arrest. She entered the garden via the back gate and spotted her grandfather digging up the last of the cabbages, parsnips and leaks from the vegetable garden. She left her bicycle and bag leaning against the potting shed and called out to him.

"My dear, we got your message from a friend of yours. So glad you've made it. Quite an adventure. We've been expecting you," Hervé Champuix hugged his granddaughter and led her into the house through the conservatory. "I'm making a soup for us tonight, with the last of winter's vegetables. Still had a few left in the ground to dig up. They're a bit slug infested, but what can you do?" He held them up for her to see. "I expect you'd like something to drink. I could make some mint tea, if you wish. We have a plentiful supply of mint in the garden. Can't stop it spreading. Bloody weed, really."

Marie-France sat down at the kitchen table and promptly began to weep. "I'm so happy to be here, believe me, but I'm in awful trouble, Grand-père."

"I see. Well, I'll call Claudette. I think she needs to hear it too." He walked into the hall and called up to her from the bottom of the staircase.

Once Claudette had descended the stairs and made a cup of tea in the kitchen, they walked into the sitting room and sat down on more comfortable chairs. Marie-France wiped her eyes and spoke slowly and softly, trying to allay any sense of anxiety.

"I'm pregnant. The father is Jean, but we are obviously not married. Maman was so ashamed of me that she wanted me out of the house. She didn't exactly say so, but the way she looked at me told me she found me repulsive. Also, for some reason, on Monday ..."

"Just one moment. Allow me to digest that," Claudette said. "How many weeks pregnant are you?"

"Fourteen."

"It won't be showing for a few weeks yet then. I'm sorry my dear, I interrupted you."

"Yes. Well on Monday morning someone painted some 'C's on the front gates. Papa said that those 'C's mean 'Collaborationnistes' and are painted by the Resistance or local villagers when they want to call someone out."

"So what does that mean? What else is going on?" Hervé said.

"Nobody knows. But I decided to leave. May be someone thought one of us was collaborating in some way, or being too friendly with the Germans. All I did was to ask a German officer to play some Beethoven at the piano in a café in Chalon one day. I was with Antoinette, an old friend from my school days. The same person who telephoned you. Is that an offence?"

"Accusations and denunciations are flying about all over the place at the moment. Most I hear, are entirely without substance. People do it mainly for money and extra food. It's commonplace and thoroughly despicable. Do you think it was against you?"

"I don't know, but I thought it best to spare the family all the indignity. And the reputation of the domaine could be at stake. I had that to consider too. There'd soon be an embargo on our wines and we'd go out of business. Papa would never forgive me."

"So you want to have your baby here?" Claudette said.

"Please, yes, I beg you. It's why I've come."

"We'll need to legitimise you or there'll be a lot of trouble," said Hervé.

"Does that mean 'Yes'?"

Hervé looked across to Claudette who nodded her approval. "The last baby to be born in this house was your father. Then of course he took over the business from your cousins, and left Lyon for Burgundy and Saubon-le-Duc."

Marie-France got up from her armchair and leant down to hug each of her grandparents in turn. She was unable to hide her tears, wiping them away with an old handkerchief. She sat down again and composed herself. "I really don't want to get you into trouble though. I'll have to hide away. I don't have any Vichy documents. And what happens when I'm due to have the baby?"

Hervé put his cup of mint tea down. "Let's not worry about the baby. First things first. We can register you here. You'll need to have your Vichy documents. Every good Frenchman knows a friend of a friend who can help with that. If there's one thing I can't stand it's having to carry a pass about upon one's person wherever one goes. I even put mine in my back pocket when working in the garden. Ridiculous. But at least it's become a habit. But yes, you're right, you can't use your German 'Ausweis' here. It's a Vichy government pass you'll need and it's in French for a start, and you need to provide a photograph, a detailed description of what you look like, and your fingerprints. Additionally, you must provide your profession, date and place of birth, and the parents' names. We'll say your husband is a POW, that's a pretty standard situation. They rarely trace it back in those circumstances."

"Should I change my name?"

Hervé frowned at the thought of it. "It'll be sad and difficult, but probably best to do so, yes. But we'll get advice on that. As far as you're concerned you'll be a new person with a new life, and regarding the Vichy, you'll be a long lost relative returning to the family."

"That sounds good," Marie-France said.

"There's some pleasure to be had in cheating these damned Vichy people. False documents are one of the ways," said Hervé, chuckling.

11

Marie-France had ample time to settle down into her new life in Lyon. Her grandfather attended to the forging of her new ration and identity cards and her grandmother organised for her everyday comforts, inspired by the thought of a young one joining them towards the end of September. By far the hardest decision was the choice of Marie-France's new name. They agreed eventually on the commonest family name they could come up with, since it was the least distinctive and the most likely to lead to confusion and traceability issues if she ever came up against civil and administrative bureaucracy, or had to deal with the police. She would henceforth be known as Marie-France Dubois.

Claudette invited their new family doctor to dinner so that Marie-France might get to know him and familiarise herself with the procedures for the birth for which they hoped he would agree to be present. Before he arrived, Hervé confirmed that although he was young, he was well-connected and reliably tolerant of all the likely scenarios covering pregnancy outside of marriage, whereas an anonymous mid-wife might be less discreet. In other words, he wasn't going to ask too many questions. Marie-France was presented as a long-lost great niece who'd been abandoned by her family owing to undeclared circumstances connected to the war. It was the sort of role to which she was adapting naturally anyway. The doctor turned out to be an affable man, easy-going and keen to help. He agreed to attend to the birth in the family home if that were Marie-

France's wish. A further check-up appointment was arranged at his surgery in town for the following month.

In those respects, Marie-France was well organised. In practical terms, it had only taken her a month or so to become accustomed to her new circumstances. However, she kept a secret of which only Antoinette and possibly one unknown other was cognisant. She still couldn't be sure if the "collabo" debacle at Domaine de Champuix had been directed at her. The uncertainty tired and worried her but, more than anything, declaring such falsehoods to her grandparents regarding the origin of her future child's father weighed heavily on her conscience. She felt the same shame concerning her parents and her family. She'd been lying to everyone when it was not in her nature to do so. Her guilt soon manifested itself in long bouts of introspection. Her grandparents considered that her depression was due to the standard anxieties associated with pregnancy, so decided not to question her or attend to her every downward mood swing when they occurred. Sometimes such indulgence only made it worse.

After a phone call to Henri, Hervé had informed Marie-France's parents of where their daughter was living, and where she intended giving birth to the child. Hervé confirmed with Marie-France as gracefully as he could that her parents had reached their own conclusion – that it was best she were out of the way in Lyon and that they had come to terms with it all.

"Are they happy to have cast me out?" Marie-France said, unable to hold back her tears. "It sounds like it to me."

"I'm not sure they see it like that, no. They expressed their sadness, especially your father who is missing you. It was more that if anyone were to enquire as to your whereabouts that they'd tell them you'd wanted to go to Lyon because it is the town closest to where the father of the child lives. You'd left home of your own volition, so to speak."

"I know that Maman is ashamed of me. She's so stuck on those silly social sensibilities and religious conventions, as if I have ruined her whole life and reputation in the community. I'm not likely to become an Anna Karenina figure, for heaven's sake."

"No. Of course not. I think it is that they've found a way to deal with the whole matter, and can move on. I wouldn't worry for one moment about your mother. She should know better. If she were a proper Champuix she'd have stood up for you."

"Thank you, Grand-père. I think that's all fine by me," Marie-France said. "At least they know what the situation is now."

"Your father, being my son, was perfectly happy with the whole matter. I tried to instil in him from a young age, a broadminded, tolerant attitude to life. I don't know what your mother is thinking, but I wouldn't get too bothered about that. Your Pa seems most sympathetic. All he really cares about is your safety and happiness. He told me so, so I wouldn't worry."

"Good old Pa. Thank you, Grand-père."

Grand-père Hervé possessed a well-stocked library at one end of the house. Marie-France soon sought solace amongst the rows of books and manuscripts, as if the doors to a whole new world had opened up before her. The library was located in a quiet area at the rear corner of the house in an oak-panelled room. The shelving was also of oak, and stacked from floor to ceiling on two sides, such that Marie-France needed a librarian's ladder to reach the top shelves. She made it her base during the long months of relative inactivity. To her it became her safehouse where she remained untouchable. There was a deep sofa upon which she could sit or lie and one large window through which she could look out onto the garden which was dominated by two impressively large trees in the background, a cedar and a tulip tree, and in the foreground there were a series of labyrinthine gravel paths bordered by neatly-clipped box hedges.

In the library, she found much to discover including, not

surprisingly, a whole shelf on viticulture and oenology. Some of the older books in this section were even in English. She picked out *A Practical Treatise on the Cultivation of the Grape Vine* by William Thomson, a first edition published in August 1862. It entertained her that her Burgundian grandfather or perhaps even her great, great grandfather should be learning about grape growing from the English. To her disappointment, she soon realised how little of her school days' English she could remember.

But what entertained her most were the newspapers which her grandfather either subscribed to or collected on the sly, some of which arrived in the house erratically, depending she assumed on their availability. Hervé kept some of them in the bottom drawer of his desk for reasons she discovered later. She was able to read about the progress of the war in detail, with her grandfather pointing out the political, economic and militaristic leanings of each of the publications. Some such as the Resistance-inspired newspapers were necessarily subjective in order to spur on support and the encouragement to rebel. The *Paris-soir,* which arrived daily, was published locally in Lyon and favoured the Vichy government. Hervé kept that on view on the hall table to "keep any visitors happy," he said. In the drawer of his desk in the library were random copies of *Défense de la France, Résistance, Combat* and *Libération,* all of which she found considerably more appealing, not least because they were supposedly both clandestine and outlawed by the Vichy government. She even found copies of *L'Humanité* and *Verité*, the communist leaning newspapers of the time. A February 1942 edition of *L'Humanité* informed its readers of the existence of the "partisans" whom patriots from all walks of life should be supporting if they were true Frenchmen. In the following month's issue, the newspaper urged people to meet and join the partisan groups to fight the "Boches." By the April 1942 edition, the *L'Humanité* newspaper was reporting daily acts of sabotage against

German soldiers and the railways and factories which favoured the war effort, as well as prompting reprisals against collaborators who needed to be called out and punished accordingly. Marie-France shuddered at the thought of it.

News of the progress of the war and especially Jean's own war of Resistance fascinated Marie-France. "There's a sort of heroism and brazen courage about these people, which I admire," she announced one evening to Hervé.

But he wasn't entirely convinced. "There are the genuine diehards who care for France and its liberation. People like Jean, although you tell me that he is also propelled by a febrile conviction for Communism which I cannot condone. But at the other extreme, there are criminal elements in the Resistance who flourish outside the law, a bandit element I would say, to whom adventure and the destruction of property probably appeals most. That sounds harsh, but it's true."

By mid-April 1942, disparate Resistance groups had organised themselves into a more formal force, composed of genuine Communist party members, those who called themselves Communists but were not, and many foreign groups such as Polish refugees and anti-fascist remnants from the Spanish Civil War. It is true that many who first joined the Resistance were simply social outcasts. They came from varied social backgrounds, rich or poor, with diverse political and religious beliefs, from towns, cities and the most remote of rural villages. And beyond the primary and general cause – the liberation of France from the Nazis – people also joined for many other diverse reasons.

Conversely, there were a small number who found it more convenient or prudent to collaborate directly – members of the establishment such as big business owners, some of the aristocracy and upper middle classes, and much of the hierarchy of the Catholic church who felt they had too much to lose by openly resisting.

The Germans called these people the "Zusammenarbeit" or the "Mitarbeit," those who worked respectively together or with the enemy.

In between these two groups were the much maligned "salonards," or "résistance de salon" types, as they became known – those who chatted or boasted with enthusiasm about the Resistance, but devoted little or nothing towards the cause of liberation.

But by far the largest group in French society, Marie-France read, were those who chose neither to join the Resistance nor to collaborate, but to abstain from any activity at all, and simply to muddle along with their lives as best they could.

*

It was the disparate members of the collective Resistance however who fascinated Marie-France more than anything, and about whom she read and attempted to learn the most, both from the newspapers and from Hervé, who proved to be a willing teacher. The differences between these diverse groups proved to be the most confusing, as was the nomenclature. The more urban-based units came to be referred to as simply the "Resistance," which confusingly was also the collective name for the entire movement. The more rural-based, forest or mountain fighters soon became known as the "Maquis" or "Maquisards," named after the Corsican scrubland so familiar to its own bucolic banditry. Other names associated with this mixed bag of a burgeoning outlaw culture – for that is what it was still known as in the early years of the war – were a general group known as the "francs-tireurs and partisans," and another group named the "réfractaires" – those who evaded the compulsory draft to work in Germany. Other groups were associated by their position in society, such as the "curé du Maquis," (the obliging village priest), the "préfet du bois," (the sympathetic rural government official) or the "mère du Maquis" (a helpful mother) and most importantly, the railway workers or "cheminots" known as the "Résistance-Fer."

By the early summer of 1942, these groups joined together and became known generically as the FTP, the "Francs-Tireurs et Partisans," representing the armed forces of the FN, the "Front National" led by Charles Tillon. The FTP had also unified three Communist organisations – the "Bataillons de Jeunesse," the "Organisation Spéciale" and the MOI, the "Main d'Oeuvre Immigrée," although fewer than half of the FTP were members of the Communist Party.

When working in the field, each group was composed of three or four men under a commander and an assistant, although the numbers varied. After each carefully planned operation the unit was trained to withdraw rapidly and return to their everyday occupations, so as to retain a level of anonymity. Their tactics relied on bluff, deception, ingenuity, subversion, surprise and mobility, avoiding any pitched battles where possible – a markedly different approach to fighting than the standard warfare of the time. There were added risks involved in this sort of clandestine combat, such as the threat of torture when captured and the risk of suicide when placed under extreme duress, but all recruits were warned and trained to handle such matters. On the plus side, there was plenty of room for imaginative thinking, including the daily tasks of writing, printing and distributing material. And there was enough creativity in the freedom of manoeuvre and the planning of tactics and strategy to satisfy most individuals, especially those with a propensity for leadership.

"Resistance" represented the struggle for liberation which remained its key inspiration. However most of those who claimed to resist were neither armed nor mobilised into active fighting cells. Many were known as "sédentaires," often working from home and tasked with a large array of administrative duties from hiding documents, to printing posters, to caching arms or providing sanctuary to airmen downed in combat. Others, such as civil servants who worked in the "mairies" or "prefectures," helped by stealing blank passes and other documents to be forged.

Favoured above all news media by Marie-France and Hervé was "Radio Londres," broadcast by the French department of the BBC in London. It distinguished itself with what became an iconic calling card, "Ici Londres. Les Français parlent aux Français." The broadcast had started life with Charles de Gaulle's 18th June 1940 appeal to all French people to rise up against the Occupation, and swiftly become the mouthpiece of the Free French Forces in London. Marie-France and her grandfather would sit listening to it on the radiogram, adjusted to a purposefully low volume so that they had to crouch together behind a sofa beside a cupboard under a bookshelf, where the radio was hidden behind false panelling. When the broadcast ended, Hervé would retune the machine to a Vichy station and wink fondly at his granddaughter as if it were their shared secret. They'd then discuss what they'd just listened to over a glass of their own Meursault, Marie-France being restricted to a half measure during her months of pregnancy.

During the months which Marie-France spent largely indoors or within the confines of her grandparents' property, she learnt that life had become much tougher outside. In May 1942, General Karl Oberg was appointed the supreme chief of the SS and German forces in Occupied France, signalling a period of increased brutality towards the Resistance and a speeding up of deportations to Germany of Jews and various resisters. In June, on Germany's orders, Prime Minister Pierre Laval introduced a scheme known as the "Relève" to swap returned French POWs for French workers. Naturally it was unpopular from the start but it turned out to be the catalyst which helped to fill the ranks of the Resistance. The following month, Marie-France and her grandfather read of the news of the "Vel d'Hiv rafle," a roundup of Jewish people into the renowned Paris velodrome, from whence they were transported to Drancy, the main French internment camp prior to being despatched to Auschwitz and other concentration camps. Hervé directed his particular disgust towards René Bousquet's French police who carried out their orders with a relish hitherto never witnessed, which included the rounding up of women and children, which the Germans had not insisted upon. The roundup comprised one quarter of the 42,000 Jews deported in that year. At least 7,000 had come from France's southern zone, confirming the suspicions that the Vichy regime and Prime Minister Laval were antisemites of the first order, and clearly complicit in the deportations of French Jews to the camps in Germany and Poland.

By early September, the Vichy government had also begun deporting French workers, conscripting men aged eighteen to fifty, and single women aged twenty-one to thirty-five, making Marie-France eligible, at twenty-one years old. At first most of those recruited came from the industrial towns of northern France and were sent to the heartlands of the Ruhr, and specifically to the Krupps steelworks in Essen. Reports soon began to appear in the newspapers that working conditions were tough and dangerous owing not least to frequent Allied aerial bombardment. Workers were housed in cramped, unheated accommodation with limited food or medical facilities, and were worked hard under an oppressive Nazi regime.

A few weeks prior to the birth of her child, which had been predicted for the last week of September, Marie-France attempted to make contact with Jean's mother in Dijon. At first she searched in vain for a phone number but ended up writing a short letter requesting Jean's whereabouts. She'd decided a few months prior to writing that it was imperative she let Jean know of her wishes for him to act as the child's father, but in the event, it was the hardest and most unusual favour she'd ever had to ask of anyone, with the result that she procrastinated until the last moment. Her main concern was that he would do the obvious – in his disgust, refuse to accept any knowledge of the child's existence.

Marie-France gave birth on 28th September in her bedroom in her grandparents' house, Clos de la Fontaine, under the supervision of the young Dr. Duplessis. The birth passed without complication and the baby was declared healthy and of average weight. Her boy was registered under the name of Gérard Louis Dubois – the adopted family name which they'd previously agreed upon, which had been a necessity under the circumstances, but with which no one was especially content. Apart from the boy's dark hair and blue eyes, similar features to Johann, she couldn't determine any others which might suggest any similar physical traits to Jean's. This provided her with a troubling sense of disconnection at a time when mothers were supposed to feel a deep joy and relief at the birth of a healthy child. She felt the pleasure, but it wasn't exactly in the proportions she was expecting. An absent and "forbidden" father was the likely cause for these conflicted feelings. She couldn't think of a better word than "forbidden" to describe Johann's status although he was not to blame and she was certain he would cherish the role of father if he ever learnt that he had a son.

Over time, Marie-France embraced motherhood and found an overwhelming desire to love Gérard. Her natural inclination to protect and watch over him provided her with her first experience of what she had imagined motherhood to be like. After a few days she was taken by surprise by the visit of Eloise and her father who arrived at the house early one morning unannounced, the news of the birth having been transmitted to them by Claudette a few days earlier.

Her father entered her bedroom with a bouquet of flowers, followed by Eloise with a distinctive glass vase which she recognised had come from the hall table at home. Henri spoke softly and placed a hand on Marie-France's shoulder, "I'm afraid I couldn't persuade your mother to come, and we've left Marc in charge of the remnants of the harvest. Naturally we're missing you and we're rather busy at the moment. Need I tell you more on that front?"

"Is it looking like a good harvest? I can imagine how busy you are … and those late nights sitting in the cellar seeing to the fermentations. I should be there, I suppose." She paused and smiled. She didn't feel guilty though. The birth of her child felt like the perfect excuse for her absence. "I suppose I might be ready to return home soon," she said eventually, although not feeling the least inclination to do so.

"What are your plans? We do miss you, you know. Can I hold him, please, if that's possible?" Eloise said, stretching out her arms towards Gérard.

"You can hold him but please don't wake him, if you can help it. A moment's peace is so welcome. I had no idea how demanding and draining it all is. I get barely a moment's rest or any time to myself. I haven't thought at all about my future. But Grand-mère and Grand-père have made me feel so welcome here, I think it's only fair that Gérard spends the first six months here at Clos de la Fontaine. It's quiet and peaceful for him too." Marie-France gestured to Eloise to take the baby. Eloise placed her hands around Gérard, picked him up, propping his head, and held him to her chest.

"Oooh, he's much heavier than I would have imagined," she whispered.

"Have you heard from Jean?" Henri asked out of the blue.

"No, I haven't. I've asked his mother though, but I haven't had a reply yet."

The flurry of questions continued. Her father and sister's visit had caught her off-guard. After a while, Marie-France could no longer summon up enough energy to converse with her family. She periodically closed her eyes and her thoughts became discursive. She feared her secret might slip if she continued talking. She ended by informing them of her disappointment that her mother had not sent her best wishes. It vexed her that Clémence could place her Catholic beliefs above the love for her own daughter. There seemed to be no sign of forgiveness or a real understanding of the circumstances. That was hardest to bear. And holding back the truth from those she loved. At one point when her father had left the room, she thought she might confide in Eloise. The truth had become increasingly difficult to hide and yet it was in Gérard's best interest that she should say nothing of his real father. Nothing. She repeated it over and over as a mantra, hoping to embed her decision deep into her subconscious. She had to think for two now and saying nothing was much the safest option.

12

News reached Lyon that the Allies – the Americans and the Free French forces – had landed in North Africa on 8th November. "Operation Torch" was in full swing. The hopes of all of France seemed to be raised in the following days, until three days later the southern "Zone Libre" was overrun and occupied by the German army, with Italian troops taking control of the south-eastern corner and Alpine "départements" of France, in an operation known as "Case Anton." The Vichy government had lost much of its autonomy in a matter of days, and was soon to lose its military wing and what remained of its navy.

Marie-France had developed a daily routine as best she could, although Gérard might often require feeding at any time, day or night. Looking after a baby was considerably harder work than she imagined. Breast feeding was uncomfortable and sometimes painful, with feeding times erratic such that like any other mother she remained short of sleep on most days. To her great relief, she at no point felt she was on her own. Claudette seemed to appear from nowhere to help with all the necessary tasks at just the right moment. And Claudette's daily help attended to the washing of nappies, sheets and clothes in the laundry room. Marie-France learnt to express milk so that she could take the afternoons off, usually to sleep, and Claudette could feed the baby on demand.

One morning she woke feeling exhausted, anxious and melancholic with no particular reason to show for it. She burst into tears spontaneously when Claudette entered the bedroom with her breakfast. Claudette drew back the curtains, sat on the side of her bed and assured her it was all part of being a mother, consoling her that such feelings would soon disappear.

"Our female hormones, my dear," she said. "Nothing we can do about that. Do you know, I think you should get out a bit. It's been over a month. You've got your passes now, if ever you're stopped in the street. A change of scene will do you good. One can often feel trapped and anxious about one's future after having one's first baby. A sense that you've lost your old life and you're in for something very different and altogether too foreboding. Perhaps that's what you're feeling."

"Yes, I do. I've been worried about what's going to happen, whether Gérard will ever see his father. I never got a reply from Jean's mother to my letter. I even wondered if I might go to his university and see if I can find some trace of him. I'd enquire discreetly, of course. He knows nothing of his child. I'm desperate to let him know."

"And Hervé has been missing your company, especially listening to those secret broadcasts together and those highbrow discussions which follow them. He has things he wants you to know. Don't think I don't know what you two get up to down there behind the sofa with your heads inside that dusty, old cupboard," Claudette said, laughing.

"Aha, yes. Well, Grand-père enjoys a good discussion. And I know, you're right. I feel ready, step by step to return to normal life. I suppose I can leave Gérard with you from time to time. Not for long of course. A few hours perhaps. I'm so glad he feels so happy with you."

Marie-France set off one morning wearing a pair of flat-soled shoes for comfort, which she borrowed from Claudette. She planned to walk across town to the university. She had no great expectations and she wasn't even sure if the university would be open. The first thing she noticed was how few people there were in the streets and those that were, were busy working, mostly delivering essential supplies such as firewood or repairing shop windows. There were no young men about. But it was early winter. Perhaps many were inside keeping warm if they could, or most likely hiding away from the "Relève."

As she approached one of the university buildings, she spotted a group of young men and women of her own age, chatting in the gardens outside one of the faculty buildings. She went up to them. They treated her with suspicion at first, explaining that the university had largely closed down owing to the number of professors who'd been arrested and deported. They explained that their own medical teaching facility was considered too important to shut down. To her surprise one of the young men knew of Jean, but only by name. He provided her with an address where she might make further enquiries. She read the note, which she was then asked to memorise and destroy.

"It's just around the corner. I'll accompany you, if you wish. My name's Marcel, by the way. These days everybody's looking for someone," he said cheerily, as they walked off together.

"That's life at the moment, I suppose. I do have an idea where Jean might be. Can I trust you?"

"That's the other thing we've had to learn how to do all over again, sadly. Trust. Who can you trust these days? Nobody knows how to trust any longer. Even instinct and intuition aren't enough. And yet trust is fundamental to life and all relationships, isn't it? So you just have to risk it. Hang on a minute." Marcel stopped and reached into his pockets and showed her his personal documents one of which was imprinted with the word "Exemption."

"I see. You seem honest. I think I can trust you. Is that an exemption from the 'Relève?'"

Marcel smiled at her. "Yes. The documents we carry reflect who we are, don't you think? Apart from me being a vital medical student, I mean. To our oppressors, we are now simply defined by our documents and the random number they allotted us. But to others? Well."

Marie-France laughed. "You are more than just your documents and a number to me … and to your friends and family, I'm sure."

"I'm not so sure. I suppose you'll need to reach beyond the mere paperwork to get to know me. Although having my identity card stamped with 'Exemption' does attract some sort of kudos and recognition. Because the next question will always be 'why you?' Not many are exempted from ordinary life as Vichy sees it." He laughed again.

At last she felt a part of her past life returning. Chatting to and walking down the streets with a young man of her own age who possessed a dry sense of humour, a hearty laugh and a resigned inevitability about the life they were living today, helped her feel more confident. In addition she found an affinity in him which reminded her of Jean.

She could be grateful for the time she'd spent with her grandparents at Clos de la Fontaine, of that she was in no doubt, but how long was she going to be living with them in Lyon, however lovely the house and its location in one of the more salubrious parts of Lyon? She needed more to life. Having a child had sent her down a path to which she hadn't yet become truly accustomed, but motherhood hadn't stunted her desire to step out into the world. She could still do that, children, or no children. For the first time, she wondered how feasible it might be to leave Gérard with her grandparents and to head off to find Jean.

They passed a dishevelled row of town houses which looked unoccupied, and walked half-way down the street before they reached an archway between Numbers 14 and 16 under which they walked, ending up in a small, cobbled courtyard. Marcel knocked on a door numbered 14bis at the far end, and waited. An elderly man called out and Marcel identified himself.

"This is my friend Marie-France. She's looking for Jean de Villeneuve."

"Who's he?" the old man replied.

"She's safe, I'm pretty sure of it," said Marcel.

"Who is Jean de Villeneuve to you?" the old man asked Marie-France. His manner was brusque but Marie-France realised why. No risks could be taken.

"He's my boyfriend. We were going to marry."

"He's not in Lyon. We keep a record of all our students. He was one of our best."

"I know he joined the Resistance and I know all about what happened to his father," she said.

"So, you know he had to leave here, right? He lived the life of a fugitive for a bit and then headed west to the Languedoc. He joined another unit. We don't ask many questions, so we don't have any answers, in case the Boches should come knocking, you understand?"

"The Languedoc's a big place, four huge départements. How on earth should I find him?"

"There are channels, ways and means. Depends how keen you are to see him. But then what are you going to do when you find him? Join the Maquis?"

"Yes, I will join the Maquis, his unit. That's what I wish to do." Marie-France blurted it out with such enthusiasm that she caught herself by surprise. This might after all be her destiny, but what of Gérard? And how tied was she? All needed careful thought.

"If you come here, same time, but on Friday next week, I'll have more information for you," said the old man.

Marie-France restrained herself from stepping forward to hug him. He looked so gaunt, he might crumble in her arms if she were to grab hold of him. "Can I bring you something? Some food, I mean. We have eggs, a few winter vegetables, leeks perhaps."

"Thank you, dear. Anything to eat, even drink, would be a feast." He smiled for the first time.

Marcel turned and addressed Marie-France. "I will stay here for now. A matter of safety. We never enter or leave by the same door. It's fine for you though. Go now. It is never safe here for long visits." He placed a kiss on her cheeks before she left.

That evening she spent a couple of hours chatting with Grand-père Hervé. She learnt that towards the end of November, Admiral François Darlan, the Vichy Secretary of the Navy, had defected to the Allies in North Africa and that his successor had scuttled the French fleet in Toulon harbour on 24th November, ensuring that neither the Allies not the Axis powers could benefit from its use.

"The French Navy managed to destroy seventy-seven of their own ships, leaving the Germans with the use of only thirty-nine small vessels." Hervé emphasised that however tragic that might be, it was important, since the Vichy government no longer possessed a credible navy, but suggested to Marie-France that he wasn't sure whether that was a good or a bad thing.

"You have to finally decide whether you have any sympathy at all for Vichy," Marie-France exclaimed after a long pause in their conversation.

"It was the crême de la crème of what was left of our navy and we destroyed it ourselves. That's a tragedy in itself. But I read that several submarines are thought to have escaped to Algeria. I appreciate the relative stability the Vichy regime has brought. Things could be worse. Your father is still able to sell our wines, for example. And be paid for them. The estate still rumbles along producing wine year after year, even without you. But I detest

Vichy's collusion in various aspects of Nazi policy such as the deportations and retributions, which I find most distasteful and un-French. This war has brought out the best and the worst in the French character. Mark my words. The noose will tighten around the necks of the worst of characters. The French people will seek their own justice if need be."

"What do you mean?"

"Well, we have in our midst devious informants, denunciators and conniving collaborators. And we have blatant Nazi sympathisers too, and then we have communist resisters whom we don't want around for ever, but who may possess ambitions for political power at some point, and then we have youthful, probably misguided, foolhardy freedom fighters sabotaging the German war effort, amongst them no doubt a bunch of undesirable misfits, hot-headed anarchists and subversives."

"You can guess where I stand," Marie-France said, looking for a reaction. "I have set my heart on the 'Jour-J' which they keep talking about, when de Gaulle and the Allies land on French soil and drive the Boches back across the border. Perhaps next year."

In mid-December, Himmler issued a decree requesting that the French police round up 35,000 "detainees for work," to be sent to Germany, which they duly carried out. It looked as though the planned target of 250,000 "worker" deportations would be fulfilled by the end of 1942. Very few had gone voluntarily, such was the mounting pressure to resist. Moods in France were changing from reluctant cooperation to outright hostility. It was clear that SS-Gruppenführer Karl Oberg, who controlled the German police in association with the French police under René Bousquet, was streamlining the necessary strategies of repression and control, especially since the German army had now occupied the whole of France.

At the end of the following week Marie-France set off to meet

Marcel and the old man. The former was waiting for her in the courtyard, sitting on a bench in the sun by a fountain.

The old man sat behind a desk over which a scruffy map had been laid out. "I have an address in the small town of Clermont l'Hérault near the opencast mines of Lodève, where I believe Jean has been agitating the miners to strike. It's a low-key Resistance area, but Jean must lie low, you understand. Clermont l'Hérault is just beyond, south-east of the Cévennes mountains. It is not where Jean lives but they can direct you, if they believe your story. It's a good 350 kilometres from here though. You'll need stamina. But if it is love which drives you, you will succeed, my dear, and with God's hand." The old man chuckled to himself and winked at Marie-France.

"Could I bicycle there?"

"No, my dear. It is far too far and you will eventually be stopped if you take the roads. They are rounding up people all the time to work in their factories. Single women too."

"Could we not get her a fake 'Exemption' stamp on her identity card?" Marcel said.

"That is a good idea. But for what reason is she exempted?"

"That is a good point," said Marcel.

"Even so, you must ride freight trains at night or hitch lifts, but sparingly. I suspect that for much of the journey, you will need to walk. You will not be following the route of the railways. Woodlands, even mountain paths will be your best cover. It could take you a month or more if you go across the mountains which I recommend, and you will find friends on the way. Come." The old man gestured to her to stand by him and study the map.

"I won't be going for at least four months," Marie-France said.

"Just as well. You see the town of St. Étienne?" The old man placed a finger on the map and began prodding it. "We can get you there quickly. That won't be difficult. Marcel could even take you."

The old man paused and glanced at Marcel.

"I could indeed. I can spare a day, I'm sure," he said without hesitation, nodding.

The old man continued. "Then on down to La Puy, Mende, Millau and Clermont l'Hérault." The old man drew his finger slowly across the map as he spoke. "The last part is mountainous. You must wait until after spring when the snows have melted, then you can sleep out. The Cévennes are glorious in the summer months, plenty of forest and garrigue to hide out in, and full of helpful partisans of course. Indeed this is the preferred, remote country of the non-conformist and the protestant. My kind of people. Rebel folks." The old man's eyes twinkled at the thought of it and he smiled again.

13

Christmas passed by with barely a hint of celebration and a token exchange of presents, inexpensive and modest in size. Marie-France accompanied her grandparents to morning church on Christmas day with Gérard, and Hervé brought up some appropriate bottles from the cellar for Christmas lunch, from which Marie-France was only permitted a sip. Two sausages were shared between three, and they made the most of the potatoes, leeks, and cabbage from the garden, with cheese to finish, which had been provided by a friend in exchange for a bottle of wine.

Meanwhile in both town and country, there was mounting unrest in the streets, with a proliferation of posters and pamphlets, with orders to reject the "Relève," accompanied by successive raids and roundups, with one such highly unpopular one in Marseilles at the end of January 1943. If once the urban resisters considered the peasantry docile and compliant, it was now clear that changes were afoot in the countryside as well, especially when as much as twenty percent of farmers' produce was now being requisitioned by the German troops. Hunger fomented unrest. A new phrase appeared in popular parlance now that the Resistance was attracting greater sympathy and wider support – to "prendre le maquis" – to take to the hills and scrubland, after which the Maquis were named. Further attempts were made to unite Resistance activities under the banner of the "Armée Secrète des Françaises Combattantes," commanded by General de Gaulle and the "Comité National

Français." They had plans to direct Maquis operations at a national level, claiming "All men of the Maquis are the enemy of Marshal Pétain and the traitors who obey him." Codes of conduct also appeared on one pamphlet Marie-France found, calling upon all citizens to sign up, "We require of the Maquis a very tough discipline, to obey all orders, to renounce all links with family and friends until the end of the war, to expect no regular wage nor to carry arms, to respect private property and the life of the local population, and to respect the opinions and beliefs of all comrades."

Marie-France read that on 24th January 1943, the 250 Resistance women who had been arrested and amassed from all over France, were due to be deported that day to the Nazi work camps for slave labour. It was the only train during the entire Occupation so far to depart from France with captured or rounded-up Resistance women on board. A week later on 30th January 1943, the Vichy government announced the creation of the paramilitary "Milice" to expressly counter the growing Resistance, and to free up the "Gendarmerie" for other work. With a limited number of men at 60,000, the police force had only ever been accustomed to general policing, and not the sort of work now required of a specialist militia.

Marie-France hadn't brought up the subject of her heading off in search of Jean again, let alone joining the Resistance. Instead she found herself confiding more in Marcel, almost a complete stranger. She met him from time to time over the weeks which followed. They met habitually in the park by the university after she'd dropped in to see the old man. On one such occasion she was more frank with him than she intended.

"It's good to feel like a woman again. When I'm with you I no longer feel like a mother. I don't suppose you'd know what I'm talking about though," she said in a jovial tone.

But it caught Marcel by surprise. "You have a child by Jean?"

"Yes I do, but that's not really what I meant to tell you. I was just saying that I feel so free when I'm out of the house. Having a child ties you down so much. I guess having children also makes you feel older than you really are. As if you suddenly have responsibilities beyond your immediate realm. It changes perspectives on life. Or it should do. Sometimes I don't always feel that way and feel a little guilty, like I didn't really deserve to have a child. I don't suppose you understand what I'm talking about." She laughed and looked at Marcel hoping for a thoughtful response.

"Like a young octopus which suddenly discovers it has tentacles and spreads them out far and wide and inadvertently comes across whole new unexpected worlds all at once," Marcel said smiling.

"Sort of, but you're making fun of me."

"Well I'm trying to find an analogy that makes sense of it."

"It's a bad one, Marcel," she said, laughing.

"Are you taking your child with you on this journey?"

"No, no. I'll leave him behind. He has a doting great grandmother who's more than capable of looking after him and I guess we'll find a wet nurse too to start with. Depends when I feel the urge to bolt. Don't get me wrong, I'll only leave if the urge becomes intolerable. I won't leave my baby unless I'm desperate."

"You know that in mid-February, Vichy introduced the STO, the "Service du Travail Obligatoire," because they failed to attract enough so-called volunteers to their 'Relève' scheme."

"Yes, I know. My grandfather is very keen on keeping us informed. He says we *have* to know what's going on. But what's the STO got to do with me leaving my baby behind?"

"It doesn't. But just wait. I'll explain. Everybody born between 1920 and 1922 has to register at their local 'Mairie.' Only miners, essential industrial workers and farmers are excluded. Fortunately, I'm just old enough to avoid it."

"Oh. I'm not, but I was a viticulturist, a grape farmer in another life."

"That's my point. You are of the age for recruitment. And you currently don't have an exempt occupation. But I think young mothers are excluded, so you should be okay. But grape farmers? I'm not sure. Anyway, the STO is helping to swell the ranks of the Resistance. The 'Relève' draft dodgers … we call them 'défaillants' or the rather derogatory name of 'réfractaires,' are now apparently looked upon as a patriotic force for good if they join the Resistance."

"Are you suggesting that it would be a good thing for me to join the Resistance. It's no longer looked down upon. Is that it? Do you think I should join?"

"Yes, I suppose I am. It's going that way, becoming the right thing to do, but it depends for what reason. For example not all these 'réfractaires' are regarded so highly. Some are just STO avoiders rather than combatants. Indeed, I believe many have no wish to fight at all. But I even read somewhere that some were threatened with being shot on their return if they went to help the German war machine. They can't win either way. What I'm saying is only join if you really feel for the cause, that it's in your bones. Do you know what I mean?"

"That's kind of nasty and threatening, isn't it, shooting them when they return?" Marie-France said.

"Better they join the Resistance, then. Collusive action, I'd say. It's already clear there's a loathing for the STO. It's just uniting all the groups of protest. And women are being separated from their men with this STO thing. It's not popular. Some women were lying on the railway tracks at the station yesterday in protest at it the other day."

"To stop the Boches deporting them?"

"Yes. I wouldn't say these people ever considered joining the Maquis beforehand, but they're doing their bit now. The STO has turned passive connivance into active contribution, I'd say. That's what STO has done." Marcel chuckled at the thought of it.

"Why don't you join the Resistance?" Marie-France said.

"How d'you know I'm not already a member? And what about you? After what I've just said, do you think there's a role for you somewhere in there? You know as far as women are concerned, only about ten percent of the Resistance are composed of women and only ten percent of those are armed. Most act as liaison agents and some are 'passeurs,' guides, leading our Allied airmen across frontiers, you know, to Spain or Switzerland. They're not especially politicised, they just dislike the occupiers. A role for you, no?"

"I think there is, yes," Marie-France said, nodding enthusiastically.

Marie-France returned home that evening, her head full of ideas. Should she tell Hervé about any of them? She wanted someone else to talk to apart from Marcel. Wouldn't Hervé be proud of her joining the Resistance? Claudette wouldn't approve of her abandoning her baby. Everything needed some more thought followed by a feasible plan. All she currently had was a route to an approximate area where Jean might be found, and the determination to find him.

In early February news began to reach them that the Germans had been defeated at the battle of Stalingrad, a fierce, relentless siege of attrition which had endured for six months, terminating in a Soviet victory and the rout of the German army which was now in the process of retreating westwards. This was greeted as a seminal victory by the communist press but it worried Hervé. How far into Europe would the Soviets now come and what were their plans? Would these Bolsheviks become the new enemy to be reckoned with? By early March, the once dreaded Demarcation Line had been opened to all, and passes were soon abolished. Marie-France could now journey north to see Antoinette or even her parents, without impediment. The postal service was also being re-established across the whole country, although sending letters by post wasn't always a safe means of communication as the Gestapo readily opened mail in transit.

By the end of April 1943, Marie-France had become increasingly frustrated with her daily life. Gérard was now seven months old and she'd successfully weaned him off her breast milk. He was growing up fast and making good progress. She enjoyed Marcel's company and left the house frequently to visit him, making the excuse that she was going out for some necessary fresh air. Each passing week Marcel spoke more vociferously of Marie-France's plans as if he were tempted to become a part of them. She welcomed his encouragement, but kept her secret. No one was to know why finding Jean had become so essential.

She decided one evening over dinner to share her ideas with her grandparents. All her plans depended on Claudette agreeing to look after her child in her absence. "I'm so keen that Gérard should meet his father. I don't think it would be fair for another Christmas to pass by without his father being present. And Jean has no idea that he's a father. I will have to look for him."

Claudette sighed. "But how realistic is that? He could be anywhere and he's in a risky place. He could die any day. Why go out looking for him? And you, a lone woman, could be arrested or charged with neglecting your child."

Hervé intervened, "Oh please, Claudette, there's no need for such negativity. It is understandable that Marie-France should want to find Jean. I wonder if we shouldn't make some enquiries for you, before you go off wandering into the wilderness. You need more direction."

"I have made enquiries. I know where to find him. It would take a few weeks. And I would feel so much happier, I'm convinced of it."

"But it's so dangerous out there, child. We are at war, don't forget. Can't we post him a letter beforehand?" Claudette said.

"He is in the Maquis. The Maquis don't have addresses. They have operational cells, liaison agents and runners," Hervé said, raising his voice and sitting up.

Claudette sighed and took another sip of her mint tea. "How on earth will she survive? On roots and sapling leaves I suppose. Oh well. Give me some time to think about it. And I suppose I will have to look after the boy."

"Perhaps Marie-France needs a rest from the daily chores, it must be depressing as a young woman to be tied down, trapped even by motherhood," Hervé said. Claudette nodded in agreement.

"I would be very grateful for your help. It won't be for long. And at least I will know where you are. I will write you as soon as I find him. And then I'll return. Do you think Gérard will be happy without his mother?"

"Some time away will do you good, I suppose. All mothers need some rest from time to time," said Claudette. "I'm sure Gérard will be fine without you. I suppose he also considers me to be his mother. He seems perfectly happy just being with me when you go out for the day. I expect he already feels that he has two mothers really."

It didn't matter that her grandparents assumed she was suffering from a bout of post-natal depression and going away for a bit would help cure her of it. That was what most likely swayed Claudette into agreeing to take responsibility for Gérard. She said as much when the subject came up again one evening, with Hervé nodding his approval. Marie-France believed it was better that way – that they'd decided a change of scenery would do her good. She'd return refreshed and fulfilled, her "depression" long since alleviated. They didn't need to know the real reason for seeking Jean. Nor that she was tempted to join the Resistance, although it had been discussed. It took her no more than a few further weeks of planning until she set off with Marcel before dawn in a small delivery lorry, the rear loaded with sacks of potatoes and onions for the restaurants of St. Étienne.

14

Marie-France had found it curiously straightforward to tear herself away from her child. It was something she was dreading but when the time came and with all the preparations for her trip occupying her thoughts, she simply hugged him tightly in her arms, kissed him on both cheeks, handed him over to Claudette and left. Her grandparents refrained from fussing over her too much prior to her departure, believing that it would only aggravate an already stressful situation. They simply wished her good luck and saw her off from the front door.

If it weren't for Marcel's obligation to return the lorry to the vegetable wholesaler in Lyon later the same day, he declared that he would have continued to accompany Marie-France on her journey beyond St. Étienne. He admitted as much shortly after they set off. Marie-France was at the wheel, as Marcel confessed to finding driving in the dark very tiring. Their papers were in order and they were expecting to cross only two checkpoints with their cargo being inspected at both. Marie-France was wearing sturdy boots and a rain proof coat and cap, and had a knapsack in which was a gourd and a few supplies – bread, boiled eggs, cured pork and a few sticks of liquorice to chew on. Sewn into the base of her knapsack was a small kitchen knife in a sheath, for self-defence should she need it. For shelter and future provisions, she was entirely dependent on the goodness of those locals she met on her path, but with no guarantees of any munificence. The old man had warned that many peasants were reluctant to shelter or feed strangers for fear of reprisals. For locals who seemed only willing to help her, she planned to identify her true credentials by showing them a small wood carving in the shape of the Cross of Lorraine with a "V" in the centre which Marcel had given her as a "good luck" charm. She kept it hidden with the knife. She carried no maps and no written information of any kind, having put all the vital information she required for the trip to memory.

At daybreak, Marcel took over the driving. They made the deliveries together and he drove on towards the edge of St. Étienne where he dropped Marie-France off on the edge of a wood. He embraced her affectionately and made it clear that they should meet again when it was all over. He waited by the roadside until he'd lost sight of her, the density of the forest foliage gradually swallowing up her meagre frame as she traipsed through the undergrowth into the darkness. Marcel remarked that the less he knew of her plight, the better, such were the conditions under which they lived. What you didn't know, you wouldn't reveal to the Gestapo under duress. On the return journey to Lyon he found himself thinking of her often and worried for her.

She followed the advice of the old man – make haste when the weather is fine, travel at night by the light of the moon whenever possible, keep warm and dry and avoid all contact with others except when ravenous or in need of shelter. Live off the land as much as possible, not that the late spring offered her much, if anything. The second stage of the route to Le Puy was distinctly rural – hills, forests, rivers and patchworks of fields of barley and wheat, still green and barely knee high. She identified the main road to Le Puy and shadowed that for most of the way, occasionally emerging from the woods to read a road sign. On the evening of the fourth day she had run out of food and approached a man tilling his field who offered her food and shelter. His wife was sympathetic if at first reticent, but Marie-France was persuasive and convincing. She had gone over in her head several times, the words that she would need to employ to court sympathy and kindness on her journey.

"My name is Marie-France. I am not on the run and I am not wanted by anyone, I assure you. I'm on a journey to visit my uncle in the south. He needs help in his vineyard so I am travelling to join him. That is all I can say. But I am hungry and I beg you most humbly for some food and a bed for the night. I will happily sleep in your barn, if I may, please."

Long journeys across the country often aroused suspicion at the random police or militia controls which one was obliged to pass through in town or on the approach roads. She did her best to avoid them. Any reasons given for travel were often followed up with a request for names and addresses of the people and places one had left and were heading for. Marie-France had no final address and luckily no one asked why it wouldn't have been easier to make the journey by train or bus. And no one she met enquired too extensively into the reasons for her journey. She did not fit the picture of a regular vagrant or drifter and she had the documents to prove it. She spoke well, confidently, and courteously, and carried her head high. She came across as an educated, bourgeois, professional woman, which is exactly what she was. She chose not to conceal this, for she was who she was, and if asked, exhibited neither pride nor shame in the fact that she was a fully-trained viticulturist and the daughter of a well-to-do, land-owning family from Burgundy.

That evening she sat by their fireplace and sipped on a thick soup of pearl barley, carrots, and chard, with a trace of mutton thrown in, making conversation in such a manner as to reveal as little as possible, but to demonstrate her gratitude for their kindness. After supper, Madame boiled a kettle of water and offered her a bucket in which to wash herself.

"Be sure to leave no trace of my visit tonight," Marie-France said. She offered to clear away the table and wash the utensils while Madame boiled her kettle.

"I wouldn't worry for us. We don't get visitors here. The Boche turned up once to steal a sheep from us, but that was all," Monsieur said.

"I suppose they could come again," Madame said.

"Yes, exactly that. It is a risk. I will sleep under the straw in the barn and be gone by dawn. The authorities are always suspicious of overnighters. I'll leave no trace of my stay."

"We have found provisions for you for at least three days. They are on the table there. Be sure to spread them out sparingly," Madame said, pointing to a loaf of bread, and some fruit and cheese.

Marie France slept solidly that night, comforted by the generosity of strangers and the knowledge that she was making good headway. She travelled when she could. If there was a burst of heavy rain, she took shelter and rested, but if there was bright moonlight and a definable footpath, she made haste. When the moon was visible and the skies clear, she marched along the roads and made the best progress. Some days she calculated that she'd managed only ten kilometres and others perhaps twenty. Marcel and the old man had counted on a journey of three weeks from St. Étienne to the Lodève area. It might take longer.

One third of the way, on a fine, warm day she stopped by a river to wash herself and her clothes, hoping the warmth of the sun would dry them out before dusk. After her washing, she planned to take shelter in the forest above the steep banks of the river, which at this point passed through a gorge in thick woodland. She was some distance and well secluded from the road. She climbed down to the water's edge, looked about, undressed and waded hastily into the water. She picked a spot which was deep enough to submerge but where the current was calm enough so as not to carry her away.

The water was cold and invigorating at first and she was tempted to cry out. She drew breath with short gasps as she lowered herself bit by bit and then sank under the bubbling current, rubbing her hands over her body and passing her fingers through her hair and over her face. She sat on a rock to dry herself, observing a heron nearby, which served as a helpful lookout. Later she got to work on cleaning her clothes, drenching them, wringing them, then starting the process over and over. She then laid them out to dry in the afternoon sun on the large boulders by the edge of the river. She saw and heard no one, surrounded only by the torrent of the river and the songs of the birds which lived by it.

She found herself falling asleep, but was aroused by the flap of the heron's wings taking off from its perch on the river bank. She covered her breasts with one arm and manoeuvred herself across the rock to take shelter behind a boulder, reaching at the same time for her sheepskin coat. Shortly she spotted an angler downstream, wading through the middle of the river, casting upstream, and approaching her step by step as he shot out a line into the current. He appeared to be a young man, no older than sixteen or seventeen. He smiled when he saw her but continued fishing. When he was level with her, he placed his rod down on a flat rock and waded towards her.

"I see you have caught a few fish," Marie France said.

"Yes. Would you like one? You look cold and shivery. You're not wearing much."

"What will I do with it?"

"What one normally does with a fish. Eat it. Cook it first. Then eat it. Are you hungry?"

"I'm extremely hungry."

"Then we shall cook two and you will eat a whole fish, possibly two. Brown trout. As natural as they come. The best you can eat."

"I should dress first perhaps."

"Ah. Yes. While I look for some kindling for the fire, you can dress. I promise you, I won't look. A good idea, no?" The boy chuckled and wandered off towards the forest.

Marie-France gathered her things, most of which were dry by now, and dressed herself, checking from time to time that the boy wasn't looking. When he returned, he gutted the fish and washed them in the river, then built and lit a fire which he fanned with a handful of dock leaves he'd picked from the river bank. While the fire burned, he stuffed the trout with sprigs of wild fennel and waited until he had enough embers to lay both fish out on them.

"Not long, ten minutes either side," he said. "My name's Jules by the way."

"Marie-France."

"Travelling alone, are you?"

"Yes. Heading south through the Cévennes." It was foolish of her to reveal her direction but the boy seemed harmless and friendly enough. "Which river is this and how far are we from Mende? Do you know?"

"This is the Haute-Loire. I guess we're sixty kilometres from Mende as the bird flies. South-west from here."

"Thank you."

"Can't blame you for taking a swim on such an evening. I spotted you when I was well downstream of you. We don't get many mermaids around here. First I've seen in my life, to be frank. Had to stop and take a good look," the boy said.

Marie-France laughed. "How much did you see?"

"Everything but your tail."

"It won't be your last mermaid, I'm sure. The fish already smells good, doesn't it?"

"Nothing like eating a fresh fish by the river. Just like our ancestors would have done." The boy removed his rubber waders and stretched out his legs. From his rucksack he pulled out a pewter plate and placed it by the fish. With his other hand he brought out a bottle, flipped the top and handed it to her. "Local cider. Very good too. Take a swig. It should be cold and refreshing."

Marie-France stretched across for it and drank from the bottle. Its fresh taste and intensely bubbly mousse filled her mouth with flavour. "Delicious. Thank you. Never tasted so good."

They sat by the river picking at the fish with their fingers, and alternately swigging from the bottle. The boy produced a chunk of bread from which they both broke bite size morsels.

"I haven't eaten so well in ages," Marie-France said when she'd finished. "My lucky day meeting you."

"Glad to be of service," the boy said. "I'd best be getting home, it's a long walk. Finish the rest, please." He left half his fish lying on the rock they were sitting on, gathered his belongings and bid her farewell.

"Goodbye, my guardian angel," Marie-France shouted out after him. He turned and smiled, doffed his cap in recognition and walked off.

She was alone again with just the endless thunder of the river filling her ears. Oh, if only rivers could talk, they would have so many tales to tell, she thought. Not so long to go now, she said to herself. She wasn't too sure how much she enjoyed the life of a vagrant, especially on her own. She'd never had to beg for food before, let alone a bed for the night.

She stopped twice more for lodgings and food before reaching the outskirts of Mende. On both occasions her first attempts were met with a rebuttal. It was better to approach the men first, she decided, having been chased off a property by a large woman wielding a pitch fork the day before. And best approach people in open fields rather than entering a farm and arousing the wrath of the resident farm dogs or the woman of the house. Men appeared to be less suspicious and took pity on her more readily. North of

Mende, high up on the plateau of the Aubrac she found a kindly shepherd who shared his wine, his local Ecir cheese and a loaf of bread with her. He offered her a bed in his shelter, where she passed the night cuddled up with his dogs which kept her warm during the cold night.

"I never knew such places existed. I suppose I was aware that the Lozère was remote but until you've been here you cannot conceive of such a place," Marie-France said, as they sat around a glowing fire.

"It's good for nothing but sheep, cattle and goats, and our cheeses. But it's a good place to be when there's an enemy about. I haven't yet seen the Boches, believe it or not."

"Oh, I have. Plenty of them. They're not all bad. Most don't want to be here at all. They just want to go home."

"Do you know anyone they've killed?" said the shepherd.

"No. I don't.

"That's lucky."

"Perhaps you can help me? I'm heading for Clermont l'Hérault and I'm confused about where I should head to next."

"I don't know the town but do you see the outline of that high peak in the far distance there? That is the Mont Aigoual." The shepherd stood up and pointed towards what remained of the amber light from the fading sun and then drew a line to the left with his hand, pointing southwards. "There. Do you see, to our south? That is in the heart of the Cévennes. But you can circumvent it. You don't have to climb over it. Head for Florac. It is the only town I know of beyond Mende. It's a long way. Be sure to sleep well. My dogs will protect you tonight."

It wasn't difficult to remember that night. It seemed a like a special moment, deep in the bosom of mother nature. She'd never experienced such wilderness, such vulnerability being so far from home. Not that she was in any danger, just that she felt a long way from civilisation, not least because the terrain was so alien to her, with the high altitude, rolling grass plains, and plentiful menhirs and dolmens dotted about the landscape to remind her of how many nomadic peoples had preceded her on similar journeys across this vast, high plateau. They sat around the camp fire well into the night while the dogs patrolled the flock which surrounded them. Occasionally they responded to a frightened bleat and sprang into action, weaving through the herd and corralling those sheep which had strayed beyond the perimeter.

"Wolves," the shepherd said. "We do get wolves up here. That's why I've got my dogs. They can tell from the tone of the sheep's bleating if it's fearful." Observing and pointing out the different stars in the still night, they both agreed it was impossible to feel further away from the cursed war.

Marie-France set off early. After two days of walking she found the road to Florac and followed it, jumping into the ditch or behind clumps of thick shrubs whenever she heard approaching traffic. On one such occasion when hearing a convoy of vehicles, she dived into a patch of white meadowsweet and surprised a grass snake. She lay there petrified, while the snake, a large adult, freed itself from under her and slithered off along the ditch. She wasn't sure who was more terrified.

She begged for food on the way and offered coins in exchange. In a few villages she found shops where she could buy bread, but with everything in such short supply, she felt she was merely depriving others less fortunate than her. Along the edge of a forest, she spotted cherry orchards and was lucky to find trees where the cherries had still not been picked. But such abundance was rare.

A couple of days later and she was in the heart of the Cévennes, a sparsely-populated, mountainous region with demanding woodland paths which meandered over high, forested passes. It was also a region which Marcel had warned her might accommodate plenty of Maquis. While they weren't going to be an immediate danger to her, the Germans and the Milice pursuing them definitely were, although as a woman she was informed that she would not be under suspicion. Apparently, this was mainly a man's war to fight. She sought help with directions when necessary and found most people helpful and biddable. There was also a tranquillity here which she found reassuring. She knew she was on the last leg and with every stride she felt she was stepping closer to Jean.

In the month of June, the hills in the Cévennes were alive with the colours of yellow broom and pink and white rock roses, the scent of wild thyme and the sound of bubbling brooks where she could wash the sweat and dust from her face and neck, and rest under the cool boughs of the sweet chestnut trees which abounded in the lower parts of the valleys. Occasionally she found edible berries growing wild, but natural food was virtually non-existent. Despite its beauty, this was harsh, unforgiving country, cold at night, and hard to endure when permanently hungry.

Outside the village of Saint-André-de-Valborgne, she found a river to wash in and fill her gourd, before walking into the village, hoping to find something to eat. She entered the first bar she came across and found a kindly woman who offered her chestnut bread, cheese and red wine from a pitcher hidden under a towel.

"My dear, you look exhausted. Where have you come from?"

"From up north. Is it safe here?" Marie-France perched on the edge of a bar stool.

"As safe as can be. Any sign of the Boches and you can run out the back door if you need to. Know what I mean?" She winked and pointed down the dark corridor. "It's true they're rounding up girls of your age at the moment to work in the factories in Marseilles and Toulon. And they'll wonder what you're doing here alone."

"I've been travelling for three weeks and so far I haven't been stopped."

"Avoid the towns and you'll be fine. They don't bother us much here except it's getting a lot busier just now. The more the Maquis get up to, the more raids and inspections we seem to get from the Milice, our own people, for heaven's sake. They removed about a dozen men only yesterday. Poor bastards. They'll be shot. But they weren't from around here. No one knew who they were or where they'd come from. They hide out in the forests, you see."

"So it's not safe here."

"The Boches won't come looking again now."

"What about reprisals?"

"Not here. There's no one here anyway. We're all old. They shot about twenty townspeople in Le Vigan, south of here, for sabotaging a truck and killing a guard. It's bad in Millau too, I hear."

"I probably need to get out of here," Marie-France said. "I'm travelling to Clermont l'Hérault."

"My dear, we will get you over the pass and Gilles, my husband, will put you on a bus to Ganges in exchange for a few sous. The bus comes once a day. From there, follow the road in the direction of Montpellier and once you meet the Hérault river turn westwards and follow it downstream all the way to Clermont."

"I'm not sure about buses. They stop them at check points and they'll ask what my business is here. My address is in Lyon, you see. I've come a long way and they don't like that."

"I won't ask what you're up to, but Gilles will certainly get you to the Ganges road tomorrow. Don't you worry. Sup with us tonight and you can be on your way at dawn. There are plenty of safe routes through the mountains here."

The woman sounded so eager to help that Marie-France became suspicious of her. Was she one of these collaborators who turned people over for a few francs? But then again Marie-France was at the end of her tether and she was still hungry. She would willingly pay for a bed around the back if one were being offered, which she assumed it was, although she was yet to meet Gilles, her guide for the following day.

Marie-France needn't have worried. She ate well that night and paid them for two additional days of provisions which she packed into her knapsack before heading to bed, a comfortable enough mattress in an outhouse at the rear of the property. The woman provided her with a blanket and quilt, and Gilles promised to wake her at 4.30 a.m. for the long journey ahead. She washed her feet and attended to her blisters onto which she dropped several drops of mercurochrome from a small bottle she'd brought with her. She'd apply a light bandage to her blisters the following morning before heading off. Only one blister on her right heel had given her the most pain and slowed her pace, but it wasn't going to halt her progress.

Six days after separating from Gilles, leaving him at the top of a col looking down onto the plains below, she arrived in Ganges having taken his advice to follow the course of the Hérault river. They had been the most challenging days of her journey and she was now into the fifth week. The constant climbs and descents took their toll on her feet and limbs. Her arms were scratched from the undergrowth when the paths tended to peter out and she had to beat her way through the inhospitable garrigue. The thought that there was only one more week to go and soon she'd be in Clermont l'Hérault making enquiries after Jean helped sustain her. Again, she was hungry and exhausted but eschewed the town of Ganges. It was too big for her liking. She stopped at a farmhouse on the outskirts and again found a friendly reception. Offering a little cash always helped. People in the south seemed poorer and yet they always had chestnut bread, eggs and maize corn to spare, for which she was most grateful.

South of Ganges she was advised to head towards Gignac and follow a road westwards to Clermont. By now she was back in wine country. The vines had flowered and small bunches of grapes were appearing on some of the vines, but they weren't going to be edible until late August. To her delight she found apricots instead, a plentiful supply, ripe and juicy. She helped herself to the fruit whenever possible, usually at night for she was effectively thieving from some unfortunate farmer's valuable harvest. But hunger got the better of her conscience on many occasions and she frequently filled her knapsack with fruit.

The day time temperatures were now sometimes too hot to travel comfortably for long so she thought it best to walk at night and rest during the middle of the day. By now she'd grown accustomed to traipsing along the verges of roads and jumping into the undergrowth if she heard a vehicle approaching. Walking on a road was easier underfoot and suited her feet better, although most roads in this part of France were not tarmacked. She decided that they were the most direct route though, as long as she found the correct direction, which wasn't always so evident. But at least there were signposts, and when she found one marking six kilometres to Clermont, she shouted for joy and sat by the roadside gorging on the last of her apricots. She estimated she'd reach the town by dawn, if she hurried.

Her journey was temporarily halted by a severe thunderstorm, common in this part of France where on occasions the warm air of the Mediterranean meets the cooler high altitude winds blowing off the Atlantic producing a sudden deluge and a spectacular lightning display. There were storms in Burgundy but nothing as ferocious as this. She found it terrifying enough, but she wondered what the small mammals with which she shared the forest floor made of it. Perhaps they were used to such a phenomenon. She hid down amongst the undergrowth sheltering as best she could. She endured two hours of spectacular lightning, thunder and heavy rain before continuing her journey to Clermont.

Marie-France sat under a plane tree in the main square as the sun rose hoping to spot someone who might help her with directions to the address which the old man had given her. She'd been taught to always ask for a street and never a house number. The sun had barely begun to rise and there were no signs that the town was about to stir into life. Feeling both elated and exhausted at having reached her journey's end, she hoped now for a long rest, although she doubted it would be easy to find Jean's exact location. It might even be the toughest stage of the journey. All depended on the stranger she was about to meet.

15

Raoul turned out to be only a little older than Marie-France, lanky and unshaven with a warm smile and a gentle, quiet demeanour. She'd expected someone older and of a more solid build, a little more battle-torn, perhaps. Apart from the boy fisherman, most of the people she'd met on her journey were scruffy, grumpy, old men, who were almost always unshaven, with the butts of old hand-rolled cigarettes hanging between their lips. Having knocked on the bare wooden door of Raoul's property more than twice, she was allowed to enter only upon answering a few rudimentary questions. She was then asked to describe Jean in unusual detail. She understood this to be a necessary safety procedure. She wasn't going to be admitted on a whim. On entering the house, she was offered some warm milk and told to sit down at the kitchen table while Raoul heated it up.

"May I remove my boots? My feet are so sore. Is it too much to ask for a little warm water? I guess that I've been walking for six weeks. What is the date and what day is it, please?"

"Ah. I see. I had no idea you'd come so far. You were walking were you? That's a long hike. Oh, and it's Thursday, the tenth of June." Raoul went to the stove, threw a log of wood into it and placed the kettle on the iron hob. "Okay, to be honest you do look a bit unkempt and unwashed and your hair is in a terrible mess. I can tell you've been out on the road for some time, but six weeks, that's a long stretch." Raoul smiled, then laughed, hoping she would appreciate the funny side of his blunt remark. "Don't worry, I have some new, clean clothes for you too, if you wish," he added.

"Thank you. A change of clothing would be appreciated. Do I really look such a mess? I don't normally look like this, you know," Marie-France said, also laughing and struggling to remove her boots, then tying her hair back. "May I clean myself up a little too? I'm sorry, so many requests all at once."

"Yes, of course, but drink your milk first. It'll help you feel better. I put some honey in it. I'll fill the tub at the back and you can take a bath and put on some new clothes. There's soap and a towel out there for you. And a mirror. Go and smarten up when you're ready. I'm heating the water."

With warm water and a good wash, Marie-France felt revived enough to ask Raoul about the last stage of her journey.

"You must head up into the Caroux." Marie-France looked puzzled. "These are the mountains on the southern fringe of the Massif Central. I can tell that you are not from around here," Raoul said, smiling and hesitating to explain further, until he'd established how much she did know of the area.

"I'm not familiar with around here at all, no. I'm sorry. I've come from Lyon. I don't know anything of this country. It's wild and beautiful though. I can see why and how the Maquis hide out here."

"I can show you a map and you can copy it, but my advice is to retain what you can in your head. The less information you carry on you, the better. There's a little village up in the Caroux called Rosis. I'll give you a name and address which you'll need to memorise, and you'll need to ask for someone when you reach the village. He'll let you know where Jean's group is camped. At the moment, they are resting up. We all need more provisions and ammunition. There'll be some food and other things I'll need you to take up there for them."

"You can trust me. I want to fight for France. I need to fight for France. Will I be able to join Jean's cell, do you know?"

"Not for me to say. Any special skills?"

"I can speak and write English. I can drive a lorry and a tractor. I can snare and shoot rabbits with a rifle."

"Ever killed anyone?"

"Oh no, I'm not that sort of person."

"You might need to learn how to, in self-defence, of course. I doubt they'll send you out with a gun anywhere. Most of our girls help liaise, beg for food, wash and tend to the wounded, and operate the radio telegraphs … that sort of thing."

"When can I set off?"

"You're not tired of me already, I hope."

Marie-France laughed. "No, no. I'm just keen to see Jean and get on with things."

"Stay the night. Leave at dawn. I'll explain the route. I'm expecting some communications tonight. We're hoping for a drop-off from England down in the valley at about one in the morning. A Lysander packed with cases of ammunition, medical supplies, several boxes of Sten submachine guns, grenades, fuses, plastic explosives, detonators, clamps and limpet mines, incendiary bombs, and most importantly cigarettes, tobacco, and chocolate."

"That's a lot of stuff."

"Some of it is going on south to the big cities. We don't need limpets here. You'll need to learn how to use one of those Sten guns. They send plenty over as they're cheap to make and we can easily get hold of the nine mil bullets for it."

"Could I help?"

"With what?

"Tonight's drop."

"No. But I can show you a Sten gun so you get the hang of how to handle it and maintain it."

"You know, I haven't officially joined the Resistance yet. What do I have to do?"

"Prove yourself, I guess, and swear an allegiance, although these days we just tend to get on with things down here. Jean is a cell leader. He'll induct you."

"But how do you know I'm not an informant or something?"

"We never know one hundred percent. But one of the Lyon cells cleared you with Jean although there was some confusion over your husband's name, Dubois. Jean didn't know you were married. And he claimed to be puzzled why you were living with your grandparents in Lyon. At least that's where and why he assumed you were living in Lyon. Otherwise you fitted the description perfectly."

"I'll tell him all when I see him. I'd like to help out tonight."

"You can start by saluting me with a raised arm and clenched fist," Raoul said. He laughed at Marie-France's first attempt. "You normally stand up to do it," he added.

She stood up and tried again. "Oh, can't I join you tonight, Raoul?"

"Sorry, you'd best stay here tonight, even though you've passed the security credentials. It's risky out there on that makeshift airfield. I can show you how to use the radio. That would be helpful. You can keep a look-out for me in the street while I'm receiving messages. The bastard Boches are using detector vans these days. But luckily they can't get down our narrow streets here. I might even have a message in English to transmit. I expect your English is better than mine. You can help me with that."

"Okay, agreed."

"It's a low grade Maquis area here anyway. Not much industry to sabotage round here. Food and arms warehouses, railway lines, a few bridges, but nothing big. It's known as a safe zone, a hideout area. The action happens more around Toulouse and Marseilles, you know, the big cities."

"Why is Jean hiding around here?"

"Oh, he's a local hero. Didn't you know? The Boches and those

Milice arses are seriously looking for him. He helped de-rail a munitions and troop train south of Lyon some months ago. Plenty of casualties. They blew up a bridge. Nice one. He had to run. Plenty of his comrades were caught and shot."

"Right. Thanks for telling me."

"Keep it to yourself. I'm already talking too much. Far too much." Raoul sighed, sat down, put up his feet and rolled a cigarette. "Oh, I've got something for you to work at. First really important thing to do. To learn the Morse code." He got up and handed Marie-France a badly scuffed booklet retrieved from the bottom of a drawer.

"Don't worry. My grandpa taught me over the winter. I don't need the booklet. Thanks," Marie-France said.

"Impressive. Well, that's a big step forward." Raoul sat down again. "Getting hungry?"

That evening after a supper of beans and one hard-boiled egg each, Raoul went through the rudiments of operating a radio. He came up from the cellar carrying a leather suitcase which he placed on the kitchen table and opened. "This is a British B2. It's how we communicate with our brothers. They dropped it off by parachute only a month ago. We were lucky to get it, so it's very precious. Basically it's divided into three units ... a receiver, a transmitter and a power supply, plus a box for spares and accessories. The transmitter is here in the centre top and the receiver below it." Raoul pointed to both in turn. "The power unit is here on the right and the Morse key under here." Raoul removed a lid to show her. Fixing the frequencies is a bit more complicated. Basically it requires some fiddling. This is for the antenna, this is for the morse key, that's the power switch and selector, volume, headphone socket and so on." Raoul pointed out each in turn.

"It looks very complicated," said Marie-France.

"Not when you know how. Next I'm going to show you

an S-Radio, which has a forty kilometre reach and we use that to communicate with the Lysanders. It's easier to use and it's quicker because it's voice operated." He closed the suitcase and carried it away with him down into the cellar, returning with a smaller box. "You actually wear this S-Radio on you, with headphones and an antenna and power supply." He placed it on the table and showed her what was involved.

"Does Jean have one?"

"No. no. We only keep them in safe houses. We use a courier to convey messages from there to our field units. Much safer. You'll probably end up helping with liaison. It's no lowly task, you know. We rely on liaison officers for everything, and women generally aren't suspected of getting involved in the Maquis, so they're a good foil."

"So we're a good foil, then," Marie-France said enthusiastically.

"You absolutely are, yes."

Later that evening, before Marie-France announced she needed to get some sleep, Raoul retrieved the B2 and switched it on to broadcast and receive a communication regarding the night's drop. He referred to what looked like an ordinary paperback from which he calculated the radio frequency for that day, checked his watch and then tuned in before transmitting his first message. A message was returned which Marie-France wrote down then translated for Raoul.

Marie-France read out the message. "Confirm weather OK. Drop timed for 1.20 a.m. No landing required. Follow drop procedure, letter 'H'. Sending Hudson, not Lysander, all cargo as agreed, parachute only." Raoul replied an affirmative for the weather.

"What happens now?" Marie-France said.

"You throw the message into the stove and watch it burn. And in about five minutes, I join some colleagues and set off for the location. When we hear the aircraft overhead the radio operator will flash the 'H' in morse. The supply aircraft will flash the confirming letter then the team on the ground will light the field, using five lights placed in an 'X' pattern to mark the drop target. The aircraft comes over the field at low altitude, almost gliding at a height of about 150 or 200 meters, reducing speed to just above stalling before releasing the cargo. Everything is parachuted in using cylindrical containers to minimise any damage And then we gather everything up quickly, concealing parachutes first. Then we carry the supplies off into the back of a lorry and leave the area as soon as possible."

"I hope it all goes well."

"If it doesn't, I won't be back tonight. Here are your plans and route for tomorrow. I'll be up to send you off. Now sleep. I can see you're barely awake." Raoul handed her some papers and a map. "Memorise it all and then chuck it in the stove. Make sure it burns, but keep the map. Write nothing on it. Goodnight."

He'd left the room before she could thank him.

16

Marie-France lay on her back unable to sleep, alert for the sound of an aircraft which she never heard. Waking at dawn with Raoul shaking her arm, she couldn't at first place where she was and yelped. Raoul muffled her mouth with his hand until she came to her senses.

"Time to go. Wash, breakfast, pack and go. Ten minutes," Raoul barked.

Marie-France had grown used to Raoul's alacrity. She decided he wasn't being unfriendly, simply brusque and necessarily business-like. "Did all go well last night? I never heard you."

"All okay. Here's some chocolate." He bit off a chunk for her. "Fresh in, and tobacco for me. I'm going to ask you to carry some grenades and ammo today for our comrades. And some medical supplies. They've got an injured Maquisard with them. Do you think you can manage that?"

"Okay. It'll take me longer than a day though, no?"

"Three, most likely, if you take the route I suggest. I dare say you could do it in a day along the roads, but you're strictly undercover, working in the shadows. You get stopped and searched and you're dead. You get me? I've packed you food for three days so you won't need to see anyone. You'll be strictly covert all the way. I'm going to show you on the map exactly how to get there. You'll be climbing for some of the way. Oh, and by the way here's a scarlet scarf to wear. It's got black spots on it like a ladybird. It's your passport, so to speak. I've warned them. If they haven't forgotten or are so battle-weary, they should check you off first by the scarf you're wearing, so don't lose it."

"I'm used to climbing and I'll be sure to wear the scarf."

"There'll be no warm bath for you when you get there," Raoul said, chuckling.

"I'm used to that too. I'm no longer an amateur, you know."

It was barely light when Marie-France set off, choosing a path into the woods as soon as she could, and as directed by Raoul. This time her pack was much heavier and her progress slower. She was still weary and her blisters began to bother her again. She reached the village of Mourèze as the sun emerged, and stopped for a rest on its outskirts on the edge of a wood, admiring the view. She could have been in another age. Not a sound stirred the air except for the barking of a dog. A clanging church bell soon confirmed there was life of sorts in this medieval village perched on a limestone ridge. Oh, for a ready supply of refreshing white wine and a few long lazy days lounging in the sun by a river, she thought.

By nightfall, she reached an area north of the town of Bédarieux. In the distance she could spot troop movements down in the valley, not much but enough for her to realise why Raoul had instructed her to keep off the roads. She walked north following the course of the River Orb until she found a suitable mass of shrubland by the river to wash and then hide for the night. She guessed she was just south of the hamlet of La Tour de l'Orb. Before she lay down to sleep she propped herself up on a rock, reached for her bag and dug down to find her notebook and pencil. She opened it, bent it over by its spine, rested it on her knee and turned to the first page. She'd brought it with her to write a day diary. Her plan was start it on the first day she saw Jean again, as if that might mark the start of a new chapter in her life. She intended it to be something worthy and precious which she could reflect upon in later years. She stared at the blank page, and placed the point of the pencil above the faint blue lines of the page, just visible by the light of the moon. A shocking thought then occurred to her. For all of these six weeks she'd barely given a thought for Gérard. She wasn't missing him. Why not? What was wrong with her? What kind of a neglectful mother was she? She picked up a smooth, round rock from the river bank, larger than her hand, and slapped her thighs with it over and over, and began to sob. She muffled her cries by burying her head in the scarf which Raoul had given her. But wasn't she doing this, this whole, wild, ghastly adventure, to find Gérard a father? And yet she had her heart set on Jean too. He was her inspiration, her motivation. She longed to be held in his arms again. She wanted to be a part of his life again, to rediscover the man she had once loved who had abandoned her for what he believed to be a higher cause, for freedom, for vengeance. She respected him for that. And she admired the loyalty he showed for his father. Loyalty was attractive to her. He had courage, and conviction, and purpose, and she now longed to be a part of it.

Marie-France slept for a few hours before becoming restless and feeling an urge to continue her journey. She stared out across the valley in the direction she was intending to travel. Somewhere amongst the hills, mountains even, in that morning darkness was Jean and his band of outlaws. Her destination today was the small village of Rosis where she was to knock on a door for further directions. She descended into the valley of the River Mare, the only way down being a steep, barely evident track. Trudging through the undergrowth off the beaten track was too much hard work. The foresters' tracks were much easier if she could find them. Her trousers were already ripped by brambles and wild roses, and the rough terrain made her blisters more painful. Where she could she found tracks in the direction she intended to travel, sometimes sheep drovers' paths, and at other times foresters' paths cut into the sides of hills, and wide enough to accommodate a small logger's vehicle.

By mid-afternoon she reached Rosis, made contact with her liaison, and camped out north of the village. Memorising the complex instructions she was given was hard work. Having left the village, she sat in a nearby wood and did what she was told not to do – make a note of the directions in her notebook while she could still remember them. From now on she was in the wild. The enemy would never find her, even if there were any soldiers within fifty kilometres of her. She climbed the hill due north towards the Portail de Roquandouire, an entirely natural wall of rock although it looked man-made. But the climb proved to be too much and she made camp by a spring under the hill upon which this landmark stood.

In the fading light, she undressed and washed her underwear. She sat on a rock and observed the bruises on her thigh which she'd inflicted on herself the night before. They'd turned purple, green and brown in concentric circles, one on each thigh – her punishment for abandoning her child. She rummaged in her rucksack, found a boiled egg and chewed on a few centimetres of sausage. She spotted a small herd of wild sheep with their distinctive, jagged, curved horns, grazing on the heather not far away. Like the heron by the river, they would act as her alarm if anyone came too close. Once again she felt herself immersed in nature's vastness. For the first time since she'd embarked on her adventure, she appreciated feeling completely alone, enough to cherish the freedom she had to stand up on a rock, naked to the world, with a cool breeze brushing her hair and the sun warming her lightly bronzed skin. It was a privilege to be here, after all the mayhem of the outside world. But this was also a barren wilderness, no good for anyone except those who sought it out. But then she wondered whether she wasn't safer here, standing fully exposed in the wide-open landscape of the Espinouse than any bustling town or city where she might be lost amongst the crowds. She dressed herself, lay down in between the rocks and boulders and rested her head on her rucksack. She wrote a few words in her notebook and paused for thought. She wasn't ready to write anything more just now. She read through what she'd written and stood up, tore the page out of her notebook along with the page with the directions to Jean's camp on it and set fire to both with her matches, stamping them out thoroughly, before lying down again and falling asleep.

At daybreak she set off up the hill. At the top she sheltered behind a rock from a cool wind which blew down from the north. She spotted the brook she was to join and follow upstream, and scrambled down the hillside through the scrubland towards it. When she reached it, she looked westwards and walked upstream until she found a large boulder upon which a solitary rock had been placed. Two hundred meters directly above this, she would find Jean. She remembered she had to remove the stone from the boulder before she left. It had only been placed there as a way marker for her. Its presence meant they were expecting her. She wanted to shout for joy at the thought of it.

Marie-France washed her face and neck in the brook, and ran her hands through her hair several times. She would be seeing Jean within the next ten minutes. She sat by the rock and sobbed. At last she'd made it. Almost. And how would he react and what was she going to say to him? Such matters seemed trivial after the long trek she'd suffered. Getting there was half the story, half the battle. She'd face what came next when it came. She gathered her things and continued slowly through the forest of stunted holm oaks and wild box, climbing steeply all the while. She slipped on an outcrop of scree, knocked her knee on a stone and almost cried out in pain. When she heard voices, she stopped. And then she heard Jean's distinctive tones and found herself almost crying out for him. Composing herself and remembering where she was, she scrambled on. She sat down again a moment later and wiped the tears from her cheeks, then got up again. She crept along slowly, on all fours at times, until she could see a small plateau under a rock face. There they were. She saw them but they failed to spot her. And there was Jean, sitting on a rock, shirtless, leaning over and blowing into the embers of a camp fire to keep it alight. A kettle which had been set upon the fire began to whistle.

*

Ma Coccinelle – And There She Was

Nothing much in life has ever surprised me, but Nelle's appearance that morning, her hands held high in the air, stumbling forward one unsteady step at a time out of the undergrowth, was one such. The boys threw their coffee mugs aside, stood up, reached for their rifles and aimed their muzzles at her. She stood there motionless for a while, swaying on her feet as if she were drunk, waiting for us to make the next move.

"My name is Marie-France. I am wearing a red scarf, don't you see? I'm the messenger with the ladybird scarf. Aren't you expecting me?" Then her knees gave way and she collapsed, some of the contents of her knapsack spilling out onto the ground, including a few apricots and a grenade, the latter rolling precariously towards the camp fire. I dived to grab hold of it before it reached the flames.

"Is this your liaison, Jean?" Bruno, one of the team, grunted. "I hope she's carrying my meds, some bloody morphine too." Bruno was lying by the fire with a soiled bandage around his right calf.

Nelle lay there for a moment in the dust and fallen holm oak leaves of our campsite before gradually weaving her hands through the straps of her rucksack and kicking it away from her towards the figure who'd requested the morphine. "There's your bloody morphine, right there, you bastard. You won't be able to thank me enough for it." Marie-France lay there a moment longer before exclaiming, "Well, is someone going to pick me up and sit me down somewhere comfortable? I've lost my legs and my feet are on fire. Can't you see?"

Some of the boys sniggered, not knowing how to react. I could tell that they'd taken to her immediately. It was most probably her impudence and resolve, evident even now, which endeared her to them so assuredly. It was obvious to me because they all dropped their rifles at once and stepped forward to help her up. We lifted her up and sat her down on a pile of our jackets that we had fashioned hurriedly into a makeshift cushion. I still couldn't believe it was her. She looked like she'd always looked but she was different too. It was puzzling. The whole strange situation was going to take time to come to terms with. No doubt she was thinking the same of me. I asked her if I could remove a ladybird resting on her nose. We handed it around for good luck and then asked her to blow it away for us. It promptly returned to her bare arm, so we left it there, and laughed again. "She's with us to stay," someone said, which made us all laugh once more. I may have already told you this, but that's when she got her name, La Coccinelle, swiftly abbreviated to Nelle.

We offered her coffee but she wanted soup, declaring she'd saved as much of the food she was carrying for us. She got a cheer for that and a gentle pat on the back from someone. We warmed the remains of last night's rabbit soup for her. It was all we ate – snared rabbit, and sometimes cherries when we could find them, and chickens, eggs and tomatoes when we could steal them.

She caught my eye as she sipped the soup, her long stare telling me all I thought I needed to know. I looked away as I didn't want any rumours flying about, at least not too early on. Soon enough they'd learn that we had a past together. You couldn't keep that a secret for too long amongst comrades you lived with every day, unless you were damn good at acting and neither of us were. And besides I wasn't having anyone else taking a fancy to her. Estranged as we'd become, Nelle was still going to be my girl whatever had befallen her.

We sat around the fire discussing our plans for the day. We had a little food and some ammunition but no further instructions except for a scruffy coded note disguised as a love letter at the bottom of Nelle's rucksack, which informed us that we were to wait our turn. But for how long? In that respect, Nelle's arrival was a morale-boosting distraction, but some of us were beginning to feel we'd been put out to grass. We were all heroes of the Lyon train derailment, on the run, and living covertly until our masters could decide what to do with us. When you're at war, which we undoubtedly considered ourselves to be, unregimented bandits as we were, and with the fire of liberation and the febrile craving for the extermination of fascism rushing through our veins, you want action. Action kept us alive. Hanging about wasn't enough, although someone had reminded us that Bruno was convalescing and we weren't abandoning him to the circling buzzards above.

Having asked for a second helping, and once she'd drunk all her soup, Nelle removed her boots and requested hot water. Three of the boys leapt up at once to help. This evident enthusiasm to attend to her every whim soon became a joke, to the extent that we established a rota, and began shouting out "Your turn now," attaching a name to whomever was next on the list to help her out. Nelle took all this in her stride as if she fully deserved all the attention. She did. We hadn't seen a soul for ten days and certainly no women for many weeks before that, and she seemed to all of us in that moment like a summertime Father Christmas bearing generous gifts but with the charm and looks of a French film star like Arletty. More than one of us had commented on how similar Nelle looked to Arletty. After all, we'd all seen and fancied that actress in the movie *Le Jour Se Lève* a few years ago. At some point such unrestrained libidinous attention was going to have to stop. But I'd leave that to her. She'd know what to say and do to quell their over-familiarity without causing any resentment.

The boys were a decent lot though. Mostly university friends, fashionably socialist in spirit even if their earlier lifestyles failed to mirror the expected ethos of a young Communist Party devotee. But all were committed to the current cause and that was the essential motive. Finding such a compelling vocation at such a young age was going to add experiences and a dimension to our lives which we would never forget. None of us had ever considered joining the military or dreamed of fighting a war. We liked to consider ourselves all future lawyers, engineers or medical practitioners. And now we all sought kudos as outlaws and brigands wreaking havoc in our own land. Blowing up that bridge just at the moment a speeding Nazi troop train was crossing over it was a wondrous spectacle no young man could ever forget. It sometimes worried me what would become of us once that blessed war ended. Where would we all go and what would we feel like after that? Like desperately displaced misfits unable to slot into the mundane existence expected of us? Probably. One of us joked he'd become a professional bank robber, such was his experience with explosives, another a professional hit-man having acquired the requisite skills of a trained marksman. How could these young men possibly adapt to sitting at a desk or production line all day when it all came to an end?

After we'd all profited from a little chocolate, coffee and tobacco which our messenger had brought us all the way from England via Rosis, someone suggested that Nelle needed an official welcome into the Maquis fold accompanied by the necessary, solemn words of allegiance, loyalty, brotherhood and so on. We agreed, but embarrassingly I couldn't remember the official text and made a botch of it. All six of us except Bruno, who could barely stand, stood in a circle, held out and grasped each other's hands to the centre and made up a few suitable words and sang a patriotic song, none of us quite remembering the last few important lines which ended in another embarrassing mumble. Much to my surprise, which reminded me that I hadn't known Nelle nearly as well as I thought I did, she came up with an apt quote from Marcus Aurelius to describe what she believed a Maquisard to be, "Justice in thought, goodness in action, speech that cannot deceive, and a disposition glad of whatever comes." She conveyed it in such a way as if she might be addressing her troops. Impressed as we were, neither I nor the boys considered her in the same way again. She was indeed going to become a much respected, thoughtful, and morale-boosting asset to our team. She later confided in me that those were the last words her grandfather had whispered to her before she left. They seemed most apposite for the times and the situation in which we found ourselves.

We got on with our duties after the formalities – checking and setting new rabbit snares, fetching water from down by the brook, collecting firewood and attending to our physical fitness. While we were confident that we were miles from anywhere where a German soldier might spot us, we nevertheless rarely raised our voices or lit a fire during the day. And every four days, we moved camp, up or down the mountain or along the valley, one of us trekking down to Rosis during the night to liaise with our coordinator, picking up the latest news and informing him of our whereabouts, as well as filling a bag with cheese, bread or whatever was available, which wasn't much.

Once Nelle had fully recovered and most importantly her blisters had died down to the extent that she no longer limped, she began to complain of the needless inactivity and a frustrating sense of redundancy. In late June, news came through that our overall leader, Jean Moulin, the head of the Resistance, had been captured near Lyon at a meeting, and tortured by the murderous Gestapo chief, Klaus Barbie, along with other Resistance members. The inference was that the Gestapo had been tipped off. Jean Moulin was executed a month later. This setback only resulted in a new sense of vigour and purpose, and only made Nelle more restless, as we had still not received any instructions.

I refer now to Nelle's notebook and some of the entries she made at that time. You will observe that each entry begins with a number since most of the time she had no clue as to the date nor even on occasions, the month:

1.Mid or early June 1943 (unsure of the exact date) up in the garrigues of the Haut Languedoc. I begin my diary.

At last I have reached Jean and here begins my story with him. He looks well, he's bearded, sunburned but fit and strong and full of bonhomie with his comrades, although I think they're bored and tired of this hanging around. They say they're in hiding until things die down and one of them mends his leg. The wound looks nasty. We could have weeks more of waiting. Everyone is talking of Jour-J, the day the Allies land on our soil again, but we don't know when or where.

I'm not so sure that he was expecting me, although perhaps his reaction was just extreme surprise. But I liked the way he delicately removed the ladybird from my nose. He's still tender and warm after all he's been through, but I suspect the rough and tumble of this war has also got under his skin. How I'd love to talk about things but I can see he's read my mind. We need to act like we don't know each other. For now. He must know of something about me. He doesn't know what, but he's tactful, clever. He'll save us from the mess Gérard and I are in, I'm sure, and that's what I need. I need a solution. I suppose I want forgiveness above all but how is that going to work out? Now that we have time on our hands, all those awful worries about what I'm going to do are returning. Acceptance, belonging, forgiveness or disgust, dismissal, revulsion, rejection and shame and banishment. All those words cause me to have the same feelings and they haunt me every day.

6.We hear from our Rosis liaison that an amphibious landing has occurred in Sicily, beginning on 10th July, Operation Husky, and that the Italians are retreating and Mussolini's government might fall. Such news lifts us. There's now talk of us sabotaging convoys travelling to Bordeaux by road, on the route west and south of here. We'll be joining others.

8.Mid July. The others have left the camp scavenging for food. They're not expected back until dawn. At last I'm alone with Jean. I decide now is the time. I've rehearsed to some extent. I'm not at all sure how well it will go.

I tell him all. After the initial expected reactions, Jean turned very silent, introspective. At least he didn't rage too much. I told him everything. He hit me across the face though. I didn't believe he'd do that. But why wouldn't he? This is just the beginning.

17

It was late-afternoon and Nelle had stripped down to a bare minimum – bra, light cotton trousers, barefoot. She wiped her face with her blouse then poured water over the blouse and dabbed her face with it as if it were a face flannel. She felt like taking everything off and saying "Here I am. Come and take me," as if inviting him to make love to her might soften the blow which was about to hit him.

The sun was exceptionally hot that day and although they were under the thick canopy of the forest, the humidity made it a stifling place to be. Somehow the holm oaks seemed to absorb the day's heat instead of deflecting it. They needed a breeze, even a warm one.

"If I put on my boots, can we go for a walk?" Nelle said.

"A walk? Now? Let's wait until dusk, when it's cooler. The boys have just left. They won't be back until the early hours. We have time."

Nelle's voice was already quivering. "We need to talk. I've got something very important to tell you. I always find it easier to talk when we're walking."

Jean raised his voice. "Can't it wait or is it that serious? Is it this rumour that you used to ride on your bike to Chalon to play the piano with a German officer? Is it playing on your conscience, having fraternised in that way? Is that why you're here? A change of heart, pangs of guilt, to try to put wrongs right, is that it?"

"So you've heard something. But it might be worse than that. How do you know about the German officer?"

"News does eventually get out about things like that. I did feel for a moment that it might have been my fault, running off, leaving you, but you'd understand that I'd need to avenge my father. Surely. You know I haven't heard a word of him. Maman thinks he's in Poland, somewhere in one of those labour camps. He wasn't in good health. The thought of him languishing there drives me onwards every day from the moment I wake. I can't wait to kill another bloody Boche, I tell you."

Marie-France was tearful and spoke slowly. "I did understand. Completely. I wished you luck and prayed for you every day. Believe me, I did. The months went by, the days drew in. I got lonely and restless but I still pined for you. Every day. There wasn't much to do but working in the vineyard, you know, after harvest, the winter pruning, tilling between the rows and so on. Helping Pa with the winemaking too."

"So is the story true?"

"Yes. I used to meet Antoinette at this bar in Chalon. There was a German officer who played the piano. I used to like that. Light relief. He played well, he was accomplished. I talked with him sometimes. I never played the piano with him."

"And then?"

"And then what?" Nelle said, sitting up. She hesitated, then stood up. "And then I got to know him better. He's a winemaker. His family owns an estate in Germany. He wasn't a Nazi. Definitely not. He just wanted to get back home and make wine like his forefathers. Like me. We had so much in common."

Jean paused before saying another word and stared at her. His face had turned red. "Don't tell me. You fucked him, didn't you? You fucked that German officer."

"One night, one night only. Possibly two, I can't remember."

"You fucked with the enemy? Are you crazy?"

Jean got up from the log he was sitting on, his face flushed and sweating. He wandered about the camp kicking out at the stones and sticks which lay in his path.

"I wanted …" Nelle started.

"Not a word more. Shut up. Not a word more," Jean shouted. "My Marie-France fucked a German officer. Well, well, well, can anyone believe that? Does anyone else know? You know what this means? It's treason. You can be shot for that. It's called 'horizontal collaboration.' That's what we call it."

"Antoinette. She knows. Antoinette knows."

"So she betrayed you for a few miserable sous. Your best friend denounced you."

"No, she didn't. It wasn't like that at all." Nelle could feel the tears rolling down her cheeks again. "I fell pregnant by him." She fell to her knees and cried out, sobbing loudly, hiding her face in her hands.

"So it gets worse," Jean shouted. He sat down on the log again. "So where is the child now? And where's the German?"

It was a long time before Nelle could answer. "Gérard is with Grand-père and Grand-mère in Lyon."

"That makes sense. So the birth was in Lyon. And when?"

"Nine … nine months ago now," Nelle said, struggling to get the words out.

"So now you want to make it all better by becoming a true patriot to avenge all the fallen countrymen and all those innocents which that German officer has killed with his army … his reprisals, his firing squads, his executions. And you feel guilty … and sorry and … wrong and dirty and … you want me to tell you it's all going to be okay. And what about your family? They must know. Why did you run away, Marie-France? Who found you out?"

"I ran because Maman didn't want me in the house. She made that clear."

"Is that all?"

"Not exactly. They painted two big 'C's on the courtyard gates at home."

Jean got up again and stamped his foot. "So you ran because you got found out and brought despicable shame upon your whole family, the business, your reputation … your poor, wretched parents. Can it get any worse? What happened to my Marie-France? However could you stoop so low? What happened to you? Goddam it. Goddam it." He stamped his foot again and raised his arms in the air.

Nelle took some time to compose herself. When she was ready, she stood up. "I don't expect your sympathy but I very desperately need your help. Listen. Listen to me carefully, please. I beg you. Everybody thinks he's your child. I told everyone that Gérard is your child, but he doesn't have your name. He's a Dubois now. That's my new name." Jean simply stared at her, his hands resting on his waist. Nelle groaned, grabbing a branch from the forest floor and throwing it across the campsite. She picked up her blouse and ran towards the path and out into the woods.

"Stop. Stop," Jean shouted. He ran to catch up with her, clasped her by the arm, turned her around, and slapped her across the face. Nelle fell to the ground, stunned for a moment. Coming to her senses, she stood up, looked him in the eye and shouted, "Yes, and now slap me again, and again. Go on, hit me. Hit me. Damn well hit me hard, you bastard."

"No. Never again. I'm sorry. I don't know what came over me." Jean stepped back and sat down on the edge of the path, propping himself up against a tree. He reached for Nelle's hand, which she pulled away. They sat without saying a word, breathless, and panting hard in the heat, sweat dripping from their brows.

"Say something, for God's sake," Nelle shouted. "Just say something. Something good. I've been waiting for two years for someone, for you, yes you, Jean, only you, to tell you the truth."

“So just like magic, I’m supposed to adopt your fascist child and be happy forever after and pretend to the whole world that I’m his father. That’s just nonsense. Have you gone mad?”

“Yes. I may very well have gone very, very mad.” She thumped the hardened ground with her fists. “Completely mad with rage and shame and guilt and hate and everything.”

“And where’s the real father? Massacring our comrades somewhere across the valley, no doubt.”

“You’re all I have. All I have.” Nelle slumped over and lay motionless across the path.

After recovering his breath, Jean got up, stepped over her and walked off leaving her lying by the path. When darkness fell an hour later, she spotted the flickering flames of a campfire through the leaves of the holm oaks. Jean was stirring a pot slowly, deep in thought. She joined him, sitting on a log opposite him. She tried to catch his eye, but his face remained downcast. There was nothing to be done except wait.

*

Ma Coccinelle – Finding a Solution

I couldn’t speak to her again that night. We ate our supper in silence accompanied by the clatter of cutlery against the metal of the mess tins. All I did say as I left her sitting by the fire, was that everything that had been said that night would remain our secret, and by the morning time we needed to have found the necessary composure so as not arouse any suspicions amongst the others. She lifted a hand to touch mine, but I couldn’t even look her in the eye.

What I had overlooked was that the whack I’d

given Nelle across her left cheek had turned into a nasty bruise which led to a blackened eye. Was anyone going to notice? Yes, of course they were. It was the first thing they remarked upon at breakfast. Nelle defended us admirably explaining that she'd slipped on the path and fallen face first onto a rock. Despite our best efforts we couldn't quell the inevitable emergence of a nasty bruise. When questioned she laughed it off, much to my delight. I would have to apologise to her again for such an angry, brutal outburst. My only explanation for my behaviour was that it was a severe reaction to shock, and a callous outburst of spontaneous anger.

We had instructions, a command at last. We were to meet up down in the valley near Saint-Pons-de-Thomières to wreak what destruction we could on a passing convoy on its way to Castres and Toulouse. We calculated a two-day hike off track to reach the rendezvous point, an auberge run by a "friend." We set off that afternoon, leaving as little evidence as we could that there'd been any previous human habitation in the area. I took up the rear, with Nelle walking a few metres ahead of me. She looked back at me a few times and I was able to raise a smile which must have brought her relief. We stopped briefly to allow a family of wild boar and their newly-born "marcassins" to cross ahead of us. I took the opportunity to rest a hand on Nelle's shoulder while the others were distracted. I felt relief when she returned a smile. There was much to resolve but we were reaching the beginnings of a peace of sorts from which some degree of understanding might result.

The going was slow although Bruno was now walking. His bullet wound was healing well but it had fractured his tibia which Hugues, a student doctor, was caring for as best he could. We had of course been deliberately rested up by our superiors for Bruno's benefit although strangely the thought had never entered my head. The disinfectant, new dressings to his wound and the morphine were doing the trick, and his pace soon quickened as he got into the stride. Hugues, Jacques and Xavier formed the rest of the cell and now with our new addition there were six of us heading off to do battle against the enemy. Spirits were optimistic, anticipation high.

Inevitably Nelle and I would have to sort our lives out. Were we going to be lovers again? Possibly. Was I going to adopt this child? No. Impossible. I didn't believe she'd expect me to, but I had to be prepared to face the possibility. So far, I hadn't agreed to act as its "pretend" father although that would be Nelle's primary objective. How long would all this take? Feelings, circumstances all change over time. And meanwhile we were putting our lives at risk every day. We were living to survive, not simply living. At least Nelle and I now both had each other's backs with any luck, although I had a responsibility for the wellbeing of the entire troupe.

Shortly before we left camp, our liaison in Rosis had passed me some news briefings. Newspapers were hard to come by so this was the best equivalent means of keeping up with the outside world. The best news was that Mussolini's government had recently resigned on 25th July, the dictator was in hiding and an armistice was surely in hand. Another boost to our morale. What I also read hidden away in the inner pages but kept to myself, was that by mid-1943, apparently 80,000 women in occupied France had claimed children's benefits from the German military authorities. So they were all at it, it seemed. That such a scheme existed in the first place seemed extraordinary to me. These women, apparently under thirty and mainly single or with husbands on STO or who were POWs, also had the right to claim German nationality for their offspring. This struck me as remarkable. However no German military were permitted to marry any women from the occupied territories, which included nearby Belgium and the Netherlands, but only presumably while the war lasted. What would happen afterwards? This would surely pose a difficult decision for Nelle, as she'd want the boy to have a father but couldn't marry the father, or perhaps she might later on. Who knew? What a damned muddle. I admit that my first thought was that she might surrender the child to its rightful father, but few mothers would willingly give away their child and walk away unless under extreme duress. I had to agree that I knew absolutely nothing about such family matters, nor had the faintest clue about the strong emotions which governed them. I became obsessed that the boy would always be in my life if I were in Nelle's. Is that how selfish men think? I was ashamed at my train of thought. I wanted Nelle, but I didn't want the child. That's what it seemed like.

At this time, Nelle had thoughts of her own. I refer you to her diary:

32.It's end-July, I'm told, but I've lost track of time. We are moving. We have orders and we are meeting up with others and we have a plan which I will only write up after the event. This morning I had terrible doubts about what I was doing and why. Do I really want to go out and kill? Perhaps I should just give myself up and throw myself onto the sacrificial altar of collaboration and summary justice, and have my limbs torn from me by an angry mob. Instead, by picking up a sword and becoming a warrior, it's my way of showing that I'm looking for exoneration and forgiveness, for my friends and family to acknowledge that I'm atoning for my sin. I'm looking for restitution, absolution and impunity (any word you want) and by so doing I'm going to save my son. But I don't know how I'm going to do this. I never even shot a rabbit, let alone a fellow human being. I can't do what these boys are doing. I'm not made for it. They have fire in their hearts and all I am is a feckless, negligent mother with a gnawing, nagging guilt. There's a big difference. And Johann isn't a bad man and a beautiful thing has happened. A child has been born out of our foolish liaison. Such awful, conflicting emotions. It's unbearable. I hoped my feelings might harden after sitting in camp all day. I need to become a cruel, ruthless, merciless savage with blood on my hands if I'm really going to show I mean something to Jean. Perhaps when I see the enemy at work, I'll feel different. Will I be able to shoot a German in the face when he comes at me? But they say I'm NOT going to be doing the killing. I'm cleaning the rifles and loading the magazines and all that kind of thing.

34.And what to do about Jean and Gérard? How am I going to persuade him to help me? I'm going to stand back and let him come round to me, slowly but surely. There's no point me making excuses for what happened. I can't expect him to understand why I did it.

18

Jean's group met up with two others at a chapel in the hills above the small town of Saint-Pons-de-Thomières, and made camp in the forest behind. There were sixteen of them, armed with two dozen grenades and each in possession of a Sten gun. The cell leaders convened later that night in a back room at Odette Belot's hotel on the edge of town. Odette was a courageous local woman who'd decided to steadfastly support the regional Maquis in their endeavours by working as a liaison and using her hotel as a storage depot for food, ammunition and medical supplies while posing as a landlady and hostess for both French travellers and German army officers.

At dawn on the following morning, German troop reinforcements and supplies of ammunition were expected to pass along the main valley road of the Jaur river in a convoy composed of an estimated four to six lorries on their way from Montpellier to Castres. The Maquisards planned to disrupt the convoy's progress by staging an accident at the intersection with a road coming up from the south, a few kilometres east of Saint Pons, where the Maquisards would be waiting in ambush. Once an adequate number of German lorries had been bombarded with grenades and consequently disabled, and a suitable number of German troops brought down by machine gun fire, a lorry would be provided for the Maquisards' immediate escape southwards on the road back towards St. Chinian, where the vehicle would be abandoned and the groups would disperse into the hills. That was the plan which had been discussed in the dimly-lit backroom of Madame Belot's auberge. Careful planning, surprise, rapid concurrent actions, followed by immediate withdrawal and dispersal were the keys to the success of such operations.

The imminent arrival of the convoy, confirmed as no more than four lorries, was radioed forward by a look out, at which point a decrepit tractor and trailer were pushed out into the middle of the road to block it. Once it had been set on fire, the Maquisards sat amongst the kerbside bushes and waited for the enemy. Nelle had been assigned to act as the driver of the escape lorry which she'd parked 400 metres down the southbound road to St. Chinian. Depending on the outcome of the battle she would either wait there in position or reverse towards the scene of the battle to collect as many Maquisards as she could, bearing in mind that many might be wounded and would need a hand. Three men had been instructed to stay behind to remove the dead and collect as much of the enemy's weaponry as they could carry, helped by farmers in the vicinity whom Madame Belot had commandeered to assist once the battle had ended. As long as all four of the German lorries had been disabled, the group's escape was guaranteed, preventing the likelihood of a pursuit.

Spotting the burning tractor and its distraught owner attempting to stifle the smoke and the flames emanating from the tractor's engine using an old sackcloth, but simultaneously sensing a potential ambush, the officer in command of the German convoy ordered it to stop some 200 metres from the tractor. Several heavily armed soldiers dismounted from each lorry and stood guard beside them while a dozen others approached the tractor from all sides. As they were doing so, a dozen of the Maquisards, including Jean's team, scrambled unseen through the bushes along the side of the road towards the parked lorries. At the command, they tossed a couple of grenades at each lorry, one upon the roof of the driver's cab and the other under each vehicle such that none of the grenades were easily recoverable and were unlikely to be tossed back before detonating.

The furious battle around the German vehicles lasted mere minutes, the massive blasts from the lorries being so intense that many German soldiers lost their lives immediately. Those who survived took up defensive positions on either side of the road. Although they were outnumbered, the Maquisards benefitted from almost total surprise, until they were left to defend themselves in a one-to-one gun battle with their better armed opponents.

Nelle observed the skirmish from the relative safety of her vehicle until the German lorries were fully ablaze. The thick, black smoke billowing from the enemy vehicles allowed her enough cover to approach the scene and drag one of her wounded comrades to safety, and then another. Two other colleagues were clearly dead so she dragged those to the side of the road. Spotting Jean with a bleeding right arm and attempting to fire his Sten gun with his left hand only, she shouted at him to take cover, which he ignored. Down to a mere eight men against at least a dozen Germans, she took hold of a redundant machine gun and jumped into a ditch beside the road. Now it was a question of picking off each German soldier before they spotted and shot you, not an easy task for Nelle who had no battle training. But no one had expected it to go this far. After ten minutes of intense gunfire, Jean gave the order to retreat to their escape vehicle. Nelle counted a mere seven who clambered on board including Jean. Most were wounded, some badly. Nelle hesitated for a moment, looking out for any stragglers before Jean shouted at her to go. They couldn't afford to collect any badly wounded or indeed the dead.

"Eleven good men lost today," Jean declared, having made a quick count.

His words were met with silence. Only the roar of the engine filled their ears as Nelle crunched through the gears, until a voice from the rear piped up, "Who's the girl at the wheel? She saved my life. Dragged me off the road to cover. Under fire too. A brave one, she is."

"That would be 'Coccinelle la Combattante,' Nelle to her friends. Never been in a fire fight until today. Directly disobeyed orders, but saved three men," Jean said, patting her on the back.

"I didn't hear that," she shouted.

"Words of praise," Jean said. "More later."

A few kilometres before the town of St. Chinian, the road cut into the edge of a steep hill and turned a sharp corner. Jean ordered Nelle to pull over, and shouted orders to the men to grab their pre-prepared food parcels and medication packs, re-group with their respective comrades and then disperse into the nearby garrigue. Meanwhile Jean and Hugues drove the lorry to the side of the road, drained it of what fuel remained, disconnected the battery, and pushed it over the edge into the ravine. As they had hoped, it broke up but failed to catch fire. Nelle, Jean, and Hugues were the only three to survive from their cell. Jean had a bullet wound to his right arm and Hugues to his abdomen, above his hip. Nevertheless, they climbed up the hill through a steep combe, stopping in a safe, thickly-wooded area by a stream to wash their faces and attend to their wounds. While both Jean and Hugues had sustained injuries which had caused extensive bleeding, it appeared that the bullets had pierced their flesh and exited leaving deep wounds, but neither had sustained bone fractures or organ damage. The best they could do was to wash the wounds, disinfect them and bandage them up to prevent infection.

"So Jean, how good are you going to be at anything now that you've only got a functioning left hand?" Hugues joked.

"It's not my hand that's wounded, it's my upper arm, you fool. I can still hold a pistol in my right hand. It's painful but I can at least defend myself. Anyway, we'll be rested up for now. Another month of boredom to recuperate, sharpening our spears and trapping rabbits, I suppose. Perhaps we'll be moved on."

"Somewhere by the sea would be nice," said Nelle.

"But I'd like to find Bruno, Jacques and Xavier. Hopefully someone's picked them up before the Boches arrive at the scene. They deserve a good burial," said Jean.

"How do we get to bury them?" Hugues said.

"We'll hear in time from the Pons cell."

"Are we going back to Rosis now?" Nelle asked.

"For the moment, yes. We report back to Rosis and hide up where we were before," Jean said, lifting his gourd and offering a toast to his fallen comrades. Nelle and Hugues duly reciprocated.

They rested up for the night several kilometres north-westwards towards the wine village of Berlou, overlooking the valley of the Orb river. The going was tough and the hills steep. The area was heavily wooded with no paths to speak of. But it offered good cover, the entire region being suitably wild and remote, unpopulated, and far away from any roads. By the time Jean had called in on their contact in Rosis a few days later, news had got about of their successful ambush. There was talk too of a German reprisal on the villagers of Saint-Pons. As it happened, retribution took the form of a series of "rafles" or round-ups for the STO in the wider area, but with limited success as most of the young people who still remained in this area were classed as "agriculteurs," working the land for the vital production of food. They were the lucky ones excused from being despatched to Germany.

The Germans had managed to capture three wounded Resistance members who were still alive. According to the Rosis liaison, they were tortured, then executed by firing squad that same evening, with the whole town being forced out of their homes and into the main square in Saint-Pons to witness it. Jean later learned that one of those executed had been Bruno. No one had come to claim the bodies overnight. They had reportedly been buried incognito the following morning in the churchyard. Graves were dug by the local undertakers and the bodies blessed by the old parish priest.

"We will give Bruno a fitting burial when all of this is over," Jean told Nelle and Hugues. "At present, anonymity is the best course, so the families aren't implicated in any way. I will get word to all eventually, informing them of our courageous, respected fallen."

"Is that part of your responsibilities?" asked Nelle. "We really are like one big family, aren't we?"

"We are indeed. We each have each other's back. That's a primary duty," Jean said. "By the way, Rosis have given us a bottle of eau de vie to celebrate. We'll drink tonight and be merry. We all need a cheer up. I don't know about you both, but I'm exhausted. Bread, sausage and cheese tonight. Tobacco and booze too."

"A veritable feast," Nelle shouted out.

They sat around a small fire in the same location up in the wooded hills which had become familiar to them over previous months, laying out their affairs, and unpacking what food, drink, medication and ammunition they had managed to bring with them. The general conclusion was that if that campsite had proved to be safe then, it most likely would be now. But it also reminded them more forcefully than ever that they were three colleagues short.

After eating, they passed the bottle of local marc around to dull the pain caused by their wounds. Nelle sat close to Jean on a log, their shoulders and knees scuffing from time to time as the evening wore on, prompting Hugues's curiosity.

"Are you two close friends now or what? I'm beginning to feel like the spare old gooseberry with you two about."

Nelle looked at Jean and nodded. It was time to inform their one remaining colleague. No harm would come of it. It was a miracle that no one had suspected anything so far but they'd both been careful and discreet enough avoid mentioning anything of their past relationship. Nelle led the way, ensuring that Hugues only heard what was necessary to hear. There was no mention of Gérard. It was up to Jean if he chose to go that far.

Hugues lay down that night on the edge of the camp, keeping to himself, while Nelle and Jean shared the night together. Jean's wounded right arm barely prevented him from enjoying the warmth of Nelle's body beside him.

*

Ma Coccinelle – Reunited

Nelle excelled that day, well beyond what was asked of her and I felt it churlish to rebuke her more than once for disobeying orders. Being the driver of the escape vehicle was not enough for her, and seeing the opportunity to help us out, she stepped into the line of fire to save a number of colleagues, some regrettably dying later. But she demonstrated to all of us that her heart was in the battle.

Such was the nature of our style of combat in those days, that we could take on the enemy in those sorts of circumstances – an ambush in remote, wooded locations – even though we were usually outnumbered. But to get involved in open battle or even lengthy skirmishes was riskier. We should have had more men at Saint-Pons, back-ups in case we'd underestimated the number of troops in those vehicles, which I have to admit we did. Having ten more of our men would have brought the resulting skirmish to a swifter end and possibly led to fewer comrades being lost. It was the concluding assessment which I sent to our superiors.

Our cell was now in need of more men to perform any further meaningful operations. We were effectively survivors convalescing away from the action, with a need to attain the necessary level of fitness before being redeployed in the field. The heat of August brought on a certain lethargy, no doubt bolstered by our lack of activity and purpose. Hugues became increasingly restless and we assumed he might have grown tired of our company, but leaving him alone for hours on end during the day might equally have compounded his boredom. Nelle and I found a deep enough pool in the stream at the bottom of the combe to wallow in the cooling waters for hours on end, drying ourselves and sunbathing on the adjacent boulders when the mountain water had cooled us sufficiently. We had little fear of being spotted. Shedding what few clothes we wore during the day seemed perfectly natural and no doubt contributed to our sense of freedom and familiarity, and that helped us rediscover the intimacy which we once enjoyed, making love day and night with the same enthusiasm as when we had first met.

Living out in the wild and off the land for months on end served to remind us of nature's proximity as if we were rediscovering a part of us we'd lost generations ago. We found the daily rituals of existence out in the wild had rejuvenated us with a palpable new energy and a natural purity of spirit. It was as if we'd stumbled upon an innate force that had been there all along, but with which we'd gradually severed our connections over the years. We felt closer to all the elements now, slotting in naturally like primordial components within the natural order of things. We often talked of how modern life had chipped away at the most basic human instincts associated with living in the natural way. And now we were able to observe everything in a new light, as if we had once again become dependent on and a part of the natural life which surrounded us, from the mighty energies induced by an electric storm, to the busy ants building a nest of pine needles beside us, as we lay on the rocks sunning and warming our bodies like young lizards in the spring.

We decided one evening over supper that it would make sense for Hugues to know that we had a son, which was a notable step forward for Nelle, as it had become clear that she'd been hoping for my acquiescence sooner rather than later. To publicise the fact also lent it some authenticity, as she later explained to me. It must have prompted Hugues to consider that as parents we were much more than passing lovers and might prefer more time alone together while the opportunity arose, for none of us ever knew where we might be next, dead or alive. It was easy to forget such dire considerations when living amongst the beauty and serenity of the Languedoc forests and mountains – that we were at war, and that life was fragile, with an indeterminate future.

Sensing our desire to indulge in each other's company while we could, Hugues announced the following morning that he'd be heading home to Lyon, but with the intention of meeting up again at some point. Nelle asked that he check in with her grandparents and convey to us any news regarding Gérard if he could.

Nelle's diary at the time is revealing:

59.August 1943 in the hills above Rosis. Jean and I have found each other again. Such a joy to lie in his arms again, to feel his warmth, to enjoy his humour and his love once more. How strange it is that I could so easily have believed that I'd never see him again. Now that we are alone, we are totally free. The lovemaking is exquisite and frequent. We cannot get enough of each other. Such desire for sexual fulfilment has caught me by surprise. We both feel it and nothing is forbidden now that we are so free and unshackled, basking in the full bosom of nature. And what ecstasy to lie close to a man again and to reach orgasm while his arms are held so tightly around me. Gone are the lonely days of pleasuring myself with his image in mind. Now I have him right by my side, every day. He's my treasure and I shan't let him go.

And yet we are at war. He has lost three mates from university: Xavier, Jacques and Bruno, all with bright futures ahead of them. I know he mourns them every day and yet he tries not to be miserable. He keeps us upbeat, ever hopeful. That's a talent, a skill.

I still feel guilty at leaving Gérard. What mother wouldn't? But I am on the way to finding a modus vivendi and I will be back in Lyon for him very soon. We have told another friend and colleague, Hugues, that we have a child. Slowly but surely Gérard will have a father, at least in name and as long as the Germans occupy our territory. And what of my friends back home and those who are not my friends at all, those who denounced me? How long are their memories? Are they still after me? Are they still looking for revenge? How long will I have to remain in hiding? Someone knows about Johann, someone saw us and someone is out for my blood. But through all this, I believe Jean will defend me, Hugues too, and the others who witnessed my resolve, my patriotism, my fervour. And Jean too knows the whole truth, namely that I need to seek forgiveness, exculpation, indemnification – whatever you want to call it. I have many words for it and not a single one is quite powerful enough on its own.

Jean will stand up for me when the time comes.

*

In September, we heard that on the 8th the Italian Armistice had been proclaimed. Subsequently, the Germans had taken over all the remaining lands in France to the east of the Rhône which the Italians had previously occupied. In early October, Corsica was liberated by the Maquis. Nelle and I finished the grape marc that night in celebration. It seemed that as the Germans were being pushed increasingly into a corner, things were getting tougher here. All men of working age remaining in France had to carry an "exemption" or "unfit" stamp in their papers to exclude them from the STO draft in Germany. 670,000 Frenchmen had gone to work in Germany and only 110,000 POWs returned in exchange. That didn't seem fair but then the Germans couldn't be trusted. Rosis was going to have to get me new forged documents as I risked being arrested without the correct paperwork.

One evening, presumably in case we should have become too blasé up in our hideaway in the hills, Nelle and I descended to Rosis for a series of intense overnight exercises. And most vitally we were to pick up brand new

IDs, resident permits and ration cards, indicating our new home in a small village outside Clermont-l'Hérault. Our new occupations were grape farming and mechanic, and you know which I was, although I frankly had not the slightest idea about engines.

That night we learnt how best to burgle a house, wriggle out of handcuffs, scale a wall, and to identify German Wehrmacht and Gestapo uniforms and ranks, weaponry and aircraft. Our Rosis contact went through the rudiments of how to operate a Eureka ground-based transponder, an "S" phone with which we were already familiar, and techniques necessary for the sabotage of industrial warehouses and factories, railway infrastructure and railway locomotives, electrical power stations, substations, and transformers. We also learnt to identify the aircraft of our British colleagues in the RAF and their various uses. Lysanders were the aircraft of choice for small drops. They also required the shortest runways. Hudsons were larger and might be used to drop off agents and collect downed airmen. And Lancasters were employed for large drop offs. None of us had ever seen or heard the legendary four-engined Lancaster, but we'd apparently know when it was coming as the ground literally shook under our feet although it was 500 feet above us.

Clearly the struggle for France's liberation had stepped up a notch. For the first time, I felt perhaps we were being prepared for something much bigger, although our Rosis man explained that we were equally valuable as part of a small network misdirecting German convoys, or helping farmers falsify quantities of produce to be requisitioned for the enemy. Equally important, we might be flyposting at night, sabotaging German and Milice vehicles, and most importantly stealing blank ID cards, ration books, demobilisation forms, census certificates, work permits, and residence permits from town halls, none of which demanded much skill but which were nevertheless vital, requisite elements of the struggle.

Before we left Rosis at dawn, an instruction came though on the radio that we were to meet in three days' time at an address in Bédarieux at midnight on 10th October, a town to the east along the valley, which I'd skirted earlier on in my travels. We were going on a mission situated somewhere on the Mediterranean coast. No further details were provided.

19

Nelle and Jean arrived in Bédarieux half an hour behind schedule, the journey into town proving to be more hazardous than expected. There, they met up with Hugues and several others, some of whom they recognised from the Saint-Pons ambush. The atmosphere was anything but relaxed. News had come through that one of the safe houses in town had been raided only a few hours earlier with the resulting loss of revolvers and explosives, and most importantly, notebooks, addresses, false IDs, forged ration books, typewriters, blueprints for attacks on trains, train timetables, fake train tickets, roneo machines, ink, stencils, and paper supplies – all the essentials required for running a Resistance cell. The whole operational capability of that cell had been compromised, and not least those who were operating it.

A man spoke up from the shadows. "My name is Bertrand. No doubt you've heard about this raid, hence the hasty change of address. Our Bédarieux colleagues were so successful that the Boches finally took revenge on them. Bravo to our comrades. For the record, in the past, their successes have included raids on food warehouses, clothes shops, wine merchants, banks, and post offices. And they've taken valuable rationing cards from smaller 'mairies' and larger town halls from all over the locality in the last few months. A good job done. But their time is now up."

"That explains why the place is crawling with bloody Boches, and why it took us so long to get here without being stopped," Jean said.

"But you weren't followed, were you?" Bertrand asked. "Are you by any chance Jean de Lyon?"

"I am Jean de Lyon, yes. And I can confirm that we weren't followed," Jean said. "And this is Nelle, a co-fighter and member of our cell." Jean put his arm around her shoulder as if to confirm that Nelle was very much part of the team.

"I have been instructed to place you in command of this operation, Jean. Please all gather round the table and I'll brief you. It's not complicated. There are six of you tonight, three in each motor car, including the young lady, Nelle, who has already earned her colours." Bertrand looked up and smiled at Nelle. "Tonight's target is two storage tanks at a fuel depot in the port of Sète. You have motor cars to get you there and bring you back, but you are to report back to Clermont-l'Hérault as things are too hot here right now. There are explosives hidden in both cars which you must locate in the vehicle and familiarise yourself with prior to leaving here. And all of you will be armed. Nelle, you will drive one vehicle, Didier the other." Bertrand pointed to a tall man standing next to Jean. "And you will carry three heavy-duty bolt cutters. Here is the map. Study it. The fuel tanks are on the shore line, clear to see, but are heavily guarded by a perimeter fence and a line of sentry posts. My advice is that only one of you enter the immediate premises and plant the explosives. The tanks are right next to each other. If you only blow one, most likely the other will go up soon enough."

"And the address in Clermont-l'Hérault?" Nelle asked.

"Right here, and memorise it," Bertrand said, passing a small piece of paper around the table. "Time to go. You should reach Sète by 2.30 a. m. And good luck. I apologise for such a quick meeting, but we must disperse before they get to us. Vive la libération."

*

Ma Coccinelle - The End of Us

I cannot be sure how Bertrand met his fate except I'm certain that he did not survive the war. Although it is said that one should never dishonour the dead, if I were to meet him again, I would surely reprimand him for a hasty and inadequately planned operation in Sète, in which my friend and colleague, Hugues, lost his life as did two others whose names I never knew.

Granted, our operation was successful but I truly believed I had lost my Nelle, who, as was now habitual, showed exemplary bravery in defending Hugues to the last as he placed and then detonated both sets of explosives. Sadly he was unable to escape the blast for which he was responsible. It was a ghastly spectacle which does not bear writing about. The oil depot was considerably better defended than we had been led to believe, such that our escape under heavy fire seemed frankly impossible. One of the cars was destroyed and our escape in the second was halted by heavy gunfire. Three of us dispersed in separate directions and I was not to see Nelle again until the war's end. I know the other survivor's name to be Gilles but I cannot recall ever seeing him again.

Nelle's own assessment is telling enough:

64.October 1943, Sète. I write this several days after the event as I was unable to scribble a word for some time. I don't expect the horror of that night will ever escape me. Jean lost a friend, Hugues, engulfed in flames from the burning oil and then blown apart by a second explosion. It's a miracle that three of us survived. Three brave lives were lost though, and I honour their memory here today.

Jean and I were lucky to escape, but in the panic and chaos we lost each other. The last I saw of him, he was running up a street in the opposite direction to the one I had been forced down. He had a limp and his leg was bleeding through his trousers, no doubt a heavy wound, that much I could see. I'd also been shot in the arm between my left wrist and elbow and I was certain the bone had been fractured. We had a rendezvous address in Clermont-l'Hérault but Jean never arrived. Gilles did though, after me, and he was able to corroborate the success of the mission with our superiors. I'm happy to say that he was full of praise for my endeavours although I was supposed to sit in the car and wait for them. As usual I couldn't resist participating. I'm not, and will never be a bystander, let that be clear, especially when I see my comrades in difficulty. We were again outnumbered, but by God what an explosion. Magnificent, especially as Sète is a significant Mediterranean port and we have given the enemy a good bashing.

Gilles and I rested up for several weeks in Clermont-l'Hérault, covering up our wounds so that they could not be spotted. We had residency and agricultural worker permits for the area, and STO exemptions, improbable as that might sound. But at least I was no imposter if it came to convincing a German sentry at a roadblock that I knew something about vines. We were surrounded by them and I felt a genuine urge to tend to them, believe it or not!

67. Clermont-l'Hérault, late October 1943. The frustrations of not knowing where Jean is finally get to me this morning. By now I like to think I'd become good friends with our contact and host, Raoul. After all he was the first "friend" I stumbled upon in Clermont before reaching Jean near Rosis, several months earlier. We get on well and I begged him today to make enquiries on my behalf, which was strictly a breach of security protocol as it might have compromised our safety and whereabouts. But I think I was convincing. We will see.

72. Clermont-l'Hérault, November 1943. News reaches us that Jean has been captured and imprisoned. I dread to think what they might have done to him. But the good news is that the local Montpellier Resistance cell arranged a road block and overwhelmed the vehicle he was being transported in. Apparently, several prisoners escaped. Jean is thought to be among them. But no one can be sure and he is still badly wounded. But where is he now? Why is he not back at Clermont with us? The uncertainty haunts me every day. Perhaps he knows better than to risk betraying our location. After all he is a fugitive and he is no doubt being hounded down as I write. I pray for him every day and wonder if I shall ever see him again. That's a terrible thought but I cannot get it out of my head.

*

My capture was somewhat inevitable as the bullet wound in my leg was painful and I couldn't run fast enough. I'm not sure why they didn't shoot me on the spot. Presumably I had a price on my head and they were thinking of extracting as much information as they could from me before finishing me off. I was duly thrown into the local Sète penitentiary. Fortunately, after a few days of constant beatings they decided to move me somewhere else. The time which passed between my capture and my escape had allowed the Maquis to concoct a plan.

It seemed to me that they had an informant in the jail, as the lorry transporting me was ambushed on the road to Montpellier and two comrades carried me off successfully, first by laying me out on a stretcher and carrying me by foot, then by strapping me onto a donkey. I don't remember much more, except my freedom came as a great relief and I was delighted to be amongst friends again, although I was left immobile and inoperative for many months to come.

I will fill you in on a few facts regarding Resistance progress at this stage as it will provide the reader with a good image of how difficult life had become. In November 1943, Joseph Epstein, the FTP Resistance Chief of Staff, was arrested and subjected to extreme torture, but revealed nothing to anyone. Bravo to him! This was followed by a major police operation that largely destroyed the FTP's Paris organisation, which came as a setback to us all. From the end of 1943 the national organisation began to intensify preparations for a nationwide uprising to support the expected Allied landings in Europe, but where it was to take place, we had not a clue. I guess that was the point. No one knew. We worked like mad with our recruitment publicity – posters and flyers were placed wherever we could. It is believed that by Christmas time 1943, the FTP were 100,000 strong. Quite an achievement.

The winter of 1943/4 was looking like it was going to be a hard one and severe shortages of food didn't help, especially essentials such as eggs, milk and meat. But by the end of 1943, the Vichy government announced an amnesty for the "réfractaires," and deportations had slowed, so the roundups for the STO became less of an issue. It depended where you were though, as we heard that some areas still suffered from arbitrary roundups by the political paramilitary group, the Milice, in cooperation with the German army and the paramilitary police, the GMR (Groupes Mobiles de Réserve) under René Bousquet, who by now had taken charge of all the national police operations against the Resistance.

In December 1943, the wretched Joseph Darnand entered the Vichy government as Secretary General and oversaw overall law enforcement. He was put at the head of the Milice, the most extreme and dominant of Vichy fascist militia groups. Among their specialities were the use of torture, extortion, summary execution and assassination. A renewed wave of deportations of Jews ensued, and the activities of the military courts intensified. Attacks against the Resistance by the German Sipo-SD, the security police forces, in collaboration with the French, became more severe with special efforts to counter the rural elements of the Resistance – the Maquis of the garrigue, hills and woodlands of rural France, which had recently become an increasingly potent force. It seemed like we were now on the map, so to speak. The Maquis had become a force to be reckoned with, and we were everyone's target.

20

Marie-France, aware of a need for a lull in her Resistance activities in order to recuperate, returned to Lyon for Christmas to the delight of her grandparents, knocking on their door one freezing night as the snow fell heavily. This time she had travelled by train as Christmas leave seemed like a bona fide pretext to travel home and no one might question her reason for travelling. She'd kept her Lyon papers so all would be in order in that respect if ever she were requested to show them.

Gérard, now one year and three months old, viewed Marie-France as if she were a stranger when she entered his room the following morning, crying out instead for Claudette. She took Gérard's reaction in her stride. It wasn't surprising, but she later succumbed to a deep melancholia. That morning's episode sparked a profound sense of guilt and a desperate yearning to spend as much time with him as she could so as to make amends, although at first she realised she risked confusing the boy. She reminded herself that she would need to become accustomed to her given name, Marie-France, again. She repeated it over and over "I am Marie-France, your mother" whenever she was with Gérard, hoping he would soon grasp who she was.

She paid a visit to her doctor to have her wound seen to – a hunting accident, she lied, upon being asked how it had happened. The same morning she clocked in at the old man's premises hoping to see Marcel again. News of her Resistance activities with Jean had been reported back to them. She was welcomed as a heroine and offered a slice of celebratory cake. Jean was discussed but no one was any the wiser as to his exact whereabouts. She was disappointed to learn that Marcel was away and wouldn't be returning until January, but she made it clear to the old man that she intended seeing Marcel again and would visit in mid-January.

Marie-France considered that six months in Lyon would be a suitable length of time for Jean to learn of her whereabouts if he should want to find her and, secondly, time enough for Gérard to bond more heartily with his mother. She spent that evening deep in conversation with Hervé. They talked well into the night, demolishing half a bottle of Poire Williamine between them. He wished to know of all she'd been up to in the Maquis although she had never once, as far as she could remember, told him she had any intentions of joining the Resistance, simply that she needed to reunite with the father of her child. She considered there was no harm in telling an old man like Hervé what she'd been up to. She surmised that he was hardly likely to be tortured if he were ever arrested.

As the months went by, Marie-France spent as much time as possible with her son. It was true however that she barely had anything else to do. She contemplated travelling north to Saubon-le-Duc but then reminded herself of the price on her head, and that her life was by no means a normal one. She still had to live an existence partly in the shadows. People out there held her in contempt whatever she might have done to atone for her former misdeeds. After all, hundreds of thousands of women had done what she'd done. In her eyes it wasn't a crime, merely a "folie de passion," or even a mere peccadillo for which she now deserved forgiveness. She visited Marcel as often as she could, principally hoping to learn of Jean, but no news of him left her increasingly frustrated and saddened. Surely someone would let her know if he'd died. The Maquis was a close enough family. No news of any kind made longing for him even harder to bear.

Marie-France learnt from Hervé that in the month of January 1944, 5,500 souls had been arrested, kept in a holding camp in Compiègne, and despatched east by train, including 1,000 women prisoners despatched on a special train to the Ravensbrück concentration camp. Things had got tough out in the field. As the Germans began to lose their grip, so their counter measures became ever more aggressive. In a February 1944 decree, Marshall Hugo Sperrle, deputy Supreme Commander for Western Europe, ordered that all German soldiers should return fire without hesitation when threatened, and all identified partisan homes should be burnt to the ground. From Field Marshall Wilhelm Keitel, in overall command of the Wehrmacht, came a further order – shoot to kill all those carrying arms. And any Resistance members not caught red-handed with weaponry, were to be arrested and sentenced to death after a hasty trial.

Meanwhile the various elements of the Resistance made further efforts to unite and coordinate their plans and activities. On 15th March a Charter of the Conseil National de la Resistance (CNR) attempted to unify all bodies under one political entity, but with limited success. Some group members, especially those members unsympathetic to the Communist Party such as elements of the Action Ouvrière (the factory workers), some of the Groupes Francs (partisans) and some Résistance-Fer (railway workers) members, united under the leadership of the CFL, the "Corps Francs de la Libération." Later in the month, General de Gaulle, in London, placed all French Forces of the Interior (FFI) under the command of General Marie-Pierre Koenig, although the FTP still maintained a measure of operational independence.

By June 1944, the official STO scheme had ended, although this did not prevent sporadic, major "rafles," such as the 500 men rounded up and arrested in Béziers in the Hérault, just as the Allies were landing in Normandy. Marie-France hoped that didn't include anyone she'd known operationally, as she was reminded that Béziers was only forty kilometres south of Rosis as the crow flies.

On 6th June 1944, Operation Overlord, Jour-J (D-Day), began, with five naval assault divisions landing on the beaches of Normandy, combining the air, land and sea forces of the Allied command. Such news was announced by a special radio broadcast that afternoon which Hervé missed. He was only alerted to it later by his highly emotional neighbour, who knocked frantically at the front door, and was barely capable of spitting out the news when Hervé received him. Hervé promptly ordered Marie-France to descend to the cellar and collect the two best bottles she could find in the house, while Hervé charged down to the chicken coop at the bottom of the garden and returned with a dead chicken, which he proceeded to pluck outside the back door. It was time for a little luxury after so many lean years. That evening Claudette brought out the best lace table cloth, napkins, bone china and silverware, and Hervé searched for their two precious ormolu candelabras which he'd hidden away from the Germans in the attic under Claudette's instructions. They sat at the dining table that evening under the light of eight flickering candles, toasting the imminent liberation of France.

Eight months had passed with no news of Jean. Perhaps no news was the best Marie-France could hope for. No one had reported his death and no one had found his body. She lived in hope that he was still alive. She surmised that a wanted man of his stature would remain in the shadows for as long as necessary. The Jour-J landings prompted Marie-France to consider taking up her duties again for the sake of France and the Resistance. She was sitting with her grandparents after dinner in early July when she broached the subject. "I'm thinking of setting off again," she announced. "I want to be part of the effort to liberate France. I cannot let it pass by without doing my part for a better France. As you know, I'm no bystander."

Hervé had something else on his mind. "I'm incensed by this 'impôt metal,' which they're talking about, this tax on copper. Have you read this?" He lifted up the newspaper to show Marie-France. "Vichy want two to three kilogrammes of copper from every household every year or you'll suffer a fine of 900 francs. Are they crazy? Are we supposed to give up cooking? Have things really got so bad that they want all our pots and pans now?" He paused for a moment, then raised his fist. "Yes, girl, go fight for our freedom and the downfall of this wretched government. I'm all for it."

Claudette shuffled uneasily in her armchair. "There is still talk that the Maquis are merely brigands and bandits … terrorists and communists. Is it really such a good idea that Marie-France is associated with that lot? Especially as the German reprisals as a result of the Maquis's actions are also becoming so unpopular with the ordinary people? It's dangerous. She might lose her life. Then what of Gérard?"

Hervé rubbed his chin. "You have a point, but it depends where she goes. Those parts of France which voted for the left-leaning Front Populaire in 1936 are far more sympathetic to the Resistance. They're even to be seen recruiting openly, and these days the rural Resistance elements, the Maquis, find a welcoming populace wherever they go. They're willingly given food and shelter. But it is true, the fighting is becoming more intense. It is dangerous."

"How do you know all this and how can you be certain? And surely it is the German army she should be worrying about, not the Maquis," Claudette said.

"I've nothing else to do but read and listen to the radio broadcasts, and do a bit of digging in the vegetable garden," said Hervé, stretching for his newspaper. "That's why I know what's going on. Besides what do you think Marie-France has been up to while she's been away?"

"I know. But it's got far more dangerous now," said Claudette.

"It says here in this article that they think we have lost 8,000 franc-tireurs in June alone, that's Resistance partisans, but I think that figure might include civilians lost in reprisals as well. It's not entirely clear. The massacres of the Maquis of the Mont Mouchet is bad enough. That particular rout left 228 killed and one hundred civilians murdered during the reprisal. 3,000 German troops were employed in those massacres, in the two villages of Ruynes and Clavières alone. That was during the second week of June. The Boches are coming down hard on the Maquis now."

"The Mont Mouchet is about 200 kilometres north of where I was in the Languedoc. It's right up nearly 1,500 meters in the middle of the Massif Central. It's a big Maquis hide-out area in the high plains," Marie-France said.

Hervé glanced at the newspaper again and said, "Despite the massacres, the Resistance are still strong. It is said that the Corps Francs of the Montagne Noires region exceeded 500 men by Jour-J, with 4,700 in the Mont Mouchet and La Tryère areas, and 4,000 men in the Vercors region. The Montagne Noires are very close to where you were in Rosis and St. Pons, no?"

"About fifty kilometres due west," Marie-France said. "But literally on my former patch, there was this incident in early June at Fonjun on the Col de Cébazan, between Puisserguier and St.Chinian. I was involved in an ambush near there last summer. I know the place where it happened." Marie-France got down onto her hands and knees and searched amongst Hervé's newspapers which were sprawled out across the floor of the salon. She picked one out and read from it. "Here we are. Young Maquis volunteers travelling from Capestang and Montady to form a group in the garrigue north of St.Chinian were confronted by a truck full of

German soldiers. Five were killed instantly and eighteen remained unhurt including Juliette Cauquil, the driver's wife. Those eighteen were hanged in the Champ de Mars in Béziers the following day. Those boys died unarmed in search of their Maquis colleagues."

"That's damn bad luck," said Hervé. "In fact it's bloody criminal."

"I know for a fact that that cell is now thriving with the help of the AS, our Armée Sécrete colleagues in St.Pons, which was one of my twinned cells. They received a parachute drop recently in the Sommail hills nearby, which I know well. So, they are now armed and regrouping. That's what a friend of mine in town said."

"Don't tell me you'll be joining them again," Claudette said sighing, but her exasperation fell on deaf ears.

Hervé continued reading out aloud from his newspaper. "And the reprisals against the innocent villagers of Tulle and Oradour-sur-Glane occurred around the same time. That's enough to make any Frenchman's blood boil," Hervé said. He let out a long sigh and put his feet up. "Oh dear. Here, let me read you this. After a successful Resistance offensive on the 7th and 8th June which killed forty German soldiers in the Tulle/Limoges area and resulted in the capture of fifty or more German soldiers, the 2nd SS Panzer Division named 'Das Reich,' under the command of SS-Gruppenführer Heinz Lammerding ended the fighting on the 9th June with a retaliative action for the earlier uprising, consequently hanging ninety-nine men from the village of Tulle and deporting one hundred and forty-nine."

Marie-France directed her gaze at Claudette, "Doesn't that make you want to go out and murder the swine? They slaughter our innocents."

"I'm afraid there is worse," Hervé continued. "Thankfully many other Maquisards had fled for the hills and escaped the German retaliation and what was to follow a day later. On 10th June, 642 civilians were massacred in the village of Oradour-sur-Glane. One of this 2nd Panzer Division's units was the 4th SS Panzer Grenadier Regiment, named 'Der Führer.' One of its staff is the regimental commander SS-Sturmbannführer Adolf Diekmann who was commanding the 1st Battalion, which committed these crimes. Women and children were locked in the village church and it was then set on fire. As for the men, they were herded into barns and sheds, then strafed with machine-gun fire. After that, the men's bodies were set on fire. It was mass murder. The youngest was a two day old child."

"That is truly shocking," interrupted Claudette.

Hervé continued reading, "Indeed. And all this was supposedly in revenge for the German soldiers' deaths in and around Tulle a few days earlier. Regarding the captured German soldiers, some say the Resistance grew tired of having to feed them, and didn't know what to do with them, so on 12th June they got them to dig their own graves, then shot and buried what remained of them. About forty men. But the Resistance deny this, saying they had to let them flee. They couldn't look after that many prisoners at once. No Maquisards are prepared to admit to these actions."

Marie-France spoke up, her voice croaking with rage. "We are not equipped to take or guard prisoners for long. What do we do with them? They are better dead. They are soldiers. As for the massacre of village innocents in Tulle and Oradour, that's pure murder, another story completely. They weren't soldiers fighting a war. And don't forget that our own Milice and GMR police forces are helping the Germans launch multi-pronged attacks like this. That's what is so desperately tragic. What have we French come to? Revenge, when it comes, will be very sweet and bloody against such traitors."

Marie-France reminded herself of her own predicament. She felt more convinced than ever that there was more she should be doing, and it could provide her with a better chance of being forgiven, if she were ever accused and brought to trial. She continued, reading aloud from the newspaper. "Do you know, Hervé, that we are triumphing against all the odds? The Germans are throwing everything at us now. They employ fast motorised response units, armoured reconnaissance platoons, and artillery regiments as well as infantry and sometimes the Luftwaffe against us. But our innocent citizens are suffering most. And it says here that Field Marshall Keitel is planning deportations of the entire male populations of villages where there's been Resistance activity."

Claudette raised her voice. "So all the more reason to stay out of it. I do insist."

Marie-France got up from her chair. "I'm going up to bed. I have too much anger and longing for revenge spinning about my head. I must rest."

That night, she lay on her back, her head propped up on the pillow, her mind racing with possibilities. It was time to press upon Marcel her need to return to the struggle against the Nazi occupiers. She wondered where Johann might be. On the miserable eastern front fighting the Soviets or as she hoped, in some quiet outpost by the sea in the south of France. And was he even alive? She soon turned her thoughts to the various options facing her, and concluded that her ultimate ambition involved joining up with Jean again. Could she work in Lyon where he might ultimately be in hiding? Was her secret safe enough in Lyon though? It would be, if Jean were around, but even so, she wasn't sure who was working against her. Perhaps there was no one. And what of Gérard? Could she call upon Claudette to look after Gérard once more? All might depend on what Marcel could come up with.

21

Marie-France put on a pair of the most comfortable shoes for walking, set out towards the centre of town, and found a bar which was open. She sat at a table in the street and ordered a pastis. It was a warm July day. She was aware of a greater police presence but nothing else seemed untoward. A man wearing a brown leather jacket, whom she estimated to be in his mid-thirties, with a dark, narrow, perfectly manicured moustache, smoked a cigarette and drank an ersatz coffee at the table next to hers. His newspaper headlines announced the establishment of special military tribunals and martial courts. In the smaller print, but nevertheless legible, she read that non-military "Courts de Justice" were to introduce a more uniform approach to sentencing crimes. So far, 5,000 policemen had been suspended and ten members of the Brigades Spéciales had been executed. These were Frenchmen being brought to justice by Frenchmen. Was her own noose being tightened?

When the man had finished his coffee, he offered Marie-France the newspaper, handing it over and casting an agreeable smile in her direction before leaving. He looked like a policeman and she hesitated before taking it from him. She continued reading it. She remarked that by June 1944, French partisans had organised summary executions of 5,238 Milice members and other "collabos," informants, and over-zealous police officials. 20,000 women, the "tondues," had had their heads shaved by the partisans for fraternising with the enemy and 9,000 communists had been killed by the Germans.

She ordered another pastis and wondered whom she should fear most – the Resistance, the rampaging mob seeking retribution, or the Germans. Such a deeply worrying prospect of being hunted down by three separate elements had not entered her head since she'd fled Saubon-le-Duc. She pondered whether she could stand up to a rowdy crowd out for her blood, who'd accuse her of sleeping with the enemy. And could she convince them she'd atoned for her one and only brief sin? She was resolved to seek the support of friends and allies. She left the bar and headed for the old man's place.

There, she found him deep in thought. "I'm worried what the aftermath is going to bring."

"Do you mean when the Germans have been defeated?" Marie-France said.

"Yes. On 28th June, Henriot was assassinated. In case you don't know, he was the propaganda mouthpiece of the Vichy government. He popularised the Maquis as bandits, outlaws and social deviants. But luckily attitudes are changing now after his death and all that propaganda has stopped. Increasingly the Maquis are seen as liberators. But consequently the Germans are becoming ever more brutal against them. Will there be any of our Resistance heroes left by the end of the war? That's what worries me. The Germans can no longer rely on us French in the local 'préfectures,' even the regional and departmental organs of government are short-staffed. Many have left their posts and fled. They are now neither collaborating with Vichy nor with the Germans. Mayors and local municipal authorities are resigning everywhere, and the Vichy government is losing men and power."

"Isn't that all good news in a way?" Marie-France said.

"The country risks turning to anarchy. People are hungry. It seems they will do anything for food. The FTP are now involved in 'ravitaillement,' requisitioning, but there are criminal elements who masquerade as the Maquis who are giving it a bad name. Vichy policing is collapsing, there are increased thefts, dislocations of people, and 'rafles' by the desperate Germans. And then we have sporadic retribution. The Maquis are targeting those who've had it easy under Vichy or who are well-known collaborators. But how can they be so sure of the guilty?"

"I want to return to Saint-Pons-de Thomières or Clermont-l'Hérault. I know that area well. I want to fight."

"What are you fighting for, dear Marie-France? Have you not done enough for your country? We don't want to lose you too."

"Do you know many who've been killed?" Marie-France asked.

"Too many unsung heroes indeed."

"I hope one of them does not include Jean de Lyon. It's the not knowing, which I find so intolerable. If I get back to my old group in the Languedoc, perhaps I'll find him again." Marie-France blinked and held her breath to stifle her tears.

"Don't cry, dear. Jean has become a valuable asset. The more revered you become, the deeper you take cover, the less you are talked about. That is what Marcel always says."

"I suppose if I were to return to my duties, he will hear about me before long."

"They are not duties. The only duty you have to your country is not to collaborate with the enemy," the old man said.

"Is being friends with the enemy also considered to be collaboration?"

"It would be by some, certainly. I have spotted a few desperate women with shaven heads begging for food here in Lyon. I'm afraid one becomes an outcast, even for accepting a drink and a meal from a German soldier. It's mainly prostitutes who've been singled out though. But at least they haven't been shot. That's what I mean when I say people will do anything for a decent meal and a bottle of wine."

"Can you blame them? Especially if they haven't seen their men folk for years. What is a solitary life, especially during times of war? Nothing but misery and hardship," Marie-France said.

"I think as a mother, if you've lost your only son to the bullet of a German soldier or a Gestapo firing squad, you might feel otherwise. You would feel disgust at the merest hint of fraternisation. And now that the Germans are murdering innocent civilians too, this German Occupation has reached new heights of savagery and cruelty."

"I see your point. Feelings are running high."

"People are going mad with the desire for revenge and recrimination. It's almost barbaric," said the old man.

At that point Marcel entered the room. The first thing he said before sitting down was, "Aha, I know that face. It's Marie-France. I expect you are looking for Jean, no?" to which she nodded.

"That, and I want to go back to the fighting, to the country I know best."

"There is talk of the Allies and Free French under de Gaulle joining forces in a pincer formation from the south, so the south might be the place to be, but I expect they'll be looking to invade and disable the ports of Toulon and Marseille first, so it'll be Provence now rather than the Languedoc where you were before."

"So you're expecting the Americans to land in the south?"

"Yes. Or you could join me up in the Massif du Vercors."

"Join you?"

"Yes. There's little going on in the area where you were previously. I leave tomorrow. The Vercors straddles the Isère and Drôme départements. There's a big Maquis encampment up there. It's like the Cévennes … remote, hilly, forested, even mountainous, and wedged between the two cities of Grenoble and Valence. Not far from Lyon either, frankly."

"Strategically placed for the main north-south route," Marie-

France said.

"Exactly, and a great hiding place. You never know, Jean might be up there. It's 150 kilometres from here, six or seven days by foot, or we could get a lift in a day. We'll be heading eventually for the village of Vassieux-en-Vercors where we've got 'friends.'"

"Do you know something I don't about Jean and you're not telling me? Don't you trust me?"

"It's not about trust. To be frank I don't know enough about Jean to give you any accurate information. It would be unfair to get your hopes up, wouldn't it? What I do know is that he was badly wounded in Sète and ordered to take a few months recuperation. I know he was in the Vercors when I last heard in April. Back on form, back in the battle. But much has happened since, and he's been promoted. The higher you get, the less others know about you, and the more you're obliged to operate in the shadows."

Marie-France's voice trembled, "I just wonder if I'll ever see him again."

"So you love him?"

"Of course I love him. Isn't that obvious?" she said, wiping away a tear.

"I'm sorry. I wasn't sure. Of course, you have a child. Silly me."

"I'd like to come with you," Marie-France said. "Oh, and by the way, I'm known as Nelle to my comrades in arms and that name applies as soon as we step out this door." She pointed to the door as if she were ready to march out with him straightaway.

22

They covered the bulk of the distance by cadging lifts, and walked the rest. They reached the high plateau surrounding the village of Vassieux-en-Vercors by nightfall on the fourth day of their travels, and camped on the edge of the forest for the night. Their liaison was located in the village itself and they both set off at dawn in search of their contact. A young woman answered the door, calling herself Krystyna.

"We have a big day today. Just as well you arrived now," she said, handing them each a glass of cold water. "You can help us collect the canisters. We're expecting an airdrop, a huge one, after which I must leave, I'm afraid. They need me and my colleagues elsewhere."

"An airdrop during the day?" asked Marcel. "Isn't that bloody risky? It'll betray all our positions."

"It's why we'll need to be quick. We have planned it carefully."

"Even so, I wouldn't hang around here for long afterwards. They'll send in the whole bloody Wehrmacht after us," Marcel said. "And who are we to meet up with? No wonder they've ordered you to run off after the drop."

"Yes. It's why we've been called out of the area afterwards," Krystyna said. "Best you do the same, but you'll first meet your colleagues this morning."

"You're not French, are you?" Nelle asked.

Krystyna sat down at the table. "I am Polish. I follow orders from the SOE in London. Trust me. We are working with you. You will meet my colleagues soon. I am expecting them any moment."

They sat in silence on the damp floor of the modest cottage, weary after their journey, quenching their thirst on mountain water which came out of a pipe from the wall and poured into a stone sink directly behind them. Following a knock on the door, a dozen or so men walked in. They were familiar to Krystyna who seemed relieved at their arrival, but she had no time to introduce them before the thunder of aircraft engines filled the room, a cacophonous rumble rattling the windows and drowning out any conversation.

"Here they are," shouted one of the men. "Jump in the trucks and do your best to load up as many canisters as you can."

Such a sudden command caught Nelle and Marcel by surprise, but they acted accordingly, jumping up, gathering their packs and following the others into the lorries which drove off at speed leaving a cloud of dust and exhaust.

It was July 14th. Seventy-two American B-17 "Flying Fortress" bombers dropped 870 canisters containing weapons, ammunition, food and medical supplies. The Germans had detected the airdrop before it arrived and responded accordingly by sending in small but nimble aircraft hoping to destroy as many canisters as possible. German aircraft flattened half the village of Vassieux-en-Vercors, with eighty-five homes being destroyed across the region in a matter of days.

Marcel and Marie-France participated in the rounding-up and loading of the canisters into the back of the lorries. They left in one of them with five colleagues with whom they weren't familiar, except for Krystyna who introduced them after a while – Huet, the local Maquis commander; Zeller, the FFI commanding officer; and two SOE colleagues, Cammearts and radio operator, Floiras. That night they hid in the forest with sixty or so other Maquisards, planning how best to counter any further German attacks and distribute the supplies which they'd successfully recovered from the landing zone.

Zeller was the first of the group gathered around the campfire to speak. "I fear that now they know where we are, and having sent in such a large bombardment, we have little to do but split into our respective units and escape as best we can. Meanwhile we will enquire about reinforcements on the radio."

"Are we to travel with you?" Marcel asked of Huet, the local Maquis commander.

"Yes. You and Nelle. Stick with me. I fear we have a battle coming like no other we have ever experienced before."

*

Such a large airdrop in daylight had the unfortunate effect of alerting the Germans to the extensive Maquis encampments in the area. Lieutenant General Karl Ludwig Pflaum, the local commander with orders to destroy the Vercors Maquis, began making extensive and rapid preparations for an attack, observed daily by the undermanned Maquis, whose preferred method of combat was not open warfare of this sort.

With eight thousand soldiers, Pflaum's troops gradually cordoned off the entire Vercors region and a week later, on 21st July, launched a major assault. German columns advanced both from the north and from the south. The troops from the south travelled up along the road up from the wine town of Die. Simultaneously alpine troops scaled the lightly defended eastern ramparts of the massif. A further two hundred airborne troops landed by glider near the village of Vassieux, supported by fighter aircraft and bombers. By that first evening it was clear that the German assault was succeeding. On that one day alone, July 21st, it was reported that 326 Maquisards lost their lives and 130 civilians had been massacred from three separate villages.

Huet encouraged his men and women to continue to fight until defeat was inevitable and then disperse into the forests and mountains of the massif, anticipating that the Germans would soon withdraw as well. By 23rd July, the remnants of the Vercors Resistance dispersed and took refuge, with Huet's superior officer in the FFI, Henri Zeller, and his SOE agents, Krystyna Granville, Cammaerts, and wireless operator Auguste Floiras all travelling south to liaise with American forces.

That evening Huet despatched a rancorous radio message to the Free French authorities in Algiers and to the SOE in London informing them of how much blood they had on their hands – blaming them for underestimating the extent of the German operations against them and failing to send in the necessary manpower reinforcements after the airdrop. What resulted had been the greatest loss of Resistance life in a single area over such a concentrated period.

*

During the battle, Nelle had been separated from Marcel, but stuck by Huet's side as instructed, so that by nightfall she found herself sitting with Huet and two of his men around a fire in the forest stirring a hastily made stew containing mostly potatoes, onions and spinach which one of the men had helped himself to from a village vegetable patch.

Huet was unhappy and said so. "This has been a most reckless and foolish adventure, which none of us fighting on the ground would have agreed to if we'd known how badly it had been planned. To engage with the enemy in such a way is not what I call heroism, especially as so many of the young men we recently recruited had virtually no experience at all. What was Zeller thinking of?"

"Such a bloody catastrophic loss of young lives," one of the men replied.

"Yes, such a waste," Nelle said, nodding, although her mind was on Marcel and his whereabouts. The thought crossed her mind that she might be in the habit of outliving comrades to whom she'd attached herself in battle. How long would her own lucky streak of immortality endure? She worried for Marcel.

"And you need to get that wound sorted out, Nelle. Come here a moment. I want to take a look. I don't suppose you're aware of quite how bad it is," Huet said, shaking his spoon in her direction as he ate his soup.

Nelle got up and walked over to him. "Let's take a look at this," Huet said as she bent down next to him. He brushed her hair away gently above her right ear. A slow but persistent trickle of blood oozed from her head and into her hair. "You're in a right bloody mess. Why didn't you say something, for God's sake?" Huet put his bowl down and got up. "Pascal, stop your eating and go and get a medic. Run, hurry. And get him to bring bandages and disinfectant. Run boy, run."

"Is it bad?" Nelle said.

"There's a nasty wound, deeper than a graze. It needs attention. I'm afraid you're going to be bandaged up for several weeks. Goes with the territory. You're a lucky bullet dodger for sure. Take it as a badge of honour." He patted her on the shoulder. The medic arrived, cut away some of Nelle's hair above her ear, cleaned up the wound, rubbed in some alcohol which made her wince and dressed the wound.

"Lucky you," the medic said as he left. "A centimetre or two closer to your temple and you'd be a corpse lying in a field down there somewhere." The man pointed in the general direction of Vassieux. It only made Marie-France worry more for Marcel. She did her best to restrain a tear.

The party sat down again and continued eating in silence. One of the men had warmed up Nelle's food for her on the fire and handed it to her. She struggled to eat what little lay in the bottom of her mess tin.

"I expect you are wondering where your Marcel is?" Huet said, after a long silence.

"I am. I lost him when we were fleeing from that barn on the edge of the village. He went one way, and I followed you. I hope he's all right, I really do. I will miss him."

"Have some brandy," Huet said, passing her a bottle he retrieved from his sack. "People have a wonderful knack of appearing again unexpectedly. I don't wish to get your hopes up though. I'm afraid I lose friends and acquaintances every day. There's a good case for leaving your heart well behind you during these times. Concentrate on the battle and driving the Boches out of our lands. That's what keeps me going and one day hoping to return to my parents, if they're still alive. But who knows? Take another swig. It'll dull the pain."

"Can you send out enquiries for Marcel?" Nelle said.

"I have already. It's not looking good. Do you know his next of kin?"

"Sort of, yes. In Lyon."

"Is that where you're from?"

"Yes. Lyon." Nelle felt a tear run down her cheek. Then another. Why him, of all the fallen? So funny, witty, enthusiastic about life. "The bastards, the bloody bastard Boches," she shouted out as loud as she felt it was allowed.

"Death to the bastards," the others replied in unison, holding up their thimbles of brandy.

Facing Huet, Nelle asked the question she'd wanted to ask for ten days. "Do you know of Jean de Villeneuve, also of Lyon."

"And what if I do? Who is he to you?" Huet's wary response

caught her by surprise and she hesitated, taking another sip of the brandy.

"He's the father of my child."

"I see. Jean and I fought together on the Mont Mouchet. He's a top chap but he's got a bad leg and can't run fast enough. They've given him a position in the high command now."

"So he's alive?"

"When I last saw him three months ago. But every day is another day. You never know what might happen from one day to the next."

Nelle had had enough of Huet's doleful tone. She stood up. "I wish you could be more positive. Jean is still alive, I'm sure of it. Where is he? I'm sure you know."

"That's the spirit, girl," said one of the other men.

"I have an idea where he is but we have a security protocol, you know. I can't just reveal names and places on a whim. And I don't know who you are, although Marcel's unit gave you high praise, it is true."

"I killed at least seven German soldiers this week. You saw that. I was with you. I'm hardly a collaborator."

"Yes. You are a good soldier, Nelle. Seems like loyalty and dedication to the cause are high on your list of priorities but the least we share amongst us, the better. You know that too."

"I'm only asking for a little kindness and help. He is the father of my child."

Huet raised his voice. "And if you are captured, raped, and tortured until you provide names and addresses? How would that go down? That's why we reveal nothing. In time, you will find Jean, if he is indeed alive. At least he's no longer in the field of battle. He's safer than us. You need to look after yourself too. You have a child to get back to."

"I know that. I was simply asking. There is room for love in war, you know."

*

Ma Coccinelle – We are Planning for Liberation

The long-anticipated Allied landings in Provence took place on 15th August. The Allied forces advanced rapidly northward, aided by the Maquis, which led eventually to the overthrow of the Vichy government in September. "Operation Dragoon" was successful from the start, leading to the capture of the ports of Marseille and Toulon by 28th August. It was a frantic time for us Resistance units in the south, and I can say with pride that we played our part in that struggle with gallantry and distinction.

Three days earlier on 25th August 1944, General Leclerc had led the FFI into Paris, and was received by ecstatic crowds. General de Gaulle announced the liberation of France by the Forces Françaises de l'Intérieur (FFI). It was as if he hadn't noticed or recognised the vast columns of Americans, Canadians, Australians and so forth, let alone those of the British forces supporting him. In liberated towns, marching columns of FFI staged triumphal parades to the "préfectures," the "mairies" and the "monuments aux morts," bearing their arms, displaying their company emblems, led by their local leaders holding their clenched fists high in salute, and carrying flags with the cross of Lorraine inside a Victory "V," the FFI insignia. And it wasn't only the French. Georgian, Croat and Yugoslav partisans marched alongside them, along with ex-Spanish civil war veterans, all of whom had played their part in France's liberation from fascism.

In those towns where the Germans had either been defeated, retreated, or had fled, a sense of liberation was evident, but in others areas, liberation wasn't going to happen overnight. Depending on where the fighting units were, liberation occurred in specific pockets, one by one, until they were all joined in one. The enemy remained very much within. I'm talking of the French traitors too – the Miliciens, the Gendarmes and members of the Parti Populaire Français (PPF). Many ran off with the Germans, others shed their uniforms and did their best to blend in. The abolition of the Demarcation Line the month before made travel much easier and especially for those who had reason to take flight.

The stench of sweet revenge was in the air, everywhere one went. It was the start of the purges, an ugly period in our French history which, although in many cases well-deserved, I admit to finding difficult to condone, especially those wild acts of cruel, personal recrimination which never saw a law court, and were known as the "épurations sauvages" – the popular convictions and extrajudicial executions. Liberation and purge had become inextricably linked. Some say as many as 6,000 executions had taken place during this period, and another 4,000 by the time liberation had been fully achieved. The "épurations légales," had actually begun a few months earlier in late June, with an "ordonnance," a directive from de Gaulle on 27th June 1944. Purge committees, "Commissions d'épurations," were set up to investigate suspects – those in the professions, government administration or those who might have profited commercially from the Occupation. They were the most vulnerable. Those who were found guilty, lost their civic rights and received a "dégradation nationale," resulting in the loss of their homes and voting rights, forcing whole families to move out of the areas which they'd previously called home. They were additionally banned from many professions and from joining any unions. Any medals, decorations, honours and pensions were also forfeited.

Additionally, on 28th August 1944, the "Chambres Civiques" were established to deal with less serious acts of collaboration such as displays of unpatriotic behaviour. Conspicuous pro-Pétain, Vichy supporters were also rounded up to be judged. Charges across the courts were varied, the newest crime being that of "collaborating with the enemy" or of "providing intelligence to the enemy," crimes somewhere on the spectrum between treason and a willing acceptance of the enemy. Death sentences were applied across the board, from the top to the bottom, and that included Joseph Darnand, the head of the Milice, and Pierre Laval, the ex-Prime Minister, eventually executed in October 1945. Revolution and upheaval were all about us.

In those inspiring, frantic and confusing days of liberation, one tended to assume the war was over, but it most certainly was not. Little did we know then that another eight months were to pass before Alfred Jodl, Chief of Staff of the German army, would formally surrender to the Allies in Reims. In many ways, life in France became more dangerous, and that wasn't just owing to the Germans, although they'd become ever more aggressive and unpredictable in the panic of defeat. I feared for Nelle and her own particular predicament as she had three enemies with whom to contend. I often wondered where she might be hiding, whether any partisans with savage vengeance on their minds might be seeking her out for punishment after her "crime," and whether she had once again been forced to reckon with my permanent absence from her life.

I refer to her diaries of the time, which provide a much better account than I could possibly supply.

101. I'm feeling elated. Yesterday, 22nd August, the city of Grenoble was liberated from German control and we, the Maquis of the Vercors, marched in the victory parade through the town. It was a fun day and people were so kind and grateful. Bottles of wine appeared miraculously from people's cellars, their contents spilling over into our open mouths as we passed by. Joy and relief filled the air. I wore a sort of uniform and we marched with the FFI flags and Croix de Lorraine held high above us. It made me feel so proud. But the streets seemed to be full of women, young and old. Where were all the young men? Then someone reminded me that her husband was working in a factory in Germany, and something like fifteen percent of German factory workers were now made up of our boys from France. So wicked. It was then that I thought first of Marcel and then of course of my Jean. Where is he? I hope he is raising a glass too, I hope, somewhere in France, at least not, I hope, being worked to death in a German factory.

Huet, my new Maquis commander, isn't being helpful in my quest to find Jean but he does admittedly have greater concerns on his mind, with the liberation of Lyon being the next major stage in Maquis activity in our area of eastern France.

112. I hang around Grenoble for a little while until it becomes clear to me that I've become somewhat superfluous so I decide to head home to Lyon and Gérard. I was excused on the grounds that I still had a young child to attend to.

113. I reach home in three days. It feels so strange writing this from the comfort of my bedroom and the little child's desk at which I'm sitting tonight. I suppose the desk might have once been my father's. And by the way, I have decided that I'm not going to take part in the celebrations around the liberation of Lyon tomorrow, September 3rd because I have no wish to attract the unnecessary attentions of any Maquisards when I'm at home with Gérard and my grandparents. It's still too risky for them. I still have good reasons to fear those who know my secret. I'm still obliged to live much of my life in the shadows, a fact which Grand-père Hervé found a little odd when I chatted with him briefly over breakfast this morning, but of course he doesn't know the whole truth. He said I should get out there and celebrate the cause, and relish all my acts of courage by marching through the centre of Lyon!! Oh dear. Had he known the stark reality, the danger I still felt of me being outed by my own people!!!

It is true too that I have been shocked into a state of semi-paralysis by the number of emaciated women I've noticed with shaved heads I've seen in the streets today, les "tondeuses" as they are called – those accused of "horizontal collaboration." And they aren't all city prostitutes, singers, actresses or bar owners, who are apparently without doubt the more vulnerable groups to be targeted.

115. Resistance men are known to be merciless towards "collabo" women, and threats of head-shaving have been made by the Resistance underground press since 1941.

But today I read that many of the men shaving women's heads are not even members of the Resistance. Many are petty collaborators themselves, seeking to divert attention from their own pathetic lack of Resistance credentials. You see what an evil, twisted mess it has all become. Where has the truth gone?

Women are almost always the first targets in the purges because they offer the easiest and most vulnerable scapegoats, particularly for those "pretender" men who joined the Resistance at the last moment and seem obsessed by randomly bringing women to justice when the opportunity arises. I'm sure that revenge on women represents a form of expiation for the frustrations and sense of impotence among males humiliated by their country's defeat and occupation. Grand-père said this lawless appetite for revenge would only get worse when forced labourers, prisoners of war and concentration camp victims return from Germany. Absurdly, many of these groups are considered to have capitulated to the Germans. As if it were their choice and they haven't suffered enough!! What a cruel, unjust world we live in.

121.The more I read, the more I'm both intrigued and worried. Often the "guilty" women are described in the press as silly teenagers who have associated with German soldiers out of bravado or boredom. Am I now one of that group? I suppose I am. But some are innocent schoolteachers who, living alone, had German soldiers forcibly billeted on them, and are now often falsely denounced for having been a "mattress for the Boches". Even crueller, many victims are young mothers, whose husbands are in German POW camps. They had no means of support, and their only hope of obtaining food for themselves and their children was to accept a liaison with a German soldier. Frankly I believe such women are often envied, jealousy masquerading as moral outrage. Absurd and disrespectful. I'm lucky in that respect, in avoiding all that.

I have no desire at all to become a "tondeuse." My poor dear Gérard is not quite two years old. Such shame for him to see his mother in such a state. And what of our future? And what of the family back in Saubon-le-Duc? We'd be living in ignominy, ostracised for evermore.

126. Passions are running high with inflamed emotions, daily revelations, arrests and executions. They keep on coming. It's relentless. These are strange and terrifying times. There is festivity, but also uncertainty and incivility, even anarchy. Jealousies and personal rivalries commonly result in false denunciations on a daily basis. Anyone seems vulnerable. Society is broken. Today I saw a horse drawing a cart slowly through the streets of Lyon. In it were a dozen women, stripped to the waist, their breasts daubed with swastikas in red lipstick, their heads shaven, their hands tied behind their backs, all to the beat of a little boy's drum, not unlike the artistic depictions of 1789. Little boys lined the streets, taunting the naked women as they passed by.

128.It is said that in rural areas where personal relations are closer, many more women have had their heads shaved, some newspapers announcing as many as 100,000 women in total throughout France, although the figure is likely to be higher by the time this nightmare has ended. Today, I'm inclined to consider the figure of 20,000 to be more realistic. The problem is that neighbour readily denounces neighbour without remorse. Petty peasant vendettas, I suppose. When will it end?

Typically during these purges, everyone in a village participates in one way or another, coming out to gloat upon others' misfortunes. But many women are simply suspects with minor infractions. The newspapers report that sleeping with the enemy was rare. Apparently they say that well fed, well-dressed bourgeois women are especially suspect, totally innocent as they might be. I hope Maman and Eloise are safe. I feel sure all the workers and neighbours will protect them at Champuix.

134. Some newspapers take a more moral line against women. In the past, head shaving had been the traditional punishment for adultery, with a deep-rooted symbolic precedent. Thus any woman who slept with a German was seen as a prostitute and needed to be cleansed of their sins in the traditional manner – a public shaving of the head. In the past it was viewed as a necessary decontamination process and apparently still is. Women accused of having had an abortion are also assumed to have consorted with the Germans. At least I hadn't gone down that route.

I was reading in Hervé's newspapers that, in the courts, women are being judged for their moral behaviour which was often not enough to condemn them, so other acts of collaboration are simply fabricated and pinned to their dossier in order to guarantee their incrimination. Often the punishment is far more severe than the crime deserves and that is what I fear most, each day that passes.

It is true that the more I feel I've contributed in battle for my fellow countrymen, for the liberation of France, the more I consider my indiscretion with a lowly, disinterested German officer of otherwise impeccable character and fine disposition, to be of minor consequence. In the grand scheme of things, my brief encounter amounts to nothing as far as the outside world is concerned. I've paid my dues, I carry the wounds to prove it, and I deserve a full exoneration. Well, don't I?

135.Only Jean knows the whole story. It would be cruel and selfish to consider Gérard as a thorn in my backside, forever present in my life, which would remind me daily that there were indelible, living consequences for my "sin," forever present, sapping me of strength like a heavy debt which could never be paid off. It was as if the slate could never be wiped entirely clean. I can only blame myself. And I know it is wrong and fatuous to blame anyone else. I am a selfish human being. And yet, neglectful, and shamefully distant mother I admit I have been so far, I am determined that one day, Gérard should stand out like a dazzling beacon, a paragon of hope for peace between former enemies. Gérard is proof that there can be love between two people of opposing, warring nations, two people who had no desire whatsoever to follow their leaders into battle, and who simply found love amongst the cruelty and futility of war. And what is so wrong about that?

Such grandiose ambitions for my little boy seem ridiculous right now as I write, serving as some deeply personal antidote to all that has happened. The song of my conscience perhaps. But one day I will disclose his Franco-German origins for all to admire. "Here is my wonderful son, Gérard, and here is his German father, my beloved Johann Schräder," I will say. And then wait for them all to work out where Jean fits in and when, how and where dear Gérard was born. Oh. Oh. I've drunk too much wine tonight. I must stop.

23

By the end of August 1944, the German army in France was in retreat and the Vichy government no longer held any authority in the land. Marshall Pétain and the ex-Prime Minister Laval refused to cooperate with the recently-arrived General de Gaulle and his Allies, so that on 7th September 1944 what remained of the Vichy cabinet fled with a puppet government to the Sigmaringen enclave in Germany, assisted by the German army.

Such news was greeted with huge pleasure by Hervé but Marie-France only feared for the worst, her thoughts consumed by the pandemonium and ominous arraignments all about them in Lyon, and throughout the rest of France.

Hervé had something reassuring to say about it. “We live at a good address in a wealthy part of town, I know that. We are vulnerable to the mob. Just keep your head down, dress scruffily when you go out, and never look like a well-kept woman. And above all make sure the bastards know how you got that wound on your head.” Hervé laughed at the thought as he pointed to her extensive bandage around her head, and tapped his own. “With such wartime Maquis credentials and such a combat record, you have nothing to fear, my dear. Now that we have a new government, the ‘Gouvernement Provisoire de la République Française,’ de Gaulle will slowly restore order, you’ll see. I note from today’s newspaper that they are even going after the black marketeers, the ‘BOFs’ as they’re called, the ‘Beurre, Oeuf, Fromage’ spivs who ripped us all off during the war." He chuckled again at the thought of it. "At least there are no bloody Boches about these days. Let's drink to that."

Nelle and Claudette raised their glasses. "It's Jean I worry for most. I haven't heard from him for a long time. I want Gérard to have a father so badly. He desperately needs a father."

"I'm sure he'll reappear very soon," said Claudette, touching Marie-France's arm.

"They're disbanding the Communist militias as we speak," Hervé said. "And de Gaulle has ordered the integration of the FTP units with the regular army under General de Lattre. It won't be long before Jean has nothing more to do."

"Does that mean the Resistance is being disbanded?" Nelle asked.

"Effectively, yes," said Hervé.

"I can't see Jean joining the army, but he knows the fight is not yet over," said Marie-France.

"Perhaps he'll go into politics. The GPRF has a Communist party element to it, agreed by de Gaulle in the interests of national unity apparently," said Hervé.

"And what are you going to do, Marie France?" Claudette said. "Return to the vineyard, I do hope. We have not heard from your parents in a long while. Perhaps it's time to return to your real home and to introduce Gérard to the family."

"I don't know what I'm going to do," Nelle said. She wasn't ready to return to Burgundy. Such a thought terrified her.

"You'd better hurry up and make up your mind before all the jobs are taken. Do you know that by the last count in early October, it was reported that 50,000 French women were working in Germany, in the factories as cleaners, as shopkeepers and so on. They'll be coming home soon. And it's estimated that 5,500 of them are prostitutes. Sleeping with the bloody Boches. Shame on them. Bloody shame." Hervé took a large sip of his cognac.

"That's surprising," said Nelle. "But I'm not intending to apply to be a prostitute." She made them laugh, but Hervé's words had shaken her.

He leaned forward in his chair. "Something better to celebrate. Two days ago, on the 23rd, the Americans, British and Soviets recognised the GPRF as the legitimate government of France, led by de Gaulle. That's quite a move forward. For some time we've known that Roosevelt preferred the Vichy to de Gaulle, but finally by October 1944, he's changed his mind when he sees the battle unfolding in his favour. This is all such good news."

*

Ma Coccinelle – The Terror of Denunciation

All in all, there were approximately 10,000 deaths by purges, of which only 1,600 were legal – those carried out by the official courts. By the end of 1945, 311,263 dossiers had been sent to the Courts of Justice. Three-quarters of those tried were given sentences. 44,000 were jailed and 46,145 lost their civic rights. The rest were given minor punishments. Approximately 25,000 state employees were penalised. But let it be known that by 1950, de Gaulle had amnestied almost all of them in the interests of national stability.

Of the reported executions, 765 were of women. I provide you with this fact so that you might imagine the precarious situation in which Nelle found herself in the autumn of 1944. At the time, neither she nor I had any idea of the wide extent of the purges, nor any inkling of the zeal with which the individuals or organisations pursued their victims. That Nelle might one day be on someone's list seemed utterly reprehensible and a gross injustice worthy of a full defence in court if it came to that. That so many of our fallen comrades were no longer with us to tell her tale, to stand up in court in her defence, so to speak, forced me to consider walking out of the shadows and meeting up with her again to support her case if need be. I inform you willingly that it had crossed my mind at the time that my association with her risked tainting my own Resistance record. But I considered that I'd reached a point of infallibility. I was irreproachable, arrogant as that might sound.

We hadn't seen each other since Sète last October. One whole year had passed by and there wasn't much hope of seeing her now either, unless I made deliberate plans to do so. It is possible too that she believed me to have been killed, but these were mere weak excuses which I placed in my path, perhaps because I was fearful. And where were people like me to go after our time in the Resistance? It was as if the bottom was about to fall out of our lives. What future did we have now that it was all coming to an end? Seeking her out and resuming our old lives seemed like a good idea. But tomorrow, I would surely change my mind, as I was apt to do in those strange, unpredictable times.

24

A visit to the old man near the university struck Marie-France as the most hopeful option if she were to find Jean. She would go and visit him one day. Not least she also sought clarification as to Marcel's whereabouts although she was prepared for the worst of news. In the afternoons, no matter the season, she was in the habit of walking with Gérard in the nearby park. He enjoyed chasing the pigeons and meeting and hugging the dogs they encountered in the gardens. His apparent affection for dogs, especially those which were larger than him, amused Marie-France and she considered acquiring one as soon as the time were right.

One day instead of going to the park, she asked Claudette if she would care for Gérard while she attended to other matters. Following Hervé's advice, she deliberately dressed down and avoided applying any make-up before she went out. It was a rainy afternoon so she borrowed an umbrella from the house and strode out into the street feeling confident and positive about her future, although she wasn't sure why.

The old man appeared vexed and restless when Marie-France made her entrance. She got to the point immediately. "Have you news of Marcel? I last saw him in Vassieux in the Vercors. We were fighting together. I expect you have heard."

"Is that where your wound has come from? I'm surprised it hasn't yet healed," he said, avoiding her question.

"It's a deep wound. But what of Marcel?"

"Marcel was my nephew. We have lost him, I'm afraid. I expect you won't be surprised. Have you come to pay your respects and offer your condolences?"

"I have, now that I know. I'm so sorry to hear. He became a close friend and was a valiant comrade in our fight for liberation. May I sit down?"

The old man changed the subject without warning. "No, you may not sit down. I won't say that I've been waiting for you, but I expected you to turn up at some point, looking for Jean. You see, it seems that you are not the person we believed you to be. And that has caused us much pain." At that point he called out a name, "Vincent, Vincent. Come in here, will you please. We have our Marie-France Champuix." A short, scruffy, well-built man appeared from down a corridor and went to stand in front of the door, folding his arms and spreading out his legs, as if he might inhibit Marie-France from dashing for the front door.

Fearing the worst, she had a feeling she knew exactly what was coming next. She decided it was best to allow some version of the truth to reveal itself, or at least the truth they thought they knew. She would correct any errors depending on the accusations. And she wasn't going to tell the whole truth unless it went to trial and she was forced to do so under oath.

The old man stood up from behind his desk, unsteady on his feet. "We have a report here accusing you of having last been spotted liaising with a German officer of the Wehrmacht on 22nd December 1941." The old man lifted a document from the desk and then dropped it. "You were spotted in his company several times before that date in and around the town of Chalon-sur-Saône and at the Café du Paix in that same town. A German officer was seen pursuing your vehicle out of the town in the direction of your family home in Saubon-le-Duc. Nine months later you produced a child which the accuser believes is the outcome of that liaison.

You will therefore be charged with treason in a court of law here in Lyon, for carrying on a relationship with a German army officer and performing acts of a sexual nature with the enemy."

"May I sit down?" Marie-France said. She hesitated before speaking. The old man gestured to her to take a seat. "The first part is true. But it was a friendship I had. It wasn't a sexual relationship. The second part is totally false. You are gravely mistaken. The child is that of Jean de Villeneuve. He will attest to that, if you can find him. I would dearly love to find him, I assure you."

"We would also like to know why you changed your name and that of your child to Dubois."

"That must be obvious. I was not married to Jean de Villeneuve and so we could not take his name. Realising and accepting the errors of my ways, and having been thrown out of my family home with accusations abounding, I needed to start a new life under a new guise. I wanted to protect my son too. As you must know, I joined the Resistance to atone for my misdemeanours which I fully accept were wrong."

"We are aware of your distinguished service in the Resistance, and I'm sure those years will count in your favour."

"And who is my 'accuser'? You must know."

"We can't divulge that here. No doubt you will be informed during the trial. An officer from the 'Renseignements généraux' or the FFI will be here shortly to arrest you."

"But what of my child? And under whose authority are you holding me?"

"I am sure you will be allowed access to the child from time to time, whatever befalls you. We are the FFI, an organisation you once served."

A loud knock at the door announced the arrival of the police. The police officer carried a rifle over his shoulder, and a younger man wearing an FFI armband carried a pistol in a holster around his waist.

Having explained their presence to Marie-France, they formally arrested her. They grabbed her arms, held them out in front of her and placed handcuffs around her wrists. "We will accompany you to your home to say goodbye to your child, and you may collect enough clothes and personal toiletries for one week."

"I don't wish to go home," Marie-France said.

"You are obliged to carry out our orders."

Throughout the journey in the back of the police van, Marie-France hurriedly went over what she might say to Hervé and Claudette. She was less concerned for Gérard. He'd only just had his second birthday although without any celebrations as such; she assumed he was unlikely to remember any of this in later life.

When she arrived in the police vehicle outside her grandparents' house, Marie-France was ordered to remain seated while the policeman knocked at the front door of Clos de la Fontaine. Claudette opened it to the officer and stood on the doorstep. To Marie-France, he seemed to take a lifetime to explain the reason for his presence. She could then see Claudette lifting her hands to her face and clasping her cheeks. She turned around and called out for Hervé. After several minutes, Hervé appeared at the door holding Gérard in his arms wrapped in a blanket. He was directed to walk across to the police vehicle with the boy. Claudette arrived a little later carrying a suitcase.

Marie-France was ordered to step out of the vehicle. She stood in the street, taking the boy in her arms from her grandfather in silence. The composed look in Hervé's eyes told her all she needed to know. What was going on wasn't a surprise to him. He seemed perfectly calm and accepting of the situation, as if her arrest and trial would merely be a minor aberration which would soon pass.

She whispered in Gérard's ear. "Maman is going away for a little while, but not for long." It was all she could manage before bursting into tears and handing the boy back to her grandfather.

Hervé clasped Marie-France's arm so tightly she wasn't sure if it was in anger or in sympathy. Then he smiled and said, "Justice will prevail, my dear. You'll see."

Before Hervé turned to leave, she grabbed him by the arm and whispered to him, "Find Jean urgently, please. Please, he's the only one who can save me. I absolutely cannot be thrown to the dogs. I'm terrified they'll shoot me. Do you understand, Grand-père? Do you?" By now Marie-France was shaking uncontrollably. Hervé nodded, held his head high and did not flinch once. He clutched her by the arm again. "Hold steady, girl. France loves its heroes and you are one of them." He turned and walked back up to the house with the child in his arms. Both her grandparents stood at the front door and lifted their hands in a half-hearted wave as the vehicle drove off.

She spent the next few days sitting in a cell in solitary confinement in the grim squalor of Lyon's Montluc "Prison Militaire," waiting for something to happen. Montluc had been a renowned centre of torture for the Gestapo until August when it had been liberated by Colonel Köenig and his FFI troops. It now served to hold inmates accused of a variety of crimes including collaboration.

"You are being put in the same cell as the Gestapo placed Jean Moulin," the guard said as he opened the gate to her cell. "You know what happened to him?"

"I know what happened to Jean Moulin. I consider it a great honour to occupy his cell. He was a French hero. What have you ever done for your country?" Marie-France said. The guard chuckled without replying, pushing her forward into the cell and slamming the heavy iron gates shut behind her, causing her to shudder in shock at the solid clash of metal against metal.

That night Marie-France prayed for Jean to appear at the trial. He would make all the difference. Where was he? She lay awake fearing the worst, that she would break down in court, admit everything, place Jean's credibility in jeopardy and worst of all leave a permanent stain on young Gérard's life. What would become of them? She cried out loud imagining her Gérard being teased and bullied mercilessly at school for having a Nazi father and a French whore as a mother. What a terrible life she was setting up for him. She punched the walls of the cell with her knuckles until they bled. She grew so weary she was unable to stand and finally collapsed onto the bed of straw in the corner of her cell.

As the days went by, she considered the advantages of the delay to proceedings – Hervé had more time to find Jean. The worst outcome would be for her go to trial and face her accuser alone without the weight of Jean's support behind her.

When she was brought to court six days later, she faced a panel of three judges and a number of court officials who administered the court's procedures and clerical functions. Looking around she seemed to have been spared a jury and questioned with her appointed defence counsel whether that was an advantage, to which she received a disinterested shrug. She guessed that that was just how things were done in times of war. The charges were read out and the questioning began. Marie-France stood up and waited for the inevitable barrage of accusations, steadying herself with both her hands clasped to the stand in front of her.

"During your liaison with Lieutenant Schräder, what did you talk about?"

"Of wine and music and the end to this war. We never discussed anything of a military nature at any point. We talked almost exclusively about winemaking and the differences between growing grapes in Burgundy and the Rheingau. Lieutenant Schräder is from a winemaking family like me, you see. That was what sparked my interest in him. It was what we shared in common, and a love of piano music as well. He told me almost immediately I met him, that he was not a Nazi, did not support the Nazi party and had no wish to be fighting the French people. That fact warmed me to him. I believed him, and he seemed sincere. He was kind and thoughtful at all times. Why wouldn't that be? Not all Germans are Nazis."

"I understand. What was the nature of your liaison?"

"It was a casual, genuinely friendly one. We never discussed politics or the details of the war, and I was never granted any favours, any special passes, and no cars or other transport were ever made available to me. I travelled everywhere with my own transport, and that was often a bicycle. We met and talked at the bar a few times and only briefly. I would go there with a friend to listen to his piano playing. It was something to do."

"Did he ever buy you a drink or take you out for dinner?"

"No. Not once."

"Did you ever meet outside the bar, in the street, in another café, on the road, or in the vineyards."

"We met once for a friendly chat one evening in my vehicle before Christmas. I was on my way home, and he followed me."

"Was there any sexual activity?"

"There was never any sexual liaison between the German officer and myself. It never seemed right or appropriate."

The judged paused his questioning, shuffled his papers and scribbled down a note.

"May I remind you that to withhold the truth in this court as in any other, is to commit an act of perjury for which the penalty will be death by firing squad."

"I am aware of that, Monsieur le Juge."

"So the child you bore was the progeny of a union between yourself and Jean de Villeneuve."

"He is my boy's father, yes. As I have told everyone a thousand times. And Jean de Villeneuve will attest to that, if you can find him."

"Thank you. You may sit down Miss Champuix-Dubois." The judge turned to one of the court officials. "Please call the first witness."

"Jean," she whispered to herself. Jean must be coming next. "Please, Jean, please come to my aid."

"May I remind the accused to remain silent unless called upon to speak," said the judge.

The sound of his name alone brought such a relief to Marie-France, whispered as it was through her own lips. She could feel her whole body shake to such an extent that she had to steady herself with her hands, even though she was sitting down. Slouching in her chair, she searched for a handkerchief in her dress pocket and leaned her head down to disguise her tears of joy.

"Please sit up Miss Champuix-Dubois. May the witness please take the stand," said the senior judge.

Marie-France looked up and wiped her tears from her eyes. "Oh no, it's not possible. It can't be possible. Not you, no, no," she cried out.

"Silence, please, Miss Champuix-Dubois. Please compose yourself," said the senior judge.

Marie-France's mother, dressed all in black like a widow, stood up. The judge began his questioning. "You attest to the fact that your daughter had begun a liaison with a German officer of the Wehrmacht and that is why you reported it to the police who reported it to the local Maquis leader in your area. And secondly, you accuse your daughter of giving birth to a child from such a liaison."

"Yes. I was aware that my daughter was engaged in a sexual relationship outside of marriage, which I cannot condone in any circumstances. I disapproved so strongly of that, that my daughter left the house in disgrace. She felt guilty from the start."

"And what proof do you have, first that your daughter was

engaged in a sexual relationship, and secondly with an officer of the Wehrmacht, and thirdly that her child's father was the German officer?"

"I telephoned Jean de Villeneuve's mother to ask of Jean's whereabouts. She informed me that ever since he'd left the Champuix vineyards he'd been in Lyon and then fled swiftly to the Languedoc and was in hiding. He was not in Burgundy at all. The child cannot be his."

"Jean de Villeneuve is a distinguished member of the Resistance. At that time, he was already a renowned fighter and patriot. You may or may not be familiar with Resistance protocol, but no one is privy to a Resistance member's whereabouts other than their immediate company. Are you sure that his mother had the slightest clue as to his movements?"

"No. I couldn't be sure."

"So your accusation stands on weak ground. Is that not the case, Madame Champuix?" said the judge.

"By chance the barman of the Café du Paix in Chalon passed by the domaine to collect a sample bottle of our white wine. Marie-France had suggested he stock our wines at his bar, you see. We began chatting. He mentioned that my daughter spent a lot of time there cavorting and flirting with a German officer who played the piano."

"But what evidence do you have of any sexual liaison?"

"The barman was convinced of it and then saw them leave together one evening."

"And what proof do you have that the child is that of the German officer?"

"The barman seemed convinced that they were having a sexual relationship."

"I see. But you have no proof whatsoever."

"No."

"Thank you, Madame Champuix. You may be seated. The witness may leave the court." The judge gestured to one of the officials to lead her out. Madame Clémence Champuix left the court without once glancing towards her daughter. "Please call the second witness," the judge said.

The barman of the Café du Paix entered the court, gazing at Marie-France before sitting down.

"Please stand, Monsieur Bave." The judge waited for the man to stand up before continuing. "When you visited Domaine de Champuix to collect a bottle of wine, did you discuss the subject of her daughter with Madame Champuix?"

"I did."

"What did you tell Madame Champuix?"

"I said that her daughter was a frequent visitor, often with a friend, and that they came to drink and enjoy the company of the German officers, one of whom played the piano."

"Did Miss Champuix ever discuss the German officer with you?"

"Yes. On many occasions. She said he was a good piano player and that he was a winemaker back in Germany. She seemed to like the man."

"How do you know that she liked the German officer?"

"It was the way she looked at him. She would flirt a bit with him too."

"How do you know they were having an affair?"

"It was obvious. You just know these things."

"Did you ever see them together engaged in intimate sexual activities?"

"No."

"Thank you." Gesturing to the court official standing behind Monsieur Bave, the judge indicated for him to be led out of the courtroom.

At that point one of the court officials entered the courtroom by a side door and handed a message to the senior judge, who read it in silence, and then looked up, "We have a last-minute witness, who has just arrived in time. I call upon the third witness," the judge said.

Marie-France whispered to herself, "Please, please God, may it be Jean. Hear my prayers, Oh Lord. Jean where are you?"

Jean walked into the courtroom and took to the stand. He was wearing a suit and tie which Marie-France had never seen him wear before, and on his right arm, an FFI armband. He limped towards the stand using a wooden walking stick to support himself. He glanced briefly at Marie-France, smiled and turned to face the judge. He was accompanied by two FFI members standing on either side of him. To Marie-France, they seemed more like his personal bodyguard. Perhaps they were. The questioning was short and to the point. Jean's responses and the manner in which he delivered them sounded like a long paean to "my Nelle," as he chose to name her when he addressed the judge. He left the courtroom in no doubt as to his feelings concerning the "total injustice and irrefutable insubstantiality of such a trial," as he described it.

Proceedings were paused at midday. Marie-France hoped to spot Jean during the break but she was whisked away to an ante-room before she had a chance, and no doubt Jean had left the court too.

The afternoon's proceedings were brief. The judge read out two charges and when he'd finished, he asked, "How do you plead to the charges?" He looked at Marie-France squarely in the eyes, waiting for a reply. "Take your time, Miss Champuix," he added.

"I plead 'not guilty' to the charge of enjoying a brief sexual liaison with an officer of the German Wehrmacht. And I plead 'not guilty' to the charge of treason."

"Do you have anything further to pronounce before the court

takes leave for its final deliberation?" said one of the senior judge's assistants.

"Yes, I do." Marie-France stood up. She spoke clearly and boldly. Her training had taught her to disguise any signs of weakness by standing erect with a tall posture, hands by her side, weight on the balls of her feet. She believed totally in the strength of her case. No one held any evidence against her. Nothing. But she was terrified. She had just this minute lied in a court of law after all. She began. "I await the conclusion from this enquiry and the decision of the judges of the 'Comité d'épuration,' but I have no fears for the outcome, as I never caused any harm at any point to my beloved country and nor did I ever intend to. Any friendship I might have had with the German officer was simply that, a friendship based on mutual respect and a shared passion for winemaking. Justice will prevail." She raised her fist in the manner of the FFI salute and shouted out, "Vive la Résistance. Vive la Libération. La Résistance sert la France. Vive la France."

Marie-France returned to the court the following day for the judgement.

The presiding judge addressed her directly, reading from a sheet of paper in his hand. "There are mitigating factors which have been taken into account in our deliberations. The case also contains fundamental weaknesses owing to a lack of sufficient evidence. Marie-France Champuix's subsequent gallant service on behalf of her country has sufficiently demonstrated that, while admitting in court that she initiated a casual friendship with a German army officer, she could not possibly have hoped to or wished to cause any harm to her country. In that respect, and recognising the inappropriate nature of a such a liaison with the enemy, one could say that she subsequently took it upon herself to both charge and punish herself, and has already admirably served her self-prescribed sentence accordingly. The evidence provided by the first two witnesses was both insubstantial and inconsequential. Neither of the witnesses provided enough evidence to suggest that the accused indulged in sexual liaisons with the German officer, nor that he is the father of Miss Champuix's child. The evidence of the third witness was sufficient to support the judgement which the court has now reached. That is, that Miss Marie-France Champuix-Dubois is found 'not guilty' of all charges, but will serve an appropriate sentence for fraternisation with the enemy. In addition, bearing in mind that Miss Champuix has a young child, the 'Comité d'épuration' and the directors of the 'police judiciare' of Lyon have decided to commute the potential charge from imprisonment to house arrest in Lyon for a period of twelve months. The case is dismissed."

Addressing Marie-France directly, the judge announced, "Such a procedure will be confirmed by the 'Préfet de Police of Lyon,' tomorrow, after which you will be released and permitted to return to your home in Lyon, where you will reside for a period of twelve months as sentenced."

25

Ma Coccinelle – A Freedom of Sorts

The way our Resistance movement as a whole, in whatever guise it took – FTP, CFL or FFI – eventually tracked down those whom it considered to be the enemies of a liberated France was admirable. I have no qualms about that. And although I admit that in the chaos of the retreat of the German army and the liberation of our country, justice often took an ugly turn, we always hoped for a fair trial and an appropriate sentence for those we'd accused of collaboration. Sometimes in the ferocity of battle, errors are made and injustices occur. Some may argue about that – war is war and all that, but certainly what befell my dear friend, Nelle Dubois, née Champuix as she was known when brought to trial, confirmed to me in retrospect that justice had found its proper course and dealt her a fair hand. I should add that I do not deny that we were both wrong to commit perjury, just that it was the only way out of a terrible situation. I believe that Nelle was driven above all by a desperate urge to spare her son.

She recounted as much as she could remember verbatim after the trial. There's no doubt she had a friendly judge. Perhaps even a Resistance man. I couldn't possibly say. But I did wonder whether he'd been deliberately lenient, whether he knew all along that the German officer was Gérard's father and chose to overlook the whole matter. Perhaps he considered that after all Nelle had proven in the field of battle, her innocent friendship, even love of a German officer seemed like a minor blemish on her record, and her reputation should remain as intact as possible. Yes, we had both committed perjury and wondered how much this might hang over us in future years, whether it would lean heavily on our consciences and drag us down. But the trial was hastily put together and took place in special, extraordinary times which most of France has preferred to forget.

The whole period was a fraught one for both Nelle and me, from the end of the oil depot sabotage at Sète to the arrest of Nelle one year later. I worried for Nelle constantly during those months. When might she be called to account and how would she be judged? Would she be spared the shame and indignity of a trial or even the worst fate of all – the death penalty? It was true that some of my colleagues felt she should be brought to trial and dealt with harshly and that the eventual sentence was a travesty of justice. But these were hardliners, burnished by years of conflict. They barely possessed a handful of compassion, with any empathy leached out of their hearts long ago. Mercifully, they were few in number.

As for me, during the time I spent in hospital in Marseille having my leg repaired in the months before Christmas 1943, word had come through to me that I would be promoted as soon as I'd convalesced sufficiently, but my future role depended on my physical fitness and that was causing difficulties. At one point, I was going to lose the leg owing to infection and I'd have ended up with a desk job, albeit in a position of some seniority. As it happened, it turned out that I would be doing both types of work – administration and active service. The assignments I enjoyed most were meeting and hosting SOE operatives and Free French personnel from London. Communication between all parties, particularly those in London, was vital and it hadn't been nearly effective enough up until now. That was probably my greatest responsibility, and after Jour-J it reached its zenith, since we had the Allied armies to contend with and to coordinate as well.

The leg mended itself to the extent that I could walk but not enough so that I could run, which was one of the requisites of active service, so I never returned to the same calibre of operations I'd been carrying out with Nelle. But that wasn't the only reason I could neither contact her nor see her. I was required to move around in and within what I can only describe as a sort of security cordon so that only a few people at any one time might know who I was or where I was. It was the same for all of us in positions which required any level of command and control.

Regrettably I was also aware of the fact that, by the spring of 1944, those people who had originally identified Nelle as a sexual collaborator back in Chalon still held her dossier and were determined to keep it open. It seemed to be the only black mark against me as I had defended her when questioned about her by my senior colleagues. However the more missions she went on and the more she excelled herself, the less the case against her seemed to retain any substance. The whole denunciation against her was like a bucket leaking water fast, but the purists in the organisation seemed determined to hold her to account one day.

It is perfectly true that reaching that courthouse on time in Lyon that day was like running for a train leaving the station, and hopping on board, exhausted, at the very last moment. That is in fact exactly what happened. I was in Paris at the time when the news of her arrest reached me. Colleagues sorted it out for me. I ended up travelling through the night in the cab of a freight train. On one occasion we were chased by an Allied bomber near Dijon. Fortunately, Nelle's arrest arrived at a time when our cell's activities were winding down and to some extent I was free, or at least not engaged on an assignment. Colleagues were dropping out, returning home or ending up joining the regular army but I'd resolved to stay on board until the last moment. I was considering returning to Lyon for Christmas to resume my studies in January 1945 at the university. On the other hand, these were uncertain times and I could easily change my mind or be forced to do so for some unpredictable reason.

I'll leave it up to Nelle to describe our first encounter after the trial, and her attempts at coming to terms with her mother's betrayal.

168. You can imagine my relief at seeing Jean in court. I can attribute his presence, his wonderful words in my defence, and the subsequent verdict as all contributing to shaping a better future for Gérard and me. I shudder to think what ghastly fate I might have endured if I'd been sent to jail. I told him all about it and he said I must have had a friendly judge because it went so well in my favour. I didn't question exactly what he meant by that.

And what of Gérard? He was also spared the shame and upset at seeing his mother jailed or worse. I have often reflected in the last few days on all of this. First, I should be grateful that the FFI to some extent protects their own. By that I mean I might have been thrown to the mob and suffered a far worse fate under the latter's summary justice. I will try and remember to ask Jean for confirmation, as I'm sure he'd know, but I suspect I could have suffered a worse fate without the FFI's intervention. In the hands of the vengeful, I'd have been shaven, tarred and taunted, paraded around Lyon and thrown into the streets. I am grateful such a destiny never befell me.

As it happens, the FFI dealt with me fairly, presented the charges, respected my defence, and the courts judged and I'm now sitting here in Hervé's salon with Gérard in my lap and looking forward to celebrating Christmas 1944 in relative peace.

I have of course had personal family matters to work out. I still consider Maman's actions to be utterly treacherous and I cannot think about her without bursting into tears, so I'm putting that aside for the moment. I have not spoken to Papa nor Marc or Eloise. Did they play a part, even a tiny one in denouncing me too? Or was it Maman acting alone, and that wretched barman? I may never find a full answer to any of this. But then I suppose I should be grateful that only Jean and I know the whole truth. True, I lied in court, and they didn't break me. I do just wonder though what that judge truly believed. Anyway he accepted both Jean and my words. So as far as the whole of France is concerned, Jean is Gérard's father.

Today, my first concern is for Claudette and Hervé. Am I putting them at risk by lodging in their house? And is

Gérard going to suffer? To date he had barely socialised or seen anything of the world beyond Clos de la Fontaine. Jean informed me on both counts, that my presence no longer posed a risk to anyone. Nevertheless, I still take precautions and I still wear my head bandage and FFI armband when I go out. I even think I might visit the old man and flaunt my innocence about his office. In reality, I want to talk to him about Marcel, and relive the times we spent on assignment. I suppose it is a kind of therapy. Something is definitely missing from my life and I think Jean feels the same way.

174.Jean had returned to Lyon from God knows where. He wouldn't tell me where he'd been lodging on the one short occasion we met after the trial but he promised to come to dinner at Clos de la Fontaine just as soon as Claudette and Hervé had come to terms with the whole debacle concerning me and the trial. That was good enough for me. Jean is still officially an FFI man and I have to respect that, and we are still at war after all.

177. It is early December. I had a good evening with Claudette and Hervé tonight. By "good," I mean that we talked thoroughly through the whole "Thing." "Thing" is the word Hervé uses to describe the combined events of my friendship with Johann, being called out as a collaborator, leaving home, fighting for the Maquis, being arrested and going to trial and being sentenced to house arrest. The "Thing" seems a harmless, non-specific word which he can handle without wincing at any particular event, any one of which except my service for the Resistance, causing him much pain. Claudette seems to follow along on the same lines, not that she hasn't an entirely independent point of view. It is clear that they'd both decided to combine their opinions, such that, mercifully I feel that I am fighting to clean my slate with only one couple, rather than two people.

Not surprisingly they take no interest in either Johann nor the love we once shared together. They tend to look to the future and what lies ahead for Gérard and me. Except that Hervé wants to know everything I've done with the Maquis which I find curiously therapeutic. That subject is likely to consume many hours during the long winter months of house arrest.

They both also want to know how the trial has gone and how I've managed to "get off so lightly," as they put it. I stalled on that one to some extent and took the opportunity to ask them if they might invite Jean for dinner one evening to explain it all to them.

179.The toughest and most intractable conversation with my grandparents concerns what to do about my immediate family, and more particularly my mother. Would a rapprochement with the family ever be possible? At this point, we left it that we had plenty of time to discuss it – eleven months remaining of my house arrest at Clos de la Fontaine. That is time enough to find a solution. I wasn't going home or anywhere else until Christmas 1945. In my own mind, I consider that returning home to Domaine de Champuix with Gérard is the most unlikely of trajectories.

Other matters also cross my mind. For example, is Jean going to marry me? Is Jean happy to adopt Gérard, and so on? And at the back of my own mind – is Gérard going to meet his real father? Would I go and live in Germany if that situation presented itself? And what of my work? Am I likely to need to earn a living somewhere? Should I start up on my own? Being a fully independent woman with her own personal wealth would certainly be a novelty, but the world will surely change for women after this war. I am reminded of Coco Chanel who has been in the newspapers recently. I won't be as rich as her but at least she doesn't have to depend on men for anything much. She is also a collaborator of sorts. Perhaps a "cooperator" would be a safer label for her. After all, during the war, we have shown the opposite sex what we can do. Women are capable and we are willing and we will fight to determine our own destiny.

181. I keep considering my future. Should I be worrying about it and how might I care for Gérard? Yes, and Claudette certainly thinks so. She has a habit of cornering me after dinner as I help her clear up in the kitchen. I take her concerns seriously but conclude that the older one got, the more one tends to worry about such things. It's as if she has become my surrogate mother so I take that as a compliment.

185. My health. I still have a limp after hitting my knee particularly hard in Sète. It isn't bad but I can no longer be certain of completing a twenty kilometre hike, especially in one day. The first move is to visit the hospital for my battle wound though, as I suspect it is causing me unforeseen problems, particularly dizziness and occasional blurred vision. The wound itself has now fully healed and my hair has largely grown back. I can now at least cover it with my mop of hair, although from time to time the wound weeps a foul liquid, which is apparently part of the healing process.

188.My visit to the hospital yields little at first and the consensus is that I should wait and see if any further symptoms appear. They have left me with a list of unpleasant ailments with which I risk being inflicted, but I have locked the list away in my chest of drawers as such things can often be psychosomatic if pondered over too closely. But I suppose I must admit that my health gives me my greatest worries as the periods of dizziness become more frequent.

189.On a happier note, Gérard is providing me with so much pleasure and joy at present. I realise of course that owing to my frequent absences, I had never really bonded with him on a continual basis since he was born, such that he must be confused having both an old and a younger mother. A mother is a mother whatever age, I'm certain of that. Grand-père has acted as Gérard's father all along and Grand-mère appears to be an excellent surrogate mother. The boy is well behaved, does not cry when he wants something or scream when he doesn't get it, but asks politely, which is a revelation to me. I'm not sure the same could have been said about me when I was his age. His apparent love of dogs and his recent craving for having one seems to have passed much to my relief. We'd have to walk the dog every day and who was going to do that? Hervé and I have set up an obstacle course for Gérard in the garden, a sort of run about as I am worried that he isn't getting enough exercise. We spend our days racing around the garden for exercise. Hervé from time to time jumps out of the bushes unexpectedly and terrifies the poor boy as he rounds a corner, but he's growing to love it nevertheless. As a child I also used to love running. Perhaps that love of exercise comes from me. I notice that Gérard often doesn't sleep during his afternoon naps. I need to find a way of tiring him out or providing him with more stimulation. How? I'm not sure. His favourite toy is Grand-père's model yacht which we sail around the perimeter of the ornamental fountain especially when the wind gets up.

The model vessel has got into such a bad state of repair that Grand-père has given up telling dear Gérard not to lift it by its mast, or to remember to wash off the algae which has accumulated around the keel and hull. These are happy times but as the winter comes, we have to find more for him to do indoors which isn't going to be easy.

192. All in all I hope I'm becoming a better mother. I am at least now permanently on the scene and I can no longer blame myself for neglecting him. In fact, the opposite. Gérard is being smothered. The bond between a mother and her child is like no other and I begin to cherish the days I spend with him, entirely devoted to his upbringing and entertainment. These days my focus is entirely on him. Some days I make a point of spending a few hours with Jean and bring the boy with me. We walk up and down the street outside the house – forbidden I know under the terms of my sentence, but no one notices us and I am never far from the house. I remind Jean that Gérard is his son when in company, and I need him to masquerade convincingly as his father. Such a role, I admit, is not easy, but I admire Jean for his fortitude and his willingness. I remind myself frequently that he is a good man. He gets full points for effort but I can tell there is some relief on his face when we have to leave. We can laugh about it though. But I must also respect his independence and his own personal ambitions. But I am relieved that as far as everyone is concerned, Gérard is still Jean's boy.

26

Owing to the shock of Marie-France's arrest, the celebration of Gérard's birthday on 28th September had been postponed until calmer times. Gérard was not to know so a weekend in early December was chosen instead. Jean arrived shortly before midday so that birthday presents could be opened well before lunch. At Claudette's insistence, Hervé had retrieved an old wooden baby chair from the attic and positioned it between where Jean and Marie-France were seated at the table. Marie-France was charged with lighting a fire in the salon and laying the table, while Claudette prepared a modest lunch with what provisions she could find. Chronic food shortages continued across the whole of France, with little meat or butter available anywhere. Hervé had worked tirelessly in the vegetable garden throughout the year, and even expanded it, so that potatoes, leeks and cabbage were readily available to them, even well into the winter months.

So much had happened in the two years since Gérard had been born, that Marie-France had to admit to forgetting whether her grandparents had ever met Jean. He had to remind her that he had never stepped inside the house nor met them. He was at first received with reservation, except by Gérard who, perfectly on cue, greeted him at the front door with a delighted "Papa, papa" much to Marie-France's relief. Jean arrived laden with goodies. There were two presents for Gérard: a second-hand iron toy soldier which Jean had touched up with paint, and a wooden toy milk delivery lorry which Gérard immediately began rolling along the parqué floor to the irritation of everyone. For Monsieur et Madame Champuix, he'd brought a leg of lamb wrapped carefully in several layers of paper. You could be mugged on the street for possessing such a luxury.

"Not from the black market, I hasten to add," said Jean as he handed it to Claudette. "My apologies, it is an unusual present to bring, but during these times of war, I hope a much appreciated one."

"So where *does* it come from?" asked Hervé abruptly.

"My uncle. He's a farmer east of here, near Éveux. He farms sheep and cattle or what remains of them since the Boches stole half his livestock."

"A very useful uncle to have, what, what?" Hervé replied. "Thank you. Very much appreciated."

"We won't be eating it without you, so you'll have to come again, in the new year perhaps," Claudette said cheerfully.

Marie-France poured out the wine and they sat in the salon until called to the table by Claudette. Marie-France assured them, "We thought we'd have our modest entrée with Gérard and then I'll put him to bed, so that we can enjoy the rest of our lunch without distractions."

Hervé was unable to hold back his interest in Jean and his Resistance activities. Such was his enthusiasm that he was determined to delay no further, beginning his interrogation before Marie-France had returned from putting Gérard to bed. "Marie-France tells me you're the equivalent rank in the Maquis these days of a regular General. Is that correct? I want to hear what you've both been up to. I presume we can talk, now that the FFI is being disbanded and we're leaving it up to the Allied armies to push the bloody Boches out of our country."

"Marie-France was being generous. The rank of 'General' is a gross exaggeration. After all we don't have any regular generals in our army aged twenty-four, do we?" Jean raised a laugh and the conversation continued in a similar vein, with Jean being bombarded with questions on the subject of his wartime activities. At appropriate moments he included Marie-France in the account of his exploits, praising her bravery, her fighting abilities and her popularity amongst the men with whom she fought. Her grandparents could not have been left in any doubt as to their granddaughter's distinguished service.

"And what of your futures?" Claudette said, addressing them both.

Before either of them could answer, Hervé intervened. "I have a letter from your father, addressed to me, but it is not for me. I'm sure it is really addressed to you. It concerns your future, Marie-France. Henri says that he remembers Jean well from the summer he worked in the vineyards, and he has suggested that you might both wish to return to the estate to take up your positions again." Marie-France hesitated. The conversation moved swiftly from offers of being welcomed home by her father, to the subject of her mother who was the main obstacle to such a step forward.

"I fear we might not be so well received by Clémence," Jean said.

"Or more likely I'd find it incredibly difficult living in the same house as my mother. She betrayed me after all, and when she was not in possession of all the correct facts. She threw me to the wolves."

Addressing Marie-France, Hervé replied, "One day you will need to find out what was on the stupid woman's mind. I have to say I never cared for her much. With all that high-Catholic doctrinal drivel, and all those inexorable anti-Boche diatribes, she's too much for me, I'm afraid to say." Hervé took a large gulp of wine and wiped his mouth with his napkin.

"Hervé, please be careful with what you say. She is your

daughter-in-law," Claudette said.

"I know that, but she shouldn't have turned in our war hero grand-daughter owing to some petty Catholic dogma about sex out of wedlock, which no one gives a damn about any longer. Especially not during a war. And then it got even worse … accusing our granddaughter of more or less procuring a child via a sexual encounter with a serving German officer. The only offended person apart from your mother, was that feckless family priest they've got hanging around their parish … Father Grosjean, or whatever he's called, cadging lunch and wine off them every Sunday. He's a deluded old fart with failed ambitions, who missed the bus to the bishopric, I'd say. I bet he was at the heart of this mess, bending Clémence's ear and tut-tutting about a child being born out of wedlock and such-like nonsense."

Jean laughed uncontrollably, until Marie-France had to stop him.

"You see, Jean 'le Général' agrees with me," Hervé said, joining in the laughter while glancing at Claudette. "And I bet that old fool of a cleric feels like a mug now, what with the whole case being pretty much dismissed and all. And might I remind you that the great Arletty was tried in Paris at exactly the same time as our Marie-France, and she's also had her case thrown out of the courts. She ended up being sentenced to house arrest in some château, I believe. And I understand the original sentence was to be eighteen months in prison."

"I think she's even been released now. Like Marie-France, she's still under house arrest, I think," Jean said.

"Hervé, who is this Arletty person?" Claudette asked.

"One of our, if not our most famous screen actresses and singers. She's done some theatre too, I believe. It's all been in the newspapers, splashed across the front pages in October and November. Haven't you been reading about it, my dear? The case no doubt helped the outcome of Marie-France's trial. Arletty had fame and talent as a mitigating factor; Marie-France had courage and service."

"Are you sure her case helped mine, Grand-père? said Marie-France, vexed at the improbability of it.

"Anyway, the woman had a most distinguished looking friend, tall and aristocratic, a German officer of the Luftwaffe no less, a friend, boyfriend, lover, who knows? He was around throughout the war. So she was charged with treason for cavorting with this man. In her defence, she claimed to have caused not the slightest bit of harm to her country."

"Ah yes. It does sound rather familiar, just like our Marie-France's experience, I suppose. I'm happy to say that forgiveness, tolerance and understanding are returning to our lives. We must never forget this war, but in time, I'm sure we shall forgive … at least a little," said Claudette.

"I'm not sure my mother ever will," Marie-France said.

"Perhaps not. But she was so close to her brother, your uncle, killed at Verdun at the tail end of the last war. One forgets how that affected her whole life. Her only brother lost at such a young age. She's always loathed the Germans after that. She never ceases from describing them as savage, belligerent barbarians. It's for us to meet her half-way, to understand the pain she has gone through too," Claudette said.

"Fair enough," said Jean. "You never told me that, Marie-France."

"I haven't told you everything, no."

"And what news of your father, Jean? Marie-France tells me he was deported back in 1941 for his political views," asked Hervé.

"He was, and nothing more has been heard of him. And I'm unable to discover a word about him. It is very frustrating. He was quite old when he was deported and not in good health. I fear the worst, I'm afraid."

"Marie-France says you may be tempted to go into politics?" said Claudette.

"I don't suppose you would approve of my politics. I am still very much a communist. Many of the Resistance fighters were communists or quasi-communists fighting against fascism and for France. There is some debate now as to whether this is the right moment to seize the political initiative while the Resistance movement is still very much in favour. We shall see. I wonder for how much longer the French people will appreciate what the Resistance did for them during the war."

27

Jean returned to his mother in Dijon for Christmas Day and expressed his intention to remain there for at least a month or two. After dropping off a Christmas present for Gérard and enjoying a modest dinner with the Champuix, Jean made a swift exit to catch a train, embracing Gérard and Marie-France and promising to return as soon as possible.

Claudette remarked that despite the triumph of liberation, Christmas 1944 at Clos de la Fontaine felt like the saddest of occasions. She believed she spoke for present company and local friends with whom she'd been in touch more frequently, when she expressed a sense of grim hopelessness, as if the country were in terminal decline. "People all about us are weary, glum, hungry and impoverished," she exclaimed.

Hervé observed that the newspapers had estimated that there had been almost two million denunciations up to the end of 1944, with varied motives. Approximately half were instigated for financial reward, a little under half in the form of objections to strong political views, and a tenth as a result of vindictive acts of petty vengeance.

Marie-France replied that she wasn't sure in which category she'd been placed. "And some people still find it acceptable to denounce anyone they know to be Jewish. Such attitudes and behaviour are contributing to the same general malaise and uncertainty in society of which Claudette speaks." Claudette nodded in approval.

Marie-France found Jean's absence difficult, but there was little she could do about it. He had obligations to his mother although she had a daughter nearby for company, and Marie-France had responsibilities to Gérard. In reality, she was finding life confined to the house oppressive at times, and she longed on occasions for the freedom she had once enjoyed, hiding out in the garrigue of the Languedoc, dangerous and unpredictable as it had been.

As the year 1945 unfolded, anti-communism became the dominant force in politics, in the newspapers and amongst the people in general. And with it came a backlash against the Resistance. Some members of the FTP and FFI were accused of extortion and were prosecuted. To many such as Jean and Nelle, it seemed like the world had been turned upside down, with collaborators amnestied in the name of national unity, while former Resistance fighters were being prosecuted. Was it time to move on? Marie-France longed for Jean to visit so that they might discuss their future. She was determined to do something worthwhile, whether it be work, or volunteering in some capacity to help in the rebuilding of her country. She needed a new sense of purpose again. She pondered her father's earlier offer of work. It might be the best way forward once her sentence came to an end. In 1944, women had gained the vote, and new employment legislation in early 1945 contributed to helping women return to work if they wished, but most women were subjugated to the same status of second-class citizen which they'd endured before the war, especially in the home, family and in society in general. What chances did Marie-France have of finding any mainstream work? Hervé had commented that the first French POWs were beginning to return home from Germany by March 1945 and they would all be looking for work as well. And there were bound to be many more coming home, as the Allies advanced into Germany and camp inmates were freed.

But there was little chance of any ex-POWs finding employment, so broken was every aspect of life and work in France.

In the spring of 1945, Hervé was still lamenting the German deportations. Addressing Marie-France and Claudette at dinner one evening, he said: "They were still deporting people from the Colmar junction in early February 1945, from the annexed Alsace zone, for God's sake, even though the military courts have been closed down long ago. And it's still going on. They're relentless, these damn Boches. When will it ever end? Oh, those most unfortunate Jews and their deportations. They've had a horrific time."

Roughly three quarters of the 330,000 Jews resident in France in 1940 survived the Nazi Occupation and the Vichy government's drive to rid them from France. This was owing in no small way to the courageous efforts of many local people who risked their lives by hiding them away in their properties. The so-called "French national Jews," as opposed to those who were simply resident in France, were the least vulnerable, and barely fifteen percent of those met their deaths. However barely one in twenty of the approximately 76,000 Jews resident in France who were deported to the camps in Germany ever returned to France.

One spring afternoon Jean appeared at the house. "I have obtained a special dispensation for you to leave your jail tonight," he announced at the front door. "And please come with me for just a second. Follow me." Marie-France accompanied Jean into the street. He stopped, took hold of her hand, then pointed to a small black motor car, and said with obvious excitement, "Mine. All mine. Ours, even."

"How delightful. Are we going to go for a spin?"

"We're going out for dinner, such as it is. A friend's family restaurant. My uncle supplies them with their food. I've managed to negotiate a quiet table."

"How lovely. So we will get to travel in your new toy."

"Yes. But not exactly new. There's a sad story behind it, which I should tell you first. It was my father's. He has not returned to us, so my mother has given it to me. The authorities believed he passed away some time ago. One day I would like to go to Germany to see if I can locate where he is buried. I believe I know which camp he was sent to."

"To Germany? I will come with you," Marie-France said without thinking.

On the journey to the restaurant, Jean announced that he was considering running for election. "I'm going into politics. My eventual aim is to be a Communist member of the National Assembly." Such news barely surprised Marie-France, and she agreed it was at least a positive move forward.

"I'm not sure about the Communist Party, but I'm delighted you've made a decision."

"I'm only thinking about it. It's not definite."

The restaurant was full and they agreed, after peering about at the other diners, that they were the youngest there. Jean had asked for a discreet table in the corner so that they were out of view.

"Oh. I suppose I should tell you now, that I haven't obtained a special dispensation for you. Nothing of the kind. It was just a ruse to get you out of the house."

"But they could send me to prison. What are you thinking of?"

"Unlikely. They're all involved with their own affairs and besides there are virtually no police around. They've all run away." He laughed at his comment but Marie-France turned her face towards the wall in case she risked being seen. "Honestly, I wouldn't worry," Jean repeated.

That evening they enjoyed a bottle of Cornas and a whole roast chicken, a rarity during such times. They laughed as they remembered the chickens which they stole from the villages they entered at night to raid for something to eat. Everything now seemed such a long time ago since those days, but they shared a nostalgia for it, and agreed it was not just about the Resistance. It was a time when they'd got to know each other on a more intimate level, a time when they really lived, when their lives surviving off the land and out in the open seemed to be so free, natural and pure. "Perfectly free, natural and pure" were the words and phrase they repeated over and over.

Jean took this moment during the conversation as a cue to ask the waiter for two glasses of champagne. As they toasted each other and sipped gratefully on the refreshing bubbles, Jean fell silent. Eventually he found his words, "Marie-France, I want you to marry me. Will you marry me?" he said, leaning across the table and gazing into her eyes.

"Marry? Marry?" Marie-France's surprise prompted Jean to reassure her.

"Yes, marry. Think about it. Don't answer me now. I know it's a big surprise and we haven't exactly discussed it. But we have been talking about our futures. Perhaps getting married is a good start to our new post-war lives."

"Goodness. Well, I'm flattered, but I'll need time. I'm sorry, Jean. I'll need to think about this."

That same evening Marie-France wrote a letter to her father, asking for his advice. She expressed her own views, that she wasn't sure she wished to be the wife of a prospective Communist member of the National Assembly and informed him that she had therefore declined the immediate proposal of marriage and begged Jean for time to consider her future. The surprise generated by Jean's proposal left Marie-France unsure of what she wanted. Part of her wished for her father to suggest that marrying a Communist was a blatant act of hypocrisy. It would be impossible for her to return to an affluent bourgeois family business selling luxury wines of high value to the wealthy citizens of France and at the same time be married to a Communist politician.

She lay in bed unable to sleep. "I hate decisions," she said aloud. "Endless, impossible choices to make. Domaine de Champuix. A life with Jean. A life with Johann. A happy family in the Rheingau. Gérard united with his father. Gérard a German. That'll be too much of a shock for everyone. Don't suppose they'll let me back into France again if I reveal the big lie I've been keeping from all and sundry. Damn it. I lied in court." She banged her fists against the headboard. "Oh, what am I to do? It's so awful."

*

Ma Coccinelle – The End of War

Was this now the right time to stop addressing her as Nelle and revert to her peacetime Christian name? But I was undecided on that one. The prospect of spending the rest of my life with Marie-France had preoccupied me for some weeks. I wondered whether ambitions to marry her might have been one of those unpredictable reactions to grief after being forced to concede that Pa had most likely passed away. I presumed that most prospective couples did at least talk about marriage openly for months before proposing. If it seemed like merely the perfect antidote or a necessary displacement activity to distract me from my grief, it was a bad decision, and I admit it should have been given more time and consideration. That's what Marie-France had thought. She wasn't ready for marriage, I could tell.

I could say the same of the burgeoning urge to follow in my father's footsteps. Was I ready to renew my membership of the PCF with ambitions to go the whole way – win an election and a seat in the Assembly as a Communist? He hadn't gone that far, but his politics were what drove him. There were days when people convinced me that this moment in the early summer of 1945 was as good a time as any. And then I read that ex- FTP members were being arrested for abusing their positions and an anti-Resistance, anti-communist sentiment was sweeping the country. Decisions at this time were difficult to make, with remarkably unpredictable consequences.

There was so much to do though. That much was obvious. And the only way to get things done was to get into politics. The Führer had taken his own life on 30th April. The Battle of Berlin had ended on 2nd May. And the German Instrument of Surrender had been signed on 8th May. And then in July, the Maréchal Pétain, the arch symbol of the Vichy years, had been charged with treason – although, like many thousands of others, he was eventually to have his death sentence commuted by de Gaulle. Everything which stank of this unholy war was collapsing about us. It was vital that the new beginnings were the right ones.

The fall out from the war and its finale was now ubiquitous. In total, 450,000 POWs would return to France. Of the 650,000 STO workers despatched to work in Germany, it is not known how many eventually returned to France, perhaps half of those who'd been transported to Germany. Many lost their lives in Allied air raids when the factories were bombed by the RAF and US Air Force. More reliable information existed for political prisoners. Of the 86,827 political prisoners deported to Germany, 40,760 returned to France, of whom 8,872 were women. I reminded myself so many times that my father was not one of those returnees.

As for the Resistance, we claimed 100,000 deaths of our comrades at the time, but in reality it was more like 20,000. 1,053 of them were eventually made "Compagnons de la Libération," the highest of honours. It was a felicitous affirmation of gratitude and recognition instituted by de Gaulle. Those who received the honour were portrayed as heroic fighters, as armed citizens, carrying out acts of sabotage or engaging directly with the enemy. But only six women were ever granted the honour. I have to admit that I put Nelle forward, but owing to circumstance with which we are already familiar, my application on her behalf was rejected. I noted that the majority of the parts played by women – messengers, radio operators, couriers, printers, distributors of banned literature, providers of safe houses, seemed not to be heroic enough, despite their sacrifices, and I was a first-hand witness to that. Now might be such an opportunity to reveal that in August 1945, I was myself honoured by de Gaulle as a "Compagnon" at a special ceremony in Paris to which I decided not to invite Nelle, nor inform her about, for the straightforward reason that it seemed so unfair that she had not been included. She would hear about it soon enough.

Many of our Resistance colleagues couldn't stand the thought of an ordinary life and it was said that 120,000 ex-members joined the regular army instead of returning home to their wives and families. One heard that same story everywhere – a general inability to return to a humdrum civilian life where there was no work to be found and little else to do. At least life in the army was something akin to how they'd lived their lives before, if somewhat more regimented.

France was in a bad way. Despite the increase in birth rates between 1943 and 1945, divorce rates peaked between 1945 and 1947, bringing misery and displacement to hundreds of thousands of families. Clearly people of all backgrounds and circumstances struggled to return to their pre-war lives, as I have suggested above. And it was no different for Nelle and me. We were wanderers, and our lives right now had become indecisive, undetermined and lugubrious.

Throughout the five years of war, 600,000 French citizens had died. Less than one third of those were actual combatants. Others lost their lives in bombardments, executions, massacres or deportations. It wasn't a fraction of the cost to human life if compared to the Soviet Union or the Red Army as I kept pointing out to Hervé, but his thoughts, like most Frenchmen, were grounded in France's own particular circumstances.

Yes, we were all in a muddle, with conflicting attitudes everywhere conflictions and guilt concerning our own particular roles in the war, and our attitudes towards the Vichy years of government. Shame and sorrow filled the air, where there was also joy and relief. By the end of 1945, it was estimated that 40,000 collaborators were residing in French jails. Gradually sentences were commuted, convictions overturned or prosecutions lifted so that by 1948 only 13,000 remained, and by 1965, all had been released. The erections of memorials and the constant anniversaries ensured that the war and its aftermath inhabited the national psyche for years to come. In the 1960s, there followed a period of national debate concerning the Vichy years, when many politicians, writers and intellectuals shone a light on the national conscience, exposing many egregious aspects of life under the Occupation, provoking much guilt and shame on both an individual and public level.

In November 1945, de Gaulle formed his second government of national unity, but he was unable to unite the country owing to the five Communist ministers and the 159 seats in the National Assembly which had been gained by the Communist Party in the October elections. De Gaulle resigned in January 1946, in despair.

The winter of 1945/6 was another tough one. There was little work, no industry, and morale amongst the people remained low. The only preoccupations seemed to be the politics of the day, the weather and an obsession with acquiring enough food to eat. Marie-France reminded me though that 1945 had been a fine vintage and even the Bordelais to the west were proclaiming it a fine one. Still, only by 1948 did the food shortages end, and the roads, rail transport and general communications begin to improve. Queueing was still commonplace well into the 1950s, especially in some types of shops. Such was the upheaval wrought upon every aspect of French society by the German Occupation of France.

28

At the end of November, Marie-France received a letter from the "Préfecture" informing her of the expiry of her sentence with a release date from her house arrest of 1st December 1945. The news induced such a feeling of relief that she immediately asked Hervé if they might open a special bottle of the family Meursault. At his instigation, she also chose a bottle of Musigny for the haunch of venison which Jean had dropped off the week before and left hanging in the cellar.

"I think it is time you reverted to your family name," Claudette said out of the blue, over dinner. "And what about the boy? He should be a Champuix too, unless you're going to marry Jean."

"These are decisions I'll need to make at some point, probably sooner rather than later I know, but I simply haven't made up my mind yet about Jean. It's his Communism which irks me most." As she said it, she realised she'd lied to them again. It wasn't only his Communism. It was simply that that was the most convincing excuse for them to hear. She hated being in such a position, having to lie to everyone. She'd increasingly wondered whether a more adventurous life might suit her better than staying at home and bringing up children. Was she the marrying kind after all?

Such comments from Claudette reminded her of a number of dilemmas which she faced. Foremost in her mind was the future wellbeing of her boy who had just turned three. Didn't Gérard deserve the right to know who his father was? Yet he was far too young at the moment to be told and would only be confused. Plenty of years would need to pass before it was right to tell him. The truth was that she was growing increasingly uncomfortable with the lies she'd been spinning. Lately she'd considered enquiring as to Johann's whereabouts. Had he survived the war? Had he been wounded? Had he returned to winemaking at the family estate? It wouldn't be too difficult to look up the Schräder family in the Rheingau, but a suitable length of time needed to pass, perhaps a year or more. Germany was also in the most terrible state. Having been defeated, she was now an overrun and occupied country much like France had been, although facing considerably greater destruction. Berlin had been greatly damaged whereas Paris remained intact. She reflected upon the irony of that fact and whether Johann might have ever thought about her since their last encounter. Yes, he had, surely. He was that sort of man, she was certain of it.

There was no one apart from Jean with whom she could talk about such matters. And now that he'd asked for her hand in marriage, discussing the boy's father with him was inappropriate. In the new year, she had other matters on her mind. She agreed with her Champuix grandparents to leave Clos de la Fontaine, admitting she'd overstayed her welcome by a year. It was Jean's suggestion that she move in with him in the centre of Lyon. There was little room in the apartment and no communal garden but they adapted quickly to their new environs. They agreed to enrol the boy in playschool and change his family name to "de Villeneuve" before the start of the autumn term, a precursor, Marie-France suggested, to marrying Jean. Finding the appropriate lawyer to facilitate a change of name occupied Marie-France's time for many months. And when they did find someone to deal with it, Gérard's papers were simply lost in a myriad of others, such was the chaos which befell France's post-war civic administration.

Jean completed his degree in June and found himself employed in post-graduate teaching in order to earn an income while he pursued his ambitions in politics, joining a local branch of the Communist party. Although the couple lived together, they spent little time in each other's company. Their favourite moments were at weekends and in the evenings if neither were too tired, and Gérard had been settled successfully to bed.

"I think I'm pregnant," Marie-France announced one evening in early July. "If so, and I haven't been to the doctor yet for confirmation, I would love to be your wife, if that's still on offer. I couldn't bear to have a second child out of wedlock. I've been thinking about it a lot these last few days."

Jean kissed her and gave her a hug, then clasped her hands. "Well, what fabulous news." He hesitated before continuing. "How can I say this?" He paused before continuing. "But I do wonder if being pregnant is a good enough reason to marry someone."

"Yes, of course it is. It's the prompt I needed. A vindication. I needed a push, Jean. Don't you see that? I couldn't go on drifting about like this in a no man's land. Now there's a justification, no? And we can become a happily married couple with a family. The height of respectability, no?"

Jean raised his voice. "What? People don't marry for that reason. What of love and passion … and trust, and respect and all the aspirations for the future together? That's why people marry. For love, not convenience."

"Of course I feel all of those things for you. I'd be lost without you. I do love you, don't you see? And besides, Gérard needs a brother or a sister. We need to become a proper, respectable family now."

"I still don't think you're understanding what I'm saying," Jean said. "Embracing respectability is barely a reason for marrying."

"I know. I know."

"Let's talk about it later. Now's not the moment. To change the subject, because I really want to talk to you about this … I've been doing some research and it seems like Papa may have gone the same way as some of our professors at Lyon University. If you remember, the university more or less had to be shut down by mid-1941 because so many staff were arrested by the Vichy scum."

"How easily do you think we'll be able to find his grave?"

"Now isn't a great time as there's so much disorder and God knows where the records are being held, if they haven't been destroyed. But what I have discovered is that as many as 80,000 political prisoners, including members of the Resistance, were deported to Germany. And they didn't go the same way as the French POWs or the Jews. They were bunched with homosexuals, murderers and criminals, as well as the Spanish and other foreign fighters deemed 'undesirables' to the Vichy regime. The Vichy and the Gestapo divided all the deportees into different groups and assigned each a separate transfer camp and a separate destination in Germany. Many went on to Poland and such. It seems that the early political prisoners were sent to work the land for food production. I can't see Pa digging up potatoes somehow, but that's probably what happened to him. But I know nothing more than that. I just hope the Allies or the Soviets didn't shoot him, thinking he was a German. He did speak Russian though. He could have talked his way out of that situation. But we don't know."

"It seems too early, my dear. You'll have to hold on another year or so."

"Papa would have been proud of the fact that Lyon became the Resistance capital of France and that I was a part of it," Jean added.

"He would be even prouder of what you're doing now."

*

In August, a few weeks prior to the harvest at Domaine de Champuix, Marie-France informed Jean that she intended returning to her family estate to lend a hand.

"I will be taking Gérard too and I'm going to tell them that we are engaged to be married."

"Will your wicked mother be there?" asked Jean.

"I don't know, but I know Papa is increasingly keen that we return to the domaine. And that includes you. He's been going on about it for some time. He's also happy for you to pursue any career you wish and admits it's none of his business what you wish to do. Just so that you know, he doesn't disapprove of you, in case you thought he did."

"I know he doesn't like my communism. There's just the impracticality initially of living so far from you if I'm in Lyon."

"I think we can come to some sort of arrangement so we don't feel stranded," said Marie-France.

"Shouldn't I be coming to Saubon too for such an announcement? For our engagement, I mean."

"I think a visit on my own first, would be best. I want to sort things out with Maman on my own. I think that's best. I need to feel fully comfortable returning home, although I'm not too sure where home truly is now after all I've been through. I've even been wondering whether this notion of home could be some sort of illusion, a myth even. Is this quest or allure to return home simply a fiction we cling to, an imperfect ideal of needing roots, an attempt to feel securely tethered when all about us is so fluid? I don't know. But I certainly need somewhere where I can feel settled after all this turmoil."

"I agree. I don't know where home is either, especially now that Pa has gone. I think what home does for you is different for everyone." Jean thought for a moment. "Home, well, it's where you make it, is it not? Where you're happiest dropping anchor. On the practical side, we'll need somewhere larger to live if you're expecting another. That's a necessity. If moving to Saubon-le-Duc would make you happy, I'm all for it. If that's going to become your true sense of finding home again."

"But would it make *you* happy, Jean?" Marie-France asked. "We won't be in the family house. There's a beautiful outbuilding that's already very liveable in. It's the one you lived in when you were helping us with the harvest in 1940. Do you remember?"

"Yes, it's going to be a much better solution to what we have now. We'll keep the flat in Lyon for me and I'll spend my weekends with you. How about that?"

With such a future mapped out, Marie-France boarded the fast train north, alighting in Beaune where her father and Marc met her. She had imagined a number of scenarios unfolding upon meeting them, and how she might react to them, but she needn't have worried. To her relief, her father and brother welcomed her and Gérard with enthusiasm. No one apart from Jean, Claudette and Hervé had so far taken so much interest in her child. How important it was to feel part of a big family. This was the first time in many years that she felt that. Her nearest equivalent had been her Maquis colleagues. At times they too had seemed like a family. Gérard was naturally overwhelmed. She put that down to the fact that he'd never travelled on a train or stood on a crowded railway platform before, with so many people of varied shapes and sizes hurrying about.

"Maman has gone to stay with a cousin in Paris, so coming home will hopefully be an easier experience for you," Marc said, as they motored down the narrow lanes towards Saubon, bordered on both sides by low stone walls and row upon row of vines which were heavy with fruit. "Three weeks," said Marc, knowing exactly what was going through Marie-France's mind, as she gazed out at the vineyards. They passed the clump of plane trees which took her straight back to that December night with Johann before Christmas 1941. How things had changed. So much seemed to have happened since then.

"I'm happy to be home," she announced as they sat around the kitchen table. Eloise had given her a genuinely delightful welcome. She reminded herself that she had suspected both her brother and sister of colluding in her denunciation, but in reality they were never high on the list. But nor had been her mother. She took that moment to consider too how unfair she'd been in suspecting Antoinette and made a mental note to get in touch as soon as the harvest was over.

"We are worried about your mother," Henri said. "She has become very unwell since you last set eyes on her. It is one of the reasons she is in Paris, seeing a medical specialist."

"Maman was right to be shocked by my friendship with a German officer. I know her reasons. She was right also to be shocked by the arrival of a child out of wedlock. Both were wrong. And I'm sorry I have caused her so much unhappiness and one day I will tell her that and apologise. I did not intend for either to happen. However, there are many good reasons for which I find it easy to argue my case, none of which we need discuss here, if you don't mind. All I do ask is that you welcome a new member to the family, and help to make Gérard feel he is most welcome here. I should appreciate that more than anything." She wiped away a tear after she'd said what she needed to say.

"We will. You have my word on that. He's such a lovely looking boy too," Eloise said. "I can't believe he's more than three years old."

"You have my word too. Gérard will be very welcome here," said Marc.

"He's very dark-haired, just like Jean. Let's hope he'll be tall like him too but any other similarities of a political nature might be difficult. I don't think we need another Communist in the house," Henri said, chuckling to himself.

"That's not funny," said Eloise. "What happens if he becomes a winemaking-loving Communist? Then you won't have a leg to stand on, Pa."

"Jean has been awarded the 'Compagnon de Libération' medal by Général de Gaulle. He told me just before seeing us off on the train this morning."

"Bravo for him," Henri said. "Pity you didn't get one too."

"He tried proposing me but it was declined. Women don't count, it seems."

"I'm just glad you're alive. Having heard about all that you've been up to from Grand-père Hervé, we're lucky you're still with us. And you might want to get that wound checked out by the family doctor in Beaune, no?" Henri said.

"I'll take her tomorrow," said Eloise.

"And one last thing. Jean has asked me to marry him and I have accepted his proposal."

"Well. Many congratulations, my girl. But you could look a bit more cheerful about it, for heaven's sake," her father said. Eloise ran towards her and hugged her.

"My sister's getting married. Wooohoo. The first of us lot too. Well done," said Marc.

*

They were married in November at Domaine de Champuix. Marie-France asked that it be a small wedding with the families and a few friends. Antoinette acted as her maid of honour and Jean's best man was an ex-Resistance fighter whom Marie-France did not know. Her mother had not returned from Paris, but the subject was barely mentioned, with Claudette making up for Clémence's absence in every way she could.

29

Ma Coccinelle – Gérard has a Sister

The delight which the birth of our daughter brought to my life took me totally by surprise. I'm not sure that men are good at preparing themselves for the arrival of a child. That is a pity, but I blame it on our genes. We are built differently. Men seem to view the whole birth thing as a woman's role. And one day, a tiny, vulnerable little creature emerges from your wife's womb and a bond between you and the child begins to materialise. First the fascination, then the urge to care and the desire to protect, then the devotion. And finally the particular love which a parent feels for their child evolves out of all that, and you become besotted.

We named her Marguerite Catherine, in honour of my mother who died a mere few weeks before the birth, at the end of March 1946. Such a sadness was met with a happy, smiling new life in our midst. I won't say it brought an end to my mourning. One can never erase or hope to assuage the death of one's mother. They live on in our memories forever. I simply regret that she never met our child.

As for Gérard, now three and a half, a little sister seemed to bring him much joy, although it was clear that he was frustrated in having a new member of the family with whom he could do little. "One day you'll be best of friends. But she's too small for you to play with just now," I heard Marie-France say so often.

Our life at Domaine de Champuix was considerably better than that of many families during the post-war years. We all tried to live modestly so as not to attract the ire or envy of our neighbours and workers. Food shortages, especially meat, were commonplace, and some items such as a new pair of shoes were impossible to find. We made do like everyone else, and anything we had in abundance, such as wine, we shared out amongst the people who worked for us. Marie-France fell back into her role as vineyard manager with gusto. It was a joy to see her happy again. There had been a malaise and a diffidence to her during the last several months which had worried me. But now she was jumping out of bed early with big plans for the day, indications to me that her unhappiness had passed her by.

My teaching at the university brought me my own distinct satisfaction in life, not only because I enjoyed it, but more I believe because there was a pleasure in observing my students' interest in their chosen subject, and then after many years of hard graft, seeing it crowned by a successful degree. I suppose I nurtured and treated them rather as though they were my own children, hoping they all might one day be potential future politicians. The job also left me in a good position to further my political ambitions. I was grateful to my father for so many people I was introduced to recognised the name and as a result I sometimes felt as if a red carpet had been rolled out in front of me, down which

I could walk with confidence. But I put in the work too. In August 1946, I'd been hired as our PCF Lyon representative's personal assistant which was a good step up from the local district work I'd been doing.

As before, our weekends were precious and I made a point of joining the family at Domaine de Champuix for as many as possible. Sometimes Marie-France brought the children to Lyon and they stayed with Claudette and Hervé, a more comfortable, expansive and less claustrophobic place for our growing family to reside.

I wasn't always sure what to expect from married life and now that I had no parents to ask and few contemporaries in the same situation, there were scarcely any reference points. Family life had its own demands. I don't suppose anything can prepare you for it. I wasn't always sure that Marie-France was entirely satisfied with her lot, but she worked the land tirelessly with its unpredictable climate and unforgiving nature, facing up to whatever came her way. Eloise devoted a lot of time to looking after the children while Marie-France was out in the vineyards but even she despaired of the round the clock attention which the children required. Eventually we employed a girl to drop in four days a week to help.

For the first time, I realised how stressful it was being a viticulturist, the worst and most demanding times being pre-harvest when you prayed for sunny, warm days with no rain. Rain early on led to rot and mildew which meant you had to discard grapes, or if it rained during harvest you ended up with diluted juice. Hail at flowering in June was a tough time too. That could wipe out the inflorescences of a whole vineyard. If you got both in one year, your crop and your income were severely compromised. But when all went well, it was a salutary finale to a year's efforts when Henri was able to taste the first wines out of the barrel after fermentation in October or November, and declare a winning year.

Roughly eighteen months after Nelle ended her time with the Maquis, her diary petered out. I include one of the last entries which, reading for the first time as I write this chapter, would explain what was to happen many years later, around July 1954. The only surprise was that it took so long.

261.Back in the vineyards of Domaine de Champuix, listening to my father's enthusiastic suggestions and seeing the smile on his face as we walk through the hectares of vineyards discussing the activities for the more important times of the year – when to start pruning, when to tie back the shoots, when to summer prune the vigorous laterals and, the most crucial date of all, when to harvest – it all gives me a lot of pleasure. This is my heritage and it is also his, both an art and a science we fully embrace together. It is "in our blood," as they say.

The children love it too, although Marguerite is far too young to fully appreciate it just now. But she enjoys sitting on the tractor with me, huddled between my legs, chugging around the vineyard perimeters, clutching and turning the heavy wheel with me. And when we were able to acquire a couple of horses again for working the soil between the rows, I can see the pleasure in her eyes each day as I harness the magnificent beasts up for their day's work. The estate has difficulties in these post-war days finding people to work the land and those we do engage are often suffering too greatly from the trauma of war to provide a full and satisfactory day's work. It is tiring managing this team and

I could do with Jean by my side. I'm not always sure I have the respect I deserve from the workers and Jean might be a better prospect as a boss. Some men just don't like taking orders from women. When will that ever change? But it becomes clear to me that this kind of work and indeed the lifestyle that goes with it has no appeal for Jean, and I at times find that disheartening.

263.I must confess that there are times when I think of Johann. He's even been here to this very place, and admired the countryside and even visited the winery. I remember him telling Papa that he too was a winemaker back in Germany, and how surprised Papa was to hear that. Really! As if the Germans are any different to us. It seems an odd portent that he'd visited Domaine de Champuix, but for all the wrong reasons. I later learnt that he'd most likely been searching for Jean at the time. I occasionally take a good look at Gérard, stare into his bright blue eyes, clasp his little face between my hands, and see an image of Johann, which pleases me deeply. I increasingly feel an urge to visit Johann and surprise him with the beautiful little boy he'd brought into my life.

I have to hide such feelings from Jean but my husband is no fool. He knows that soon enough I'd want Gérard to meet his real father, but when and how, I could not possibly know.

30

July 1954

With the summer holidays upon them, Marie-France once again cajoled Gérard into helping her out in the vineyards. It was where she could best keep an eye on him. He was reluctant at first, preferring the company of his village friends, but the promise of extra pocket money soon helped him change his mind. Racing a bicycle around the country lanes was more fun than helping out his mother, but being called on for a few days a week to please her and his grandfather proved to be no great sacrifice.

Marie-France discussed the activities of the day over breakfast. "Today we're green pruning in Genevrières. It's only half a hectare, it won't take long, and we've got four others helping us."

"But you said I didn't have to prune because it's boring and repetitive and my hands are too small for the secateurs and then they ache, and I can't write or do my homework or do anything after that," Gérard said.

"Yes, I know that. So you can take the horse with Marguerite and collect all the shoots we've cut off as we go along the rows. Can I trust you with a pitch fork?"

"Yes, of course," said Gérard.

Gérard, now twelve, had begun to take an interest in everything equestrian. He was taking riding and dressage lessons twice weekly at the stables in the village. His mother soon realised that he was happiest in the vineyards if he were working the horses. At such a young age, it was obvious to Marie-France that little else regarding winemaking was likely to interest him however much she tried to teach him the rudiments of running a vineyard.

"Laurent is setting Daisy up in the courtyard with a cart. You can take the reins and drive us all down to the vineyard with her. How about that?" Marie-France told Gérard.

"Marc promised me he'd show me how to drive the tractor," Gérard said.

"When did he promise that?" Jean said.

"Last night when we were having supper at the big house. Grand-père also nodded his approval."

"Well not today. It's a fine day and we're pruning excess shoots off. It's an important job," said Marie-France.

"Do as your mother says, please Gérard. Be a good boy. She has a lot on her plate at the moment," Jean said. "I'm late for work. I must go." Jean kissed Marie-France and patted Marguerite on the head before leaving.

It was Gérard's first year at helping them out with the winemaking. Maric-Francc knew he was too young but, at her father's instigation, she'd begun to tempt him with the sort of tasks which might attract his boyish fascination. The latest expected arrival, for delivery in the autumn, was the Farmall Super, a tractor made in France from largely imported American components. The tractor company had begun a new line of narrow-axled tractors for vignerons which Henri had been quick to research.

"What with our labour shortages, mechanisation is the only way forward," Henri had announced one morning. "Come with me to Dijon, Marie-France. We need to go to the new agricultural equipment show." That same day, Henri had put in an order for it, although Marie-France had insisted that she was perfectly happy with the old Labourier.

The day was going to be a hot one and Marie-France insisted on sunhats all round. Such was the heat that they were obliged to stop frequently for water. The small crew worked their way methodically along each row and then the next and so forth. They stopped and sat down for a bite or two from a baguette at the end of each row. Progress was slow and methodical.

"I knew we should have done this last week when it was cooler," Marie-France said, after they'd stopped for a rest.

"Maman, there's a man standing at the end of this row. Look. Up there," Marguerite said, pointing. She was sitting on Daisy, the mare, and had the best view up the row of vines. The Champuix plot in the Les Genevrières Premier Cru vineyard was on a mild convex slope such that if you were at the bottom it was difficult to see the top.

"I don't see anyone," said Marie-France.

"Yes. He's still there. He's not moving. He's very thin and tall and has a wavy moustache and he's leaning on a stick," Margeurite said excitedly.

"Let me see." Marie-France slipped through the trellis wire and stepped up onto the cart. "Hold Daisy steady please, Gérard. Let me have a look."

"Right there," said Marguerite, pointing to the silhouette of a man standing tall against the bright sky.

"I see him. I see him. All of you continue with your work and I'll go up and see what he wants." She climbed down, picked her sunhat off the ground and strode up through the rows of vines towards the stranger, who was standing 400 metres away towards the top of the slope. Before she reached him she straightened her dress, checked her cleavage, ran her fingers through her hair, tucked any loose strands behind her ears and straightened her posture.

She was panting when she reached him, and tried to suppress her shortness of breath with long, slow inhalations. She removed her sunhat and stood deliberately with her back to the sun so that she could savour his face in the sunlight. He held out his right hand and clasped her forearm, steadying himself with his stick which he held in the other hand. She took a step forward. They both spoke at once, hesitated, smiled, then he gestured with his hand for her to speak. She said the first thing that came into her head, "A good day for working in the vineyard, wouldn't you say?"

"Agreed. A wonderful day for working the land." He gazed upwards and waved his hand across the horizon.

"Are you passing through by any chance?"

"I've been advised to take some time off and walk as much as possible. I must exercise my foot, you see." He pointed down to his left foot.

"What happened to it?"

"Mysteriously, I received a wound to my head so my foot doesn't work." He chuckled and explained further. "The bullet wound affected my nervous system. I lost all feeling in the left side of my body for six months but it's all coming back, slowly but surely. It is really only my left foot now which does not function properly. Anyway you really don't want to hear about all that nonsense, do you?"

"Yes, I do. I want to hear about *all* your nonsense. So you walked all the way here from the Rheingau to exercise your foot? Is that what you're telling me?" Marie-France said, smiling and withholding a laugh. Johann laughed and clutched her forearm again. His palm was warm, his clasp strong. This time she held the knuckle of his left hand which held his walking stick. "So what are we to do Johann? Have you come to see me? I also have a wound to my head, by the way." She clasped some strands of her hair and lifted them away for him to see. He peered down at the side of her head above her ear.

"Seems like we both narrowly avoided death then. And yet

here we are now standing in a vineyard in Burgundy ten years later," Johann said.

"It does seem like we avoided death, doesn't it? Thank God it is all over, but it's been a struggle. I can't tell you how lovely it is to see you. I can't believe it's really you. It's so strange. And after all these years. Did you miss me?"

"Indeed, it has been a long time. I still have your photograph. Do you remember? The one you gave me before we parted. You kept me going through the last years of the war. But to answer your question, yes, I have come to see you, but if this is all you can see of me, a brief encounter in a vineyard, I apologise for my intrusion. I will have to accept the fact that your life has moved on and I am too late. Perhaps you are married, you have children, you are extremely busy or your family chooses not to speak to Germans. I have come across many who feel that way on my travels here."

"Well indeed, I am married and I have children but no one here is especially hostile towards Germans. We can still be friends. Good, close friends even, I'm sure. The only person who couldn't accept Germans was my mother, but she died in 1948. I have so much to tell you, so much."

Johann shuffled, shifting his weight onto his left side and adjusted his sunhat. "I have much to tell you too. Can we not meet in that little bar, the Café du Paix I think it was, in Chalon? At the end of the working day, perhaps? Around six-ish."

"That bar is still there. The piano too. Yes, I'm sure that will be fine. I will tell Jean that I am collecting supplies. It's easy to make an excuse. Jean, my husband, works so hard, I barely see him these days. And we don't see him during the week normally. He works in Lyon but he's around just now. You will like him. He was decorated for his courage as a Resistance fighter."

*

Johann leant forward. “Perhaps it is best that we don’t talk of the war too much in a place like this. It is too public. The walls hold too many memories. I would just like to say though that we Germans are making great efforts to face our past head on, you know. We call it ‘Vergangenheitsbewältigung.’” He whispered the word across the table as if he wished to conceal his German accent. Marie-France was tempted to ask him to repeat the word, as she hadn’t been able to grasp it. “I don’t know how else to translate it. It’s a process, a necessary process of admitting guilt and making amends for past evils, I suppose.”

“But you were never a Nazi. I do distinctly remember you saying that.”

“Absolutely true. I was not a Nazi. Heaven forbid. I have always abhorred it. But it’s a sort of collective guilt trip in which we must all wallow. It’s a national obsession at the moment in Germany. I think it’s important that the world knows of it. That the new generation comes in peace.”

“I see. But for how long do you need to atone? It’s been nine years since peace was signed.”

“We might have to hold our heads down in shame for generations. Although I don’t see the Americans doing that over Japan after they dropped that atomic bomb,” said Johann.

“No. Calling it ‘Little Boy’ has to be the euphemism of the century.” Johann laughed at her comment. “Perhaps they should apologise, I don’t know. But it was also a peacemaker.”

“Yes. I guess the bomb is still holding the peace. Meanwhile, there are reparations, tribunals, war crime trials, bilateral agreements, treaties, all that sort of thing is still going on as a result of the war. We call it ‘Wiedergutmachung,’ literally meaning to make all good again. That’s the point … to try and wipe the slate clean… a quest for the tabula rasa, to start all over again with nothing, but memories are long and cross generations. We’ll probably never get there. And we have another word, 'Schlusstrich,' which means trying to allow bygones to be bygones. Big German words for a big narrative of national guilt, and it's everywhere about us."

"It's the price Germany has to pay. You've certainly found some big, long words for I suppose some big, long problems," she said.

"Yes. You noticed. We love to string words together." Johann laughed again.

Marie-France leant across the table and whispered, "Everyone has a story of guilt to tell during that war. Me too. But I will tell you later. You seem almost weighed down by this 'guilt' thing though. Have you not found your own peace?"

"I don't feel guilty on a personal level but I feel like I have to carry it for all Germans, because I am a German. It's a collective responsibility. It'll take a whole generation to come to terms with our past. At least that long. We call it 'Aufarbeitung,' meaning confronting the past, I guess to absolve ourselves. I feel like doing that. But others feel no guilt for their pasts, or what they did during the war. I cannot understand that, especially if they were Nazis, but they really can't see why they should. Sometimes I almost feel like I don't want to be a German any longer and I should go and live somewhere else."

There was a natural pause in the conversation and Marie-France decided it was time to change the subject. "How is your property? Is the family still making wine?"

"All that is going well. I thought we might make some red wine too. Plant some Pinot Noir. It is partly why I'm here. To enquire about a supplier of Pinot Noir rootstocks who is based in Dijon. Perhaps you could help. How is your family business going?"

"We've had a string of excellent vintages in Burgundy post-war. We've been blessed. The war nearly brought bankruptcy upon us, you know. I suppose it was the same for you. It's been a struggle ever since, but we've paid off our debts now."

"I expect you enjoyed the same fine years as in the Rheingau."

"I don't know. 1945, 1947, 1949, 1952 and last year," said Marie-France.

"Exactly that," said Johann.

"I can't say for certain how 1954 will turn out but 1953 is stunningly good in barrel. We're not drinking it yet.

"It would be good to come and taste, if I'm allowed."

"I'm sure we could arrange that. But before that, I have a surprise for you, but I honestly have no idea what you will think. It could be quite shocking and very emotional for you. But you need to know. It's time you both knew. And I fear there will be consequences, even sacrifices."

31

Ma Coccinelle – Meeting my Nemesis

The day Marie-France insisted on me meeting her "amour perdu" came as a surprise, not only because I believed his very existence to have been long lost in the ether of post-war chaos but because I could not have imagined the swift and profound changes that came about in Marie-France's life. I believe she herself was also bowled over by the suddenness of the effects his reappearance had on her.

It began gradually with her mentioning almost haphazardly that he'd arrived in Burgundy to buy grapevines and rootstocks and that she'd met him in Chalon for a drink the same evening. She talked about him and his plans for growing red grapes on his estate in laudable terms as if he were going to revolutionise red grape growing in Germany, a land principally of white wines. It was clear to me that she was merely thrilled to have him return to her life, irrespective of what he was up to. Matters progressed rapidly from then onwards. She saw Johann more often and she talked of him to her father, adding increasing levels of detail as the weeks went by without revealing the whole truth regarding Gérard.

Then on her chosen day, "revelation day" as I called it, Marie-France spewed out the whole truth at once as if it were an act of absolution. Gérard was duly informed that he had a second father and that his name was Johann and that he was a winemaker living in Germany and that he was about to meet him because he was in fact his real father and he'd arrived in Burgundy. From Marie-France's point of view, it was best that she present the whole truth on a plate for all to see. She'd told me several times how much she loathed all the lying. I'm not entirely sure whether Gérard understood it all though. She left it up to me to inform him that I was not his "biological" father – probably one of the cruellest things I've ever had to do. Gérard was left sitting at the table dumbfounded. I did all I could to comfort him, and told him I wasn't ever going to leave him, but I could tell he felt betrayed. He wouldn't look me in the eye any longer and then began to avoid me completely. The poor boy was growing up quickly but still at an age when he was hardly equipped on an emotional level to absorb such revelations and the inevitable changes which would ensue. Things he'd known about for all his years were now suddenly not so, from that day on.

I dreaded Johann's forthcoming meeting with Gérard and the effects that might have on Gérard and the Champuix family. I wondered what Marie-France's mother would have made of it. Once Marie-France had told the family, to their credit, she was not thrown out of the house. Instead, she was accused of having lied to everyone and therefore persona non-grata at the dining-room table for a few days and nights, until her father grudgingly admitted her back. I believe I was even chastised by Henri for keeping the secret to myself for so long although family disapproval was so subtle it was almost imperceptible. They must have balanced their disapproval with the fact that I'd done an admirable job as a surrogate father for so long.

Henri had perhaps thought ahead more than any of us when he admitted one evening that "There will be significant and damaging consequences, mark my word." We had conveniently forgotten the trial and the fact that we had both committed perjury. How long might it take for the authorities to put two and two together? Perhaps not at all. Unless Johann were to claim Gérard as his own and change both his name and his nationality. Such complications began to weigh heavily upon me. Opening up the case again would bring disgrace and shame upon us both and tarnish our reputations concerning our Resistance pasts, Marie-France more so than myself. Both Marie-France and I would surely be found guilty of perjury in a re-trial. I put the matter to Marie-France but such was her mood, that she dismissed the impending situation outright.

All of this put a strain on my relations with Marie-France. Over those couple of weeks, I was being taken for granted and felt like I counted for nothing. There wasn't even so much as an apology or time for a sympathetic discussion about it all. Marie-France seemed to have lost her sensitivities. Part of it was no doubt an expression of relief, that she could finally rid her conscience of the deception she'd kept so close to her chest for so long. And secondly that Gérard had finally met his father, which was undoubtedly going to lead to a moderation of the feelings of guilt which had weighed her down for all those years. But I wasn't sure whether she had adequately thought through all the repercussions which were likely to arise both for the boy and ourselves. I assumed she'd got carried away with it all, the relief and her sense of liberation being evident to all in small acts of frivolity and light headedness. She often returned home late, plied friends with too much wine and wound up the gramophone in the middle of the night. Despite the initial family opprobrium, it seemed that her life had lit up and all the enthusiasm and energy of youth had returned to her. She couldn't keep still for a moment and hurried about with a permanent smile on her face. It was a joy to observe, but harder still for me as I sensed I might be losing her to someone else.

The love of wine, the vineyards and everything with which Marie-France occupied her day, were second nature to Johann, and admittedly of increasingly less interest to me as my political ambitions grew. I freely agree that I'm not one for working the land. My inspiration is not derived from the countryside and all that entails. Even so I found Johann to be an affable, well-mannered fellow, impressively educated and even talented on the piano. And I believed him to be a man of goodwill. I can understand why Marie-France had fallen in love with him back in 1941, but surprised that it had endured through the war years into times of peace, after all she'd been through. But who am I to judge another one's love, even my wife's?

Johann was staying in the best hotel in Beaune, and he drove a beautiful new motor car, so I surmised that he had wealth. His attempts to sign a contract with a Pinot Noir grape supplier in Dijon had been successful and to his credit he extended his stay and spent the rest of his days in France with Gérard. When not with his son, he busied himself with getting to know the vineyards of Burgundy. He bought a second-hand motor cycle to visit the famous names of Burgundy, preferring to leave his open-top Mercedes in the hotel car park, after being pelted with tomatoes in one village he passed through. Germans weren't always welcome in France, even a decade after the war.

I considered the nature of forgiveness in all the many guises in which it might apply to us – first the forgiveness which Marie-France had sought for her own misdeeds, secondly in the way her family might view her behaviour, and then the general one with which we were faced as a nation, if cooperation with Germany and the building of a more stable Europe were to evolve. How far and in what ways were we ready to pardon the Germans? Forgiveness is a hard one to concede, and highly subjective to feel. No one has the right to admonish someone for lacking the ability or the will to forgive. It must emerge naturally from within, from a deep conviction, and not from arbitrary, external inducement. For instance, how could a mother forgive the murderers of her innocent son by a German firing squad? I know several mothers who cannot be reconciled and I never took it upon myself to intervene in their grief although in each case their boy had been one of my comrades, and I his commander. What can one do but express a few fond words of condolence for your colleague in arms and commiserate their loss with his parents? Such grief is not always easily assuaged. Yet others appeared to have suffered considerably less from the war and its aftermath. They were the lucky ones. France herself was coming to terms with the fallout after the German Occupation of their country and the Vichy years of government. Like Germany to some extent, people were examining and questioning their past and their role in it. This was all happening against a backdrop of renewal and reconstruction. The mid and late 1950s were a time of rapid mass industrialisation in France and workers needed their unions and the Communist Party more than at any other time. I was busier than ever. Amongst all the mayhem which had erupted in my personal life, I had a career and a job to think of, in which to be honest I felt much appreciated.

So what was I to do about Johann and his presence in our lives? Marie-France and I still shared a bed at weekends and occasionally during the week and yet her mind and heart were elsewhere. And was I to terminate my role as a father to Gérard forthwith now that he'd magically found a new one? Such matters needed discussing and yet Marie-France and I spent so little time together, perhaps things would have to find their natural way on their own without our joint input. But for how much longer could I put up with this? Johann had been amongst us for three weeks now and seemed in no hurry to return to Germany. This new turn in their fortunes had left Johann as enthralled as Marie-France with their new situation. There were no signs of him leaving us alone. On my own personal level, could I forgive either of them?

As for Gérard, he refused to discuss the matter with me which made me suspicious that his mother might be behind his silence. And my dear Marguerite. Had anyone taken her into account during this whirlwind of events? What effect was such an upheaval to have on her? And yet I was in no position to attend to her daily requirements as often or as dutifully as her mother. I was out of the picture to a large extent. Being rejected and abandoned at such short notice hit me hard. I buried myself in my work and hoped for a better outcome.

*

With Marguerite's help, Marie-France busied herself with preparing a picnic that morning. Gérard was intent on assembling his fishing rod and tackle, declaring that he preferred fishing to swimming. Johann was to meet them at eleven at the house and drive them to the river for a day's outing on the water. On the way Marie-France pointed out the old guardsmen's posts of the Demarcation Line and Johann suggested it was time they were taken down. He declared that such vestiges of the war depressed him.

"These are times of renewal and joy, of progress and new ideas. We should not be looking back. All is in today and tomorrow," he said.

"Wish me luck for today to catch a fish," Gérard shouted excitedly from the back seat.

"I'm going to swim with Maman," said Marguerite.

"And what are you going to do Papa?" said Gérard.

Johann lifted his foot from the accelerator and glanced at Gérard through the back mirror. Their eyes met and Johann smiled. He felt a tear run down his cheek. Hearing himself being referred to as "Papa" came as such a shock that he forgot that he was in control of a vehicle.

"Do you think it's wise to stop here, my love?" Marie-France said, clutching Johann's arm as the motor car almost reached a halt.

"Ah yes, sorry, I didn't mean to stop. Let's hurry on. There's a river to fish, water to swim in and a picnic to eat, and lots of fun to be had by everyone, n'est-ce pas?" Johann applied his foot to the accelerator and the Mercedes roared off, the sudden increase in speed blowing their hair about, requiring them to clutch the edges of their seats as if they were strapped into a rollercoaster at the fairground.

"Yes, yes," shouted Gérard. "Let's go faster and faster, Papa. I love windy cars with no roof." He leant his head out to catch the full strength of the blast.

Marie-France turned around briefly to check the children were still there and shouted, "You two sit firmly in your seats and hold on in the back there."

They found a familiar spot on the river bank amongst the reeds and bulrushes by an inlet where the water was shallow and where a couple of rowing boats were moored to an old wooden jetty under the shade of a clump of alder trees. Marie-France laid out a couple of rugs and cushions in the sun and left the picnic hamper in the shade until they were ready to eat. "We have shade and we have sun. Take your choice, children. No one is to swim without first letting me know, and no one is to go anywhere near the main current of the river. Stay close to the bank. We'll eat in ten minutes," said Marie-France.

The Saône is a wide, slow-moving river at this point around Chalon, flowing from north to south, eventually converging with the River Rhône in Lyon. This spot had served many generations of the Champuix family during the summer months as a place to entertain guests and clients, to cool off and relax, and enjoy the riparian pleasures.

Marie-France kept an eye on the children as they paddled in the little bay but her attention was on Johann. He opened the bottle of wine which had been sitting in an icebox and poured out two glasses. He handed one to Marie-France, and stretched out on the rug beside her. "Times like these seem almost unreal. I suppose it's because we were at war most of the time we were seeing each other before. Life was so different. It was no way to live, was it? I wonder if peace is a luxury, something we need to savour when it's here amongst us."

Marie-France laughed at the thought of it. "Peace is normal, Johann. We should take it for granted. You talk as if peace is fragile and ephemeral. Here today, gone tomorrow."

"Peace in Europe must surely be a certainty, but the world will change rapidly. It already is. Look at Japan, a rising economic powerhouse in the East, and America is now the most dominant economic power in the world. That will bring changes."

"For the better I hope."

"They may not have a history like Europe but at least the Americans believe in democracy, freedom and the rule of law," said Johann. He took a sip of wine and continued. "We now have half of Germany under the yoke of a socialist government under Soviet control, and they have none of the freedoms we have. Poor bastards. How lucky we are."

"I'm going to change the subject."

"Okay," said Johann.

"So you have plans to plant a few hectares of Pinot Noir. Are you sure you have enough sun to ripen them fully?"

"I'm not entirely sure. We may end up with just a rosé but we are forever experimenting. The more Pinot Noirs I taste here, the more obsessed I am with growing this grape … such subtle, complex wines, they bring tears to my eyes."

"They're a winemaker's nightmare. We bought a few hectares in Santenay a few years ago and Marc's still finding it challenging."

"I don't know your family apart from a few brief encounters."

"Marc is my younger brother and helps Pa with the winemaking. I expect Papa will invite you for dinner one evening but I think Jean should be there too, so it will need to be this coming weekend. It's the only one possible. I'm not sure if Eloise will come with her husband. She's my younger sister. Probably not.

They have two young ones. Marc might be there. It's difficult. I think they're still upset that I wasn't honest with them for so many years, but what could I do?"

"What would you have done if I hadn't shown up?"

"I had it in mind to do exactly what you have done. To track you down. I think I would have brought Gérard with me …and prepped him well in advance, of course."

"Are you sure?"

"Yes. I'm perfectly sure. I never just wrote you off, Johann. Surely you know that, no?

"I know. I can tell from how much time we have spent together."

"Do you love me, Johann?"

"I do, but what good will it bring either of us? There are plenty of lovely women in Germany. But strangely, I am in France, in Burgundy, and sitting by the Saône with you."

"Yes." Marie-France leant up against him on the rug and lifted a leg over his. She made herself comfortable and wiped the hair from Johann's brow so that she could see the whole of his face. "What future do we have?" she said, without thinking. She hesitated, then said, "I love you too."

"Who knows what will become of us? I suppose Gérard is the little person who brought us back together again. Don't you think so?"

"That is probably so, yes. I have something to tell you which you need to know. Are you ready?"

"I'm ready."

"Once I knew I was pregnant, and knowing it was obviously your child, I had to find a father, so I sought out Jean to ask him to take on the role. It all seems so improbable now, looking back on it."

"Yes. Quite a favour and an obligation to thrust upon of your ex-boyfriend." Johann chuckled.

"He agreed eventually. He turned out to be an excellent father and Gérard feels very close to him…"

"And now Jean feels like he's been used, and he's going to lose his boy, and he's quite understandably very upset I suppose," Johann said.

"Yes. Exactly that. That is undoubtedly the case but, there's worse than that. I was denounced for collaborating because of my friendship with you and I eventually had to face a trial during the purges in 1944. I will explain all the details another time. Anyway, at the trial, Jean was brought in as a witness and he swore on oath that he was Gérard's father. And during the trial I denied having had any sexual relations with you whatsoever. So I lied too."

"And now everyone knows you both lied in court. Is that right?"

"No, wrong. They don't because they don't know the details of what was said in court. Only the court records will hold that evidence. I hope they have long since been burned. But the worry is that some busybody will drag up the records and ask for a re-trial and we will both be tried for perjury and I might well be threatened with the death sentence again."

"Are they still really going to such lengths? All the post-war trials you hear about these days are for Nazis and the simply awful crimes of mass extermination which they committed. I wouldn't worry. You're small fry compared to that evil."

"I do worry because the French have long memories. At least the two people who denounced me are dead."

"So you found out who they were?"

"Yes. That's a story for another time."

32

Marc and Eloise remembered the calm, polite, but authoritative German officer who insisted on searching the premises with his troops on that freezing morning at Champuix back in the late autumn of 1941. They were searching for Resistance fighters, Marc reminded them, "And one of them was Jean. What a strange coincidence that my sister should now be proposing that the same man should be invited here for dinner at some point in the next few weeks."

Eloise had been the first to bring up the matter of Johann's return over supper with her brother and father, after Marie-France had announced Johann's reappearance in Burgundy a few weeks ago. "Just as well Maman has left us. I don't suppose she would ever have allowed his presence anywhere near the family. And Marie-France would have been ordered to leave home once again. Yet again Marie-France has surprised and confounded us all." Eloise chuckled at the thought of it.

"And deceived us," Marc said.

"There is a certain fate in this coincidence which puzzles and intrigues me," said Henri. "If I were being generous and sanguine about it, it would be as if the wheel of fortune has turned full circle. As if this man were meant to be here. I still chuckle to myself that his son has been living here amongst us for several years and none of us knew. Almost like the lieutenant despatched a scout or herald ahead of time to check out the zeitgeist. All most strange to me.

There is indeed something propitious about it all though. And I'm prepared to embrace it."

"So you feel no anger with Marie-France?" Eloise said. "And you hardly fell off your chair when she told you who Gérard's father was. Like you half knew. And that Jean had been lying to us too."

"Hervé, your grandfather had suspicions long ago, I should add, which is why I wasn't so surprised to hear the news. I respected the fact that Jean was protecting Marie-France because he loved her. He had also taken on the boy as if he were his own, knowing full well that his father was an officer of the Wehrmacht, an army which he was fighting and which had murdered hundreds of his colleagues. That's a brave, magnanimous choice to make. He loved Marie-France. Frankly, who would have done that unless they loved my daughter? There are always two ways of looking at things. You must balance all the elements before judging people."

"You are a very reasonable and understanding man, Pa," said Eloise. "I am grateful for that, you know. You're a good man."

"And believe me, Eloise, I have had all my anger out with your sister when she first broached the subject. Yes. I felt insulted and betrayed and I told her so, just like you did. Then she did her usual by bursting into tears, and then I did what I always do with you two girls …"

"Yes, Pa. You capitulated," said Marc.

Henri recalled Johann's comments in the winery. "I do remember him saying he would like to return here to get to know the wines of Burgundy. I thought that strange at the time. But it was also genuine, I believe. I didn't feel he was one of Hitler's boys, simply a pleasant young man carrying out orders in which he had no interest at all."

"Do you think there is some sinister plot going on between those two, to place an heir on the Champuix throne and to buy us out one day or something? Is Gérard the intended new generation, do you think?" Marc said.

"Logically he would be, as Gérard is the son of my first born," Henri said. "But a sinister plot? No. Don't be so absurd. Things just happen how they happen."

"Sometimes I think you forget that it was Jean and his comrades that the German officer was searching for that morning. That was Jean's big coup. Blowing that bridge and destroying that troop train. It won him loads of kudos with the guys in Lyon. He was promoted rapidly after that. We shouldn't forget where Jean came from, what he went through and what he did for France."

"Yes, I did know that and I do appreciate Jean and what he did for France's liberation," said Henri. "Oh, and his name is Johann not 'the German officer.' You need to be careful. And also, I do not need educating concerning Jean's pedigree, his track record and his rightful place among us here."

"I'm sorry, Pa, but you seem very resigned to this whole thing. You know, having him visit and so forth, walking the vineyards with him, tasting wine with him and Marie-France, just like he was some kind of prospective client or even a new member of the family," Marc said.

"You are referring to Johann, I assume. Marie-France knows exactly what she is doing. She's a Champuix through and through … never afraid to push the boundaries, takes all the alternatives into account, she weighs things up, never takes 'No' for an answer, and then she gets stuck into it. I have confidence in her. Perhaps Johann will simply come and go. Or he will stay and cherish his son. And we will accommodate him somehow."

"And what of Jean? There cannot be a threesome," Eloise said, raising her voice.

"Jean will sort himself out. He has never cared for the domaine and he has almost no interest in what we do here. He's a man for the city, an intellectual, and now an agitator with his politics and workers' rights stuff and the Communist Party. I know he means well and he will be successful in that world, but he does not have wine in the blood like us."

"That doesn't mean he doesn't love, and can't love Marie-France," Marc said.

"The problem is … he's not here much. We don't see him. He's absent," said Henri. "And that cannot be good for anyone's marriage. You might consider whether Jean loves his work or his politics more than he loves his wife and family."

Eloise joined in. "How can you say that? They have a daughter together. Marguerite cannot be forgotten. What of her? And how do we know Johann isn't going to break up the family? It's all gone so well and happily for several years since the end of the war. I'm honestly not so sure I can condone this Johann man's return."

*

Marie-France could hear the rumble of Johann's motor car as it entered the courtyard. She was running late and hadn't yet bathed or changed, but dinner was ready and simply required being kept warm until they sat down. She welcomed Johann into the family sitting-room, then made her excuses and went across the courtyard to her house to change, leaving him with Henri and Jean.

When she returned, Marc had joined them. The subject under discussion happened to be future Franco-German relations. To her relief the conversation was lively and jovial. She needn't have worried about any animosities. Johann expressed his beliefs freely and diplomatically. "We are two great nations, neighbours with so many common attributes and interests. First, we need cooperation in foreign policy, and then economic and military integration."

"And we need strong international labour unions," Jean said, smiling. "Let's not forget the workers," he added.

"You and your unions," Marc said. "Do you think we should invite union membership on the estate? I suppose you do."

"I won't be having any unions at Domaine de Champuix," said Henri, grunting.

"Let's go in for dinner," Marie-France said.

"Not me, I'm afraid. I've got things to do," said Marc, excusing himself.

"You're not staying?" Marie-France said, surprised.

"No, sorry. Important things to do."

Dinner passed off successfully. Marie-France was delighted to see how much interest her father and Jean took in Johann. The war was only mentioned briefly, and Johann was able to inform them convincingly that he had had no truck with national socialism.

"Where did you get your war wound?" Henri asked.

"After Burgundy, I was moved to southern Italy. An American sniper shot me early one morning. Well, I believe it was an American. I was washing myself in a river. A sitting target, as they say. Luckily either his rifle jammed or he was shot by a colleague of mine. I'm not sure. But he couldn't aim the second vital shot to finish me off. I was lucky to receive medical assistance swiftly. But that was it for me. My war ended towards the end of 1943 near Salerno with a bullet skimming the top of my head that wrecked my nervous system. Then I spent six months lying in a hospital in Wiesbaden, not far from my home. I was lucky I suppose. But I'm not sure I can climb a ladder to clean out a vat any longer. Or work a vineyard for long. I get painful cramps."

"I suppose we have all been forced to pick up the pieces after the war and live with what we had left," Henri said. "I'm sure your leg will improve and you'll be back to normal soon."

"Well, it's been ten years and my leg has improved over the years, but it's slow progress. I think we were lucky to have something to do, an employment I mean, when so many didn't. I believe there will always be a market for wine. People will always want wine, as long as it is well made, and the styles move with the times. The Germans want red wine now, so I will grow red grapes and see how I can do. We are in a good, but tough business. We have a future. I'm confident of that."

"Let us drink to that," Marie-France said. "And many great vintages to come."

33

Gérard shook his mother's shoulder until she woke. "Quick. Quick. There's a police officer at the door, Maman. He's asking for you."

Marie-France rolled over. "It's very early. Is it important? Did he say what it was about?"

"No, he said he wanted to speak to you most urgently."

Marie-France put on her dressing gown and went downstairs to the front door.

The solemn expression on the police officer's face left Marie-France cold. The officer stood alone at the front door, peering in. "My name is Inspector Merveil. Madame de Villeneuve, would you please join me in the courtyard. I have an important matter to discuss with you, alone." Marie-France accompanied the officer into the middle of the courtyard, out of earshot of the house.

"Do mind that puddle there. It looks like oil," Marie-France said. She leant down and put a finger in it and smelled it. "Odd. Not sure what that is or how it got there."

"Are you familiar with a certain Johann Schräder?" the Inspector asked.

"Yes. He's a friend of mine and the father of my son, Gérard." She pointed to the front door where Gérard was still standing in his dressing gown by the open door.

"We found your name and address in his car."

"That would make sense. He was visiting us last night and might have needed to ask for directions. He doesn't know us well."

"I see. I have to inform you that Johann Schräder was killed last night in a road accident. There were no other vehicles involved. He appears to have been unable to slow down, missed a corner and came off the road. He hit the side of a house. We believe that he would have died within seconds from the wounds he incurred. I am so sorry to inform you." Marie-France stared at the officer without saying a word. He continued. "You say he was at dinner. Did he drink much? Do you think he may have been drunk?"

"No, that's not Johann. He didn't drink like that. You say that he is dead?"

"Yes, ma'am. I'm sorry to inform you. Johann Schräder has passed away."

"Where is he?"

"He is in the mortuary at Beaune hospital. Do you know any next of kin? They will be in Germany, I suppose. I have ascertained where he was staying and his home address and telephone number were given to us by the hotel. We will require you to formally identify his body today. I hope that will be convenient."

"And what of his son, Gérard?"

"What do you mean, ma'am?" The officer hesitated for a moment. "I wonder if you have anyone to comfort you. You don't look at all well, ma'am." Marie-France let out a cry so loud that the doves sunning themselves on the courtyard cobblestones launched into flight en masse. A moment later, she collapsed to the ground like an abandoned marionette, the police officer catching her head before it hit the cobbles. Within seconds Gérard and Jean had joined her.

"What is it?" Jean asked the Inspector.

"Her German friend is deceased. A car accident, I'm afraid. Late last night."

"Gérard, your father. I'm afraid your father. No. I will tell you later," said Jean.

Gérard appeared not to understand what Jean had meant at first. "What is wrong with Maman?"

"She's not well, she has had some bad news." Jean comforted the boy but he chose to sit on the ground next to his mother. She held out her arms for him and drew him to her side, grasping him.

Henri, hearing the commotion, appeared in the courtyard and approached the officer. "What is going on here, officer?"

"I have been obliged to inform the lady …"

"Yes, my daughter," Henri interjected.

"I am sorry to bring you bad news. I've been obliged to inform your daughter that her friend, Johann Schräder, died in a car accident last night on the road to Beaune. No one was able to save him and no other vehicle was involved, so we have ruled out anyone else to blame. An unfortunate accident, I'm afraid."

Marie-France spoke quietly and clearly. "Pa, that's where Johann's car was parked last night. I saw him off from there. That spot. Over there." She pointed to a dark puddle on the cobblestones. "What is that oil in the cobblestones there? Is it engine oil or something else? Could his car have failed him?"

Henri walked over to the puddle, stuck a finger in it and smelled it. "Brake fluid. That's brake fluid. Officer, do you hear me? That's brake fluid." Henri again pointed to the mess in the courtyard. Did his brakes fail, officer? Have you checked the brake lines?" The Inspector leant down to sample the fluid.

"Indeed, there is no sign of him braking. We have no skid marks on the road. Simply a smashed-up Mercedes motor car. I'm afraid I'm not sure I can put it any more delicately than that. We assumed he may have fallen asleep or he was drunk and failed to take account of the corner. It is a sharp one there."

Henri addressed the officer. "Well then, make a note of this mess down here, won't you. Could someone have sabotaged his vehicle? It was a common trick during the war, you know. This may not be some 'unfortunate accident' as you suggest."

"I will have the vehicle inspected thoroughly when I return. It is in the compound by the police station. Meanwhile I would ask that you accompany your daughter to the mortuary to identify the corpse."

"Very well," said Henri. "In due course. My daughter and my grandson will need to compose themselves first. Later this afternoon, I expect."

*

When Marie-France, accompanied by Henri, had verified Johann's body, she was handed a message requesting that she meet the Inspector at the police station afterwards.

"Our suspicions are aroused," said the Inspector. "It seems that the brake lines leading from the hydraulic pump and master cylinder under the bonnet to the wheels were snipped with some heavy-duty bolt cutters, most likely."

"Are you certain?" said Henri.

"The model is a 220 Sedan and we have asked our German counterparts to confirm the layout of the brake lines supplying the braking components on the wheels. They confirmed the locations on the vehicle with our mechanic this afternoon, from the pump along the chassis and to the axle and wheels. Our mechanic believes they were not destroyed in the accident but had been systematically cut beforehand. A loss of hydraulic fluid would result in immediate brake failure."

"So that is most likely the cause of the accident?" asked Henri.

"I'm afraid so, yes. So we have opened a murder enquiry," the Inspector said.

"So Johann was murdered?" Marie-France said.

"That is the most likely scenario. We would of course like to question you about Mr. Schräder, your relationship with him and so forth. I'm afraid we will have to consider everyone as a suspect and in due course, ask you all in for questioning. It is very possible that the person who perpetrated the crime was simply paid to do the job. Who actually ordered for the German to be murdered, is a different matter."

"I suppose it could be revenge," Henri suggested.

"We will have to study his war record, if that is what you mean. Did Johann Schräder have any enemies in this part of France?" the Inspector asked.

"All we know is that he served for several months here. He was an officer, a lieutenant, but not a career soldier, nor a Nazi. But I do not know his regiment. He hated the war. He was not a natural soldier. I'm sure he would have tried to avoid offending everyone," Marie-France said.

*

On the journey home, Marie-France's mind began to race. Who was going to kill a harmless man like Johann? Such a thing was preposterous. It would have to be something to do with his past. Possibly even way back, before the war. Perhaps something about him or his family of which she had no inkling. She reminded herself of what little she knew of him in reality.

She turned to her father who was driving them home. "It's like they got to me in the end, like I deserved it. If their form of justice couldn't reach me, they'd kill Johann instead. It was the Resistance. It must have been the Resistance." She paused for a moment to draw breath. "They took out their revenge on Johann instead. The cowards. The damn cowards."

"Do you think Jean was behind it?" said Henri, sighing.

"Or even Marc, who excused himself that evening, saying he

had things to do. Do you remember?"

"Your brother, Marc? I can't see my son doing something like that. But leave that one to me. I expect he'll have an alibi. As the officer said, we are all suspects. It becomes more complicated when the motives are blurred. Who was behind it? They are the guilty ones, not the man with the bolt-cutters."

"It may have nothing to do with us. We don't know, I don't know what else Johann did here when he was posted in this area. Perhaps he organised or personally oversaw retributive firing squads or round-ups of villagers and whatever. It could have been a villager taking revenge. There have been so many petty vendettas since the war. When will this end?"

"We need a time for reflection, my dear, some peace and quiet for a bit. I'm behind you. I will do all I can to bring justice for Johann," Henri said.

"Do you like him?" Marie-France asked tearfully.

"I did. You meet people throughout the course of your life, whether perfectly at random or by formal introduction, it doesn't matter. Very few whom you meet do you take to immediately. Johann was one of the few."

"Thank you, Pa." Marie-France wiped her tears and leant up against her father, clutching him under his arm with both hands. "And we must be extra loving for Gérard. So confusing for him. He only knew his father for four weeks. It's wicked. So cruel. It's unbelievable."

"I think you will need to ask Jean, first. I suspect he will know something of it," Henri said.

"I can't believe he would have done that."

"Do you want me to ask him?"

"No. I will ask him."

34

Ma Coccinelle – Under Months of Suspicion

I spent much of July and August 1954 under suspicion and not just from Marie-France. As far as she was concerned everybody had wanted Johann out of the way except Henri, who remained above suspicion. Once Marc's alibi had been confirmed and Eloise had sworn her absolute innocence, the suspicions were once again directed at myself for arranging Johann's "assassination," as Marie-France had chosen to call it.

Inspector Merveil had decided that I and my accomplices from the old Resistance days were surely culpable, even if I had not directly given the order. There were good reasons why I should have wanted Johann gone from Burgundy, but dead, no. I hardly knew him, but he had a wonderful son who would once again be fatherless and, besides, Marie-France would never forgive me for such an act. I might declare that I am not the "murdering kind" as I swore to Marie-France so often, but then she would remind me that I had killed, if not murdered many German soldiers less than ten years ago.

The wrangling continued for weeks and weeks. But Inspector Merveil could not pin any evidence on anyone. Johann's death had been announced in the local newspapers the day after the accident accompanied by a picture of the wrecked Mercedes and a mug shot of Johann. At the end of the piece, the Inspector had added some words of his own, requesting that anyone who had any knowledge of the crime should come forward and provide evidence in confidence. Not a soul had declared themselves after six weeks, after which Inspector Merveil decided to temporarily close the case.

There were periodic news items of many other killings thought to be related to the war and not necessarily involving Germans visiting France. The British were also vulnerable. The "Affaire Domenici," for example, in August 1952, comes to mind. Gaston Domenici was the suspected culprit who had supposedly murdered the eminent British scientist by the road side, Sir Jack Drummond, with his wife and daughter. He was sentenced to death but released from prison in 1960 on humanitarian grounds. No one believed he was the killer and the Maquisards amongst others had again been implicated in the crime, but no credible evidence came to the fore. The Maquis were frequently given a hard time as if the whiff of brigandry had never left us.

I was disappointed in Henri who gave me the cold shoulder whenever I should bump into him, and I was no longer welcome in the main house for family dinners. Marie-France insisted she still loved me but we slept in separate bedrooms in our converted barn next door. I believed she had not thrown me out completely from Champuix because Gérard badly needed a father and I was expected to return to my duties once again as a surrogate. It didn't work though. Gérard had been brainwashed, he became distant, and I remained the man who might have killed his father, whom, let's be frank, he had hardly had the time to get to know anyway. Nevertheless, living under such conditions was bound to take its toll before long.

After the murder, I spent more than a few days wondering whether people might have thought I'd bumped the man off so that there was less risk of the "perjury issue" emerging in a re-trial. We were both implicated, indeed we'd both lied under oath in December 1944, and I had a reputation to uphold and Marie-France had even more to fear. The logic of their thinking and my presumed motive was that if Johann was out the way, suspicions regarding who was the real father of the child would be less relevant and unlikely to emerge as a talking point. A re-trial for perjury would indeed be much less likely. I put it to Marie-France. She seemed to agree and she had indeed discussed it with her father, which resulted in me having to defend my innocence once again. Difficult days indeed, but I felt optimistic that the "perjury issue," as we began to call it, would quictly disappear, although it still haunted me from time to time. However, the decade of the 1950s came to be defined increasingly in the national conscience as the years of amnesty when as much about Vichy and the Occupation was hidden away and forgotten as was remembered.

Before I decided to quit Domaine de Champuix and take up permanent residence in my flat in Lyon, Marie-France announced that she was travelling to Wiesbaden with Gérard and Henri to meet the Schräder family. It had been the latter's idea and the invitation was heartily welcomed. The small party left in the family motor car in late August, merely weeks before the harvest was due in Burgundy. It was my cue to leave the estate too, so that when they returned, few vestiges of my presence would remain. We did not discuss divorce or anything so dramatic as that at this stage, and we were both very mindful of Marguerite who was sent to stay nearby with her cousins, Eloise's girls, while her mother was away.

*

Henri Champuix remained undecided as to exactly why he had accepted the invitation to the Schräder home but agreed with Marie-France that it was for a number of reasons, one among them being to act as chauffeur and chaperone to his loved ones. At the top of Henri's list, consideration had to be given to Gérard and what might best suit him. A visit to his father's family home seemed like a sensible move – there had been discussions at the time about attending the funeral but it was considered too complicated. Secondly, Henri decided that a visit to Johann's home was going to be helpful for his daughter's grieving process. Thirdly, he felt an urge to pay his respects to the family of the deceased. And lastly, he desired to satisfy his own curiosity as to Johann's origins and the wines his estate produced in the Rheingau. He appointed himself as the main driver, having taken the motor car down the road for a service at the local garage the day before, for a precautionary inspection. He himself inspected the correct functioning of the brakes before they left. Days earlier, he had bought a Michelin road map and planned a 500 km route due north-west with Marie-France. There had been difficulties obtaining the boy's passport, and with it arriving a day late, their arrival in Wiesbaden was delayed by the same.

None of the party had been to Germany before, with Henri suggesting that although he did not care greatly for German wines, it was worth noting and appreciating their grape-growing culture which had developed entirely independently from that of their neighbour, France. Then he admitted that that might not have been quite true, as the Germans had planted some of their own varieties in Alsace-Lorraine during their occupation of that disputed region in the last century, so there had surely been an exchange of knowledge. Marie-France then reminded him that there had been grapes growing in Alsace since Roman times, and in Germany too. While Henri was unable to admit that there might be lessons to be learned, he commented that it was worth making observations. Marie-France had other ideas and their conversation turned into a heated discussion which occupied them for much of the journey.

"I am not clear, Pa. Is the Riesling a French or a German grape? One thing which I do know … in France, Riesling is only grown in Alsace. Perhaps the Germans put it there or we planted it there and they stole it?"

"I expect they stole it from us," Henri said.

"Can we ask the Schräders, do you think?"

"If we do, I think we should begin by assuming that we are grateful that their Riesling grows in Alsace, although that could enflame relations as Alsace-Lorraine has been subject to many treaties and a frequent thorn in Franco-German relations."

"Perhaps we should drop the topic."

"No. I wish to know," said Henri. The discussion continued until they reached the German border.

They crossed south of Saarbrücken and then traversed the river Rhine south of Mainz before turning westwards and entering the Rheingau wine country, motoring along the north bank of the river through the wine villages of Eltville, Hattenheim, Oestrich, and lastly Rüdesheim where they stopped in the main square to read the map.

"I do believe we are very close," announced Marie-France.

"How exciting. It is so beautiful here," said Gérard. "Such big castles and churches and things."

"Indeed, it is," said Henri. "Observe how most of the vineyards are planted on the north bank, sloping downwards and facing south across the river. Why might that be, Gérard?"

"For light and heat, for sugar, flavour and alcohol."

"Well done, boy. Spot on. Let's proceed, Marie-France. Do you have directions worked out for me?"

"I think it is right here, through these gates." She pointed across the square.

"Those gates. Are you sure? This looks very grand. Makes our motor car look rather shabby. Hope the butler doesn't send us around to the tradesmen's entrance."

Marie-France laughed loudly. "Why shouldn't it be grander than ours, Pa?"

Henri entered through the gates and slowed the motor car, raising a cloud of white dust from the gravel which took a while to settle. He stopped opposite the front entrance, a semi-circle of white stone steps which led up to large, ornate wrought iron double doors, one of which had been left open. "Good to hear you truly laugh again, my dear," Henri said as he got out of the car. "Well. We'd better see if there's someone here to greet us."

After the formalities which involved Gérard meeting in turn his grandmother, grandfather, two aunts and his uncle who resembled his father so completely that he addressed him as "Papa" at one point, they decided to set off to the winery for a tour which had been Henri's special request. The cellar and grape receival halls were built into the hillside directly behind the house, a four-storey, half-timbered, baroque-style, turreted building in the centre of town. At the front of the house, there was a secluded lawn and garden with a half hectare of woods and parkland. Benches and tables were situated in the shade under the larger trees, and to one side of the house there was a conservatory with wide, white painted doors which had been left open to reveal a long table which had been laid for dinner.

Ursula, Gérard's younger aunt, took to him immediately, exclaiming how much like Johann he was, and remarking too, how tall he was for his age. "And I will take you to your father's room after tea, if you wish. Perhaps you would like to come too, Marie-France. Then we can leave our parents to chat alone."

"I'm not sure my father speaks much German. So I'm relieved that you all speak such good French."

They sipped tea and ate cake in the garden, in the shade of the low boughs of a mature weeping ash, after which Ursula walked Marie-France and Gérard up to the house. Gérard went on ahead while Marie-France confided in Ursula, "You will understand how hard this is for me, won't you, Ursula? And as for dear Gérard, it must be very confusing and heart-breaking for him too. I note he's already called your brother by his father's name. Poor fellow, he must be confused."

"We know. We all know. It is hard for us too, but it was necessary. This meeting was my mother's idea. We only learnt that Johann had a son when he was listed on the paperwork when the body was returned to Wiesbaden train station, and the lawyers had got to work on clarifying the matter. I think Gérard will have been considered as an heir of sorts, as the family solicitor was involved too. I know that Gérard was discussed a lot and my mother said we absolutely must meet him if he is going to be a part of the family. So that's how your visit came about."

Gérard went on ahead, opening doors and exploring each of the rooms in the house while Marie-France and Ursula followed on, chatting. "Gérard has a half-sister at home, Marguerite, but I'm so glad he has met his German family. Now he has siblings and a family on both sides."

"Gérard has German cousins too. Agnes, my elder sister, has

two sons. We may meet them tomorrow depending on how you feel. We didn't want to overwhelm you straightaway."

"Are Freddy and Johann twins? They seem so similar," Marie-France asked.

"They could be, but no. There was always a lot of rivalry between those two. Always friendly though."

"Who is the eldest?"

"Johann, by sixteen months."

"It's lovely here and you have all been so kind and welcoming. I expect Gérard will want to visit again. Perhaps he could be persuaded to work two harvests when he's old enough." They laughed at the thought of it.

"Gérard, where are you?" shouted Marie-France down the corridor. "Gérard, Gérard."

"He has probably found his father's room. It's at the end here." When they reached the room, they found Gérard sitting on Johann's bed staring at a photograph of his father standing with a young man wearing a black uniform, saluting to a bust of the Führer situated on a piano in a drawing room.

"Is that Papa?" Gérard said.

"Yes, next to his wayward, estranged schoolfriend, Günther," said Ursula. "I think they are playing the fool, but Günther was already beginning to take his Nazism seriously."

Marie-France recognised the uniform from her Maquis days. "That's an SS uniform, which that young man is wearing, isn't it?"

"Yes, I'm afraid Günther became a fanatical Nazi and joined the SS. We don't know if he survived the war. Johann completely disassociated himself from him. They ended up hating each other, I think. They were poles apart by the time Johann was compelled to join the army a few years later."

"It's funny how best friends can go their separate ways so easily and suddenly," Marie-France said.

*

Dinner that evening was formal but lively. Gérard was allowed to stay up for the first course. He was poured wine and encouraged to taste and comment on two Rieslings from the estate, after which Ursula offered to take him to bed.

On her return she reassured Marie-France. "I have put him in a room next to you. There is an adjoining door to the rooms. You're on the second floor. I've left the door open between your rooms."

"Was he happy?"

"Very happy. I could not stop him talking, but when his head hit the pillow, that was it. Straight off. Oh, how very sweet and charming he is."

Johann's father, Peter, sat at one end of the table. They talked a little of Johann, the circumstances of his death and the war. Peter's voice was stark and loud. Even so he was naturally inclined to bellow believing that most of his guests might be deaf. The table was not as long as he believed it to be, so for those seated close to him, it was a tiring experience. "I do often wonder what hidden effects that war has had on all of us, the people whose lands we invaded and destroyed, and the German people as a whole, the eventual, humiliating defeat and the years of misery and poverty which ensued, particularly with all that inflation and so forth. And it will not just be our generation. The effects will filter though into the psyche of the next generation and perhaps further on to the next. Prejudices have a habit of passing from one generation to the next unfortunately."

Henri grunted and put his glass down. "We cannot ever allow such a war again. Such a catastrophe no longer seems conceivable amongst civilised European nations, or indeed on European soil ever again. Let us hope that we have learnt our lessons, and that we've progressed from uncivility and barbarity, to new times of cooperation, tolerance and understanding. I suppose the new dangers are from the east, the Soviets and the Chinese. We need unity in our defence, not division."

"Hear, hear," said Sonja, Johann's mother, and everyone raised their glasses.

"To a lasting peace in Europe," Peter bellowed.

Freddy lifted his hand as if he required his father's permission to speak – or perhaps it was to prevent him dominating the conversation. "I agree that we need to reinforce our peace. It requires time and effort. In the years after the war, the Americans and their allies tried to introduce a comprehensive purge of former Nazis, but I'm not sure it was entirely successful. I'm afraid that there was much resentment of the Americans. They confirmed some of the worst fears concerning victors' retribution, when carrying out their policies."

"Interesting. How was that done? Do you think it succeeded even a little?" asked Henri.

"It operated through the infamous 'Spruchkammern,' which were local de-Nazification courts. They made a point of processing individual cases. Effectively all those over eighteen were required to account for their political pasts. It was quite a task. It is fair to say that there was a fair bit of resentment regarding the de-Nazification process among Germans at that time."

"Why resentment?" asked Marie-France.

Freddy turned and faced Marie-France. "I think it was fear. Fear of retribution. A fear of being stripped of all dignity and possessions beyond what shame and defeat had inflicted upon them already. It was what defined defeat. We were an exhausted, depleted, vanquished people. Fear served both as a veiled expression of guilt and as a defence mechanism against it. I would say that within a few years, the people of Germany were fully informed of the extent of the Nazi crimes and encouraged to carry the guilt for them. That in turn led to fear over what the victors might hand down as a punishment or retaliation."

Peter spoke up, "It is possible that in many cases, fear and anxiety hampered a more extensive self-reflection and general admission of guilt, which after all, was what was needed."

"Johann often talked to me of the collective guilt and how Germany was addressing her past in terms of the national consciousness," said Marie-France.

"Yes, he was very mindful of it," said Freddy. "There was a period of national stasis, because I think the real and imagined consequences of this guilt appeared too severe to many Germans. Many chose not to confront it. In this way, fears of retribution delayed a more extensive confrontation with the catastrophe which Germany, and more precisely the Nazis, brought upon the millions of their victims in Europe and the Soviet Union."

"Do you know, we are having our own debate about the Vichy years?" Marie-France said.

"Collaboration, do you mean?" asked Freddy.

"Yes. As you know I had my own spot of bother with that. Go ahead. You have my permission to laugh about it now."

Freddy was the first to respond. "The war has stained us all. Let's be honest and frank about it. I'm not excusing anything that happened during the Third Reich, but I do wonder what was so especially bad about the German people that national socialism could only have happened here. Could the British or the French, also downtrodden and brow-beaten after the First World War, have also supported an equally charismatic leader like Adolf Hitler and been swept off their feet by the promises of a better future?"

Marie-France made one last contribution before making her excuses and heading for bed. "Perhaps you are correct. A war changes people and causes them to do terrible things out of character. People and leaders become monsters. Who knows how great are the emotional wounds within us after five years of war? After all, we cannot see them."

"A good point," said Freddy. "Some of the wounds have not yet emerged. I'm sure."

35

Marie-France walked up the wide, creaking staircase to her bedroom, checking on Gérard on the way. She opened the windows in her room and stared out into the night. She could hear a low rumble from a barge making its way down the Rhine, its lights shimmering across the water as it made its way upstream. The only other sound was an occasional rustle in the trees from a gentle breeze. She lay down that night with Freddy's words echoing in her head. What a thoughtful, well-mannered man and so like Johann. It was uncanny, she thought.

Not long after the Champuix left Rüdesheim-am-Rhein, the Schräder family received an anonymous letter from an organisation calling itself the AS, the "Aryan Sturmabteilung." It read, *"Your son, Lieutenant Johann Schräder, honourable officer of the Wehrmacht and servant of the Third Reich has recently met his death by our hand. His crime was to defile the blood of the Aryan race by consorting with the Jewish Untermensch while serving his country in a time of war."*

Peter Schräder made a point of telephoning Henri Champuix that same evening to discuss the matter. Speculation amongst the family suggested that Johann's erstwhile childhood friend, Günther Brandt, may have been a member of the AS and could have been responsible. It was their only conceivable lead.

"I have told the police and asked them to investigate Johann's murder, supposedly by these AS people, and to find out more about this terrorist group. Could you please provide me with the name of your investigating officer, the case number, and any other details so that I might hand it over to our police team here."

Henri was left speechless. After clearing his throat and sighing, he said, "Do you mean this terrorist group murdered Johann for having relations with my daughter, a woman whose heritage barely contains a drop of Jewish blood?"

"This is what they are claiming. I must say I have never heard of these people, but there are still many vestiges of the war which have not yet been stamped out. Of that, I am entirely certain. They are still here to haunt us, I'm afraid to say."

"Good heavens, It's unbelievable. First, we suspected the French Resistance, and now we have the neo-Nazis to contend with. As we were discussing at dinner last week ... the casualties of that war continue manifesting," Henri said.

That same evening, Marie-France received a phone call from Ursula. "Pa has shown me this letter which arrived this morning. I expect your father has told you."

"Yes, he has. We're talking about it now. It changes everything. As I think I told you, I had blamed my husband and his Resistance friends all along. And now I feel guilty."

"Well, this neo-fascist organisation claim that Johann died because he was consorting with a Jewish woman. Please understand me, that I am not judging you for being Jewish. I just need to try to understand the motives behind Johann's death, that is all. Understanding is part of my grieving. I hope you understand."

"Yes. I completely understand. First you should know that I am not Jewish, Ursula. I have remote Jewish ancestry on my mother's side. But I would not claim to be Jewish. I'm a French Catholic."

"How Jewish is Jewish? Do you really think that's why they killed Johann?"

"My mother's mother was half-Jewish, but totally non-practising. Maman wasn't brought up with any religion but converted to Catholicism when she met my father and before they married. You couldn't have met a more devout Catholic in my mother. If this is all true, I think they really have stretched their case for murdering Johann on the weakest of pretexts. Perhaps there was another motive, don't you think?"

"Yes, it seems like they falsely murdered Johann for sleeping with a Jew, when that was hardly true or accurate. And I would add that it should have been irrelevant," said Ursula, sounding distraught. "It shouldn't have made the slightest difference. We are not antisemitic in this family, I can assure you. It was the regime. The damned Nazis who tried to contaminate us all with their propaganda."

"My father says that in the eyes of these crazy antisemite neo-Nazi fanatics, I must have been considered a Jew. He said that my mother's children, that's us … me, Eloise and Marc, would always be Jewish by blood. I never considered it. I'd never given it a second thought."

"It's crazy to be persecuted for that," Ursula said.

"Yes. It's crazy and you would have thought that all that Nazi extremism would have ended by now. The detritus of that war will stretch far into the future," said Marie-France. "So if I can grasp this … it feels like the Jews were condemned by both our peoples. They were damned from the beginning. And that's not to forget Pétain and his antisemitic Vichy government, especially that Prime Minister Laval. You know I think they sent nearly one hundred thousand Jews from France to the camps in Germany and Poland."

"I didn't know that," said Ursula.

"Oh, yes. France was … perhaps still is, institutionally antisemitic."

"We think we know who might have ordered Johann's murder," said Ursula. "It could be Günther Brandt. Johann and he were such close friends. They did everything together. But after school this chap became an Aryan fanatic. At the first signs of him going crazy, we began to distance ourselves. Eventually Pa refused him entrance to the house and Johann began to hate him. He sent Johann nasty letters saying he wasn't a real German and he needed to fight for Germany to restore the dignity of the fatherland. All that sort of stuff. Then Günther began to disrespect Johann for his pacifist views. Johann was a pacifist. Did you know that?"

"I didn't realise he was an ardent pacifist, but I knew he loathed Nazism and hated the war and just wanted to go home. I know why he joined up too. He had to, but he didn't want to."

"Those who didn't want to but were eventually drafted in, suffered humiliating consequences, even within the Hitler Youth. Johann just went off to war hoping not to kill anyone. That was our lovely Johann."

"Such a tragedy. I'm so glad I came to see you all in Rüdesheim." Marie-France reached for a handkerchief in the sleeve of her cardigan and blew her nose.

"Me too. I'm glad you came. You know, Günther Brandt, like many Nazis, was arrested after the war and interned. I guess he never lost his Nazi credentials. Perhaps he was even more defiant and more determined than ever after he was released. I do worry that these revanchist attitudes might rise up once more, as they did here in the 1930s," Ursula said.

"I don't believe that. The world has received such a shock by this last war. I even remember telling Johann that I thought the invention of the atom bomb would act as the final peacemaker."

"Let us hope so."

*

Ma Coccinelle – Difficult Months

The whole Johann affair and his untimely death brought with it a great deal of unhappiness for all of us, as well as consequences which no one could have predicted. Marie-France only spent five days in Germany, and two of those were travelling, but it was enough time for me to carry out my plans, which we had discussed together beforehand. I moved out of the house but I was now welcome there any time I wished, not least to see Marguerite whom I visited on weekends. And occasionally she would come to stay in Lyon.

Despite myself and my Resistance colleagues being absolved of any culpability for Johann's death, the damage had already been done. It seemed like my leaving the Champuix household was unlikely to be reversed. Additionally, Henri, Marie-France and Gérard had returned from Germany full of the joys of Rüdesheim, and with a fondness for the Schräder family, for which everyone could only be grateful. And this was mainly for Gérard's sake. He now had a family in Germany which was happy to welcome him back at any time.

As the months went by and Christmas 1954 came and went, everyone became accustomed to the new situation. Marie-France and I talked of divorce but agreed it might only happen if we should meet someone whom we wished to marry. Our young family was no different to many in the 50s and 60s, a time when divorce rates were going up and old family traditions and morals declining, leaving divided families and multiple relationships. Not everyone survived the emotional turmoil which these situations provoked. Inevitably it was the children who suffered the most from the broken homes. Marie-France and I did our best for Gérard and Marguerite. Gérard had become almost obsessed, certainly distracted by his "new" German family and Marguerite was mercifully still perhaps too young to suffer the worst of the consequences of a split home. But we were aware that as they grew up, strong emotions would be ever present and forever fluid, and we should be there when our children required a sympathetic shoulder to lean on.

Henri confided in me during a family gathering at Easter in 1955 at Domaine de Champuix, that he was afraid of losing Marie-France if Gérard should prefer his German family to that of the Champuix. It seemed unlikely to me that Marie-France should want to live in Germany. Her lot at the domaine was a good one. She had a career she loved and a family home which would always be her family home. Henri had argued that she might equally find herself running the vineyards at the Schräder estate. I suggested she could conceivably do both, which I now admit is unrealistic.

Henri's anxieties were stirred again, after Marie-France and Gérard visited Rüdesheim shortly after Easter. They had taken the new high-speed train from Dijon to Frankfurt, Marie-France declaring that Rüdesheim was now merely within half a day's reach of Saubon-le-Duc. And what an easy, convenient journey it had now become. Their visit had been such a success that Gérard had refused to come home. Johann's brother, Freddy, seemed to have graduated from the status of uncle to that of surrogate father. Once again, Gérard had got into the habit of addressing him as "Papa," which Freddy claimed not to mind in the least.

I remarked to Henri while discussing the future of our family, that his prophecy might come true. Perhaps we were indeed to be split between Burgundy and the Rheingau. Everyone had ceased to view these two geographical regions in national terms and began to define them by their common viticultural entities. Soon we were talking of Meursault and Rüdesheim as if they were part of the same winemaking map, separated only by a short train journey.

36

The fine summer of 1955 bade well for the harvest in Burgundy. Quality expectations were running high, and certainly if no rain were to fall prior to or during the harvest, scheduled to start in early September, it would turn out to be a fine vintage. It was also the case for the Rheingau. Everything looked good there too according to Freddy who'd got into the habit of writing frequently to Gérard. After much discussion, dates were confirmed for an August visit to the Schräders. A longer stay than usual had been requested by both Gérard and the Schräders. This time it was agreed that Gérard's mother would leave him in Germany for most of the month of August since she was unable to take the whole month off work to accompany him.

Although the Rhine was a larger and busier river than the Saône, the Schräders were lucky enough to possess much the same facilities on the river as the Champuix, with a private picnic spot and their own adjoining boathouse and jetty. On the second day of their visit, Gérard had asked Freddy whether they might embark on a river trip in the Schräder motor launch one day. The boat was more of a modest cruiser, with a deck awning and a small cabin below, but it was comfortable and powerful enough to negotiate an upstream current.

"Could I come too?" asked Marie-France, overhearing the proposal.

"You are very welcome. We'll make a day of it. It's also a great way to learn about the vineyards in the Rheingau, that is if you're interested," Freddy said.

"I certainly am," said Marie-France.

The day before, Freddy had given her a tour of the winery. They'd spent a couple of hours tasting from tank and barrel, both the 1953 and 1954 vintages, of which they agreed the former had been the superior. Freddy explained that the domaine was based in Rüdesheim-am-Rhein but the family had owned small parcels in several of the renowned vineyards in the region for several generations.

"It is much like chez nous," she said. "We own plots in a few Meursault Premiers Crus and a little red in Santenay. Talking of red, what happened to Johann's Pinot Noir vines which he bought from that 'pépinière' in Dijon? Do you know about that?"

"Yes, we're planting them. I can take you to see them, if you like. It's only an experimental hectare. 4,000 vines. It's become a sort of tribute vineyard, well, more of a memorial vineyard. We've called it 'Clos Johann.'"

"Lovely. Yes, I'd love you to show me. Such a good idea. Gérard must come too."

"Yes, it's a bit of a pilgrimage site, as you can imagine. Whenever my parents go missing, I know they've gone off to that vineyard. Sometimes they take a picnic and sit there all day, reminiscing. We won't get a vintage yield for three or four years, but it's symbolic. That's what counts."

"Perhaps I could come and make the wine for you?" Marie-France said, catching herself by surprise.

"Why not? You have more experience of Pinot Noir than any of us. Here we call it Spätburgunder. It's not new here, but it's not common except in Assmanshausen not far from here, where they seem to like it. Johann would surely give the thumbs up on that. I can see him persuading us we couldn't find a better winemaker than

Marie-France." They laughed at the thought of it. She felt an urge to kiss Freddy there and then. Instead she found herself grabbing his arm as she temporarily lost her footing moving out from behind the cask from which they'd been tasting a wine.

"Oooh, be careful," said Freddy. "I'm sorry, there's not much light in here."

"I should be used to that in the cellar. Shall we go and join the others?" Marie-France said, feeling mildly embarrassed.

Towards the end of the week, the three of them set off on their boat trip to discover the Rheingau vineyards. Ursula had decided that she also wished to accompany them. Gérard stood up front with Freddy at the wheel while Marie-France and Ursula sat on the bench in the stern and chatted as the boat chugged upstream.

"How happy Gérard seems to be," Ursula remarked to Marie-France."He does seem to love Freddy. It makes me so happy to see them together. Uncle or father, what does it matter when a man can relate to a boy of their own kin and vice-versa, especially after such a tragedy for everyone?"

"Yes, these visits to Rüdeseim have all been such a revelation. I couldn't have hoped for more," Marie-France said.

"Does Gérard miss your husband?"

"I don't believe so. He seems to have simply found Freddy, as if he's become the new father figure, magically, just like that. Freddy seems to be enough for him. It's quite extraordinary really."

"It's lovely to see. My parents are delighted about it too. It's been remarked upon, I can assure you." She chuckled, then hesitated before asking another question. "And what about you? About Freddy, I mean? You said you were leaving Gérard here last week. Did Freddy persuade you to stay on?"

"Oh. How strange. I never considered it. Did I say I would leave after a few days?"

"You did. And you're still here, and much of that time has been spent with Freddy. I don't suppose you noticed that either." Ursula laughed this time.

"How strange."

"How wonderful, I would say," said Ursula. "Why don't you tell Gérard to come and sit with me. Go up and stand with Freddy at the wheel. He can help you with the sightseeing. I think he's really keen to show you our vineyards. They're very beautiful, you know."

"Should I?"

"You should. Go on." Ursula gave her her hand and lifted her off the seat to encourage her to move to the front.

Marie-France stood by Freddy. She held onto a rail as he pointed out the various vineyards of the Rheingau. When a passing barge left a wide wake, the launch rolled violently and Marie-France lost her balance. Freddy placed his spare hand around her waist and drew her to him to steady her. Ursula laughed at the two of them.

"That's the future," said Ursula, under her breath, pointing to the two of them.

"What?" said Gérard.

"I think your mother likes Freddy and vice-versa. Look, he has his arm around her."

"I like Freddy too."

*

Ma Coccinelle – Nothing is Impossible

As I finish Nelle's memoire in the cold, dismal winter of 1974, we have strikes and power cuts and we still have an oil crisis, which has led to inflation and high fuel prices. My Paris flat is so cold, sometimes I wonder how I can still tap at these keys without my fingers dropping off. And then I recall our glory days, when every day was a fight for survival and we had a cause, and we had "us." We were a couple who were more dependent on each other, and more loving of each other than we'd ever been before. I do not eulogise the war, only the strong ties and the camaraderie it nurtured.

I can't help thinking that things were better twenty years ago. Even so, in the spring of 1956, I lost my wife and her son to the Schräder family. "Lost" is too strong a word but I suffered from a form of grief which I had not expected. We had been estranged, yes, but when your wife confirms for the last time with such a sobering measure of sincerity that she is leaving you for another man, which translates as "for a better man," you feel no larger and no less vulnerable than the spider you happen to observe making its way gingerly across the floor by your feet.

We were divorced a year later but in an amicable, respectful manner for which I should not be resentful and with which the children coped admirably well. Marie-France married Freddy Schräder and took Gérard with her to live in Germany. Marguerite stayed with me but was never marooned from her mother for long. We maintained a satisfactory fluidity amongst ourselves and our children. Gérard and the new Madame Marie-France Schräder often returned to Burgundy during Gérard's school holidays.

I won a seat in the National Assembly in the 1958 elections. The beginnings of my political career at the highest echelons coincided with the debut of the Fifth Republic.

To her credit, Marie-France, or Nelle as I so frequently preferred to call her, never let go of the years we spent resisting the Germans and their occupation of our country. She attended each of the reunions, which usually took place in a little bistro in the Marais, with a regularity that earned her much respect. We could count on mustering a dozen or so of us every five years or whenever it took our fancy, quite often after one of us had passed away. Then we'd call it a "memorial meeting" but it was always celebratory. It is true that a surprising number of us died young, in our fifties and early sixties.

There is a part of me which will forever love Nelle, evident enough in the words I have written on these pages over the past year. She did after all bestow upon me the greatest of honours – to tell her story and to insist I be placed at the heart of it. I suppose in that respect she never let go of me either. I heard from her last in the summer of this same year, just before her fiftieth birthday when she informed me that she had advanced breast cancer. She would never see the publication of our story. She wouldn't have me visit her when she was unwell, but instead insisted I read her what I'd written over the phone as she lay dying in that hospital in Wiesbaden. We spent hours over it. She often laughed, reprimanded me too, and reminded me of significant snippets which I should add, which I'd foolishly forgotten.

I have kept her final entry in her notebook until last. It reads as follows:

270. If you have never lived under the yoke of an occupation by a foreign army, you cannot imagine it, and you are not equipped to judge those who have, and the things they got up to. The fear, the terror, the hunger, the cold, the grief, and the depravity pervade your entire life, from one day to the next, not knowing who to trust, leading a life of profound trepidation when love might turn to hatred over a few words, when a friend denounces you for a loaf of bread, and when a knock at the door might lead to deportation and death. You are not living. You are barely existing, but in all that hell there is a light, a hope and a love which pours forth from those special souls with whom you share the misery of it.

Other publications by Tim Holmes

Novels

Tyranny of Faith (2018)

All the Singing (2020)

Short Stories

Put Me Back Together (2018)

Heft & Piffle (2020)

The Potterer & Joey the Swimmer (2022)

The works of others which have informed this novel

BIBLIOGRAPHY

Non-Fiction

In Search of the Maquis – Rural Resistance in Southern France 1942-1944 – H.R. Kedward (1993)

I Chose the Storm – Marie Chamming's (1965, trans. Clare Vining 2022)

The Vichy Syndrome – History and Memory in France since 1944 (Henri Rousso, trans by Arthur Goldhammer, 1987 and 1990)

Women and the Second World War in France 1939-1948 – Choices and Constraints (Hanna Diamond, 1999)

A Train in Winter - A Story of Resistance, Friendship and Survival in Auschwitz (Caroline Moorehead, 2011)

Vichy France – Old Guard and New Order 1940 – 1944 (Robert O. Paxton, 1971, 2001)

Marianne in Chains – In Search of the German Occupation 1940-45 (Robert Gildea, 2002)

Odette – Secret Agent, Prisoner, Survivor (Jerrard Tickell, 1949)

Village of Secrets – Defying the Nazis in Vichy France (Caroline Moorehead, 2014)

Collaboration Horizontale (Illustrated Cartoons, Navie et Carole Maurel, 2017)

FILMOGRAPHY

Cinema

La Bataille du Rail (1946)

Now It Can Be Told (1947)

Army of Shadows (1969)
Le Chagrin et la Pitié (The Sorrow and the Pity) (1969)
Lucie Aubrac (1997)

Television/DVD
Un Village Français (2009-2017)

About the Author

Tim Holmes was born in London and brought up in Geneva, Switzerland eventually embarking on a thirty-five year career in the international drinks industry, having learned his craft in Bordeaux and Burgundy as a *stagiare* winemaker during university vacations. After establishing a wine distribution business in Zürich, and during a long career as a professional wine buyer, the author took time off for privatisation projects in eastern Europe working for the EU's PHARE programme as an international wine marketing expert. He now lives in the Languedoc and Exmoor where he dedicates his time to knocking Little Englanders on the head, rejoining the EU, writing, and opening bottles of wine for friends.

Printed in Poland
by Amazon Fulfillment
Poland Sp. z o.o., Wrocław